LITTLE WHITE LIES

A NOVEL

MELISSA HILL

ONE

CHLOE KNEW she should be concentrating on her driving, but she couldn't help it. She just *couldn't* look away.

There it was glistening attractively in the afternoon sunshine, newly polished and extraordinary, adorning the third finger of her left hand. Was there anything in the world more exhilarating than an engagement ring – *your own* engagement ring?

"So what do you think I should wear on Sunday?" her best friend asked. Lynne had been rabbiting down the phone about her latest shopping trip for the last twenty minutes.

Chloe loved a good natter as much as the next girl but she just wasn't in the right frame of mind for discussing the merits of see-through strap bras as opposed to strapless – not today.

"Hey, I have to hang up – there's a patrol car ahead," she mumbled, deciding she'd better pay attention to the road. And Lynne was boring the pants off her.

"Oh, OK." Her friend sounded disappointed. "I suppose I'll see you at Alison's – you and Dan are going, yes?"

"Should be," Chloe replied. "Talk to you later ... and wish me luck!"

After they had said their goodbyes, she hung up and tossed her phone onto the passenger seat.

Of course she and Dan would be at the barbecue on Sunday. She had picked up a badass Rachel Zoe top to go with her cropped white jeans especially for the occasion, and she would be damned if she was going to miss the opportunity to show it (and her toned ass) off.

She shivered with excitement as she approached the dinky little town. It was a shame that Dan couldn't come with her today, but he'd laughed when she suggested that he take the morning off to do this.

Typical...

She weaved through busy main street; she hadn't expected the place to be so thronged. Attempting to negotiate a narrow stretch between cars parked on each side of the street, Chloe was horrified to find that, not only had she clipped the Rav4 wing mirror, but hers had actually shattered the mirror of an Astra parked on her right.

Yikes ...

Heart pounding, she sped on. There was no one in the car and she didn't think anyone had seen her, so if she could get away with it ...

Anyway it was the driver's fault for parking on double yellow lines, so what else did he expect? She was no rally driver *and* she was in a hurry. She could always pop back later and leave a note and her number on the windscreen or something.

Maybe.

Dammit though, a broken mirror of all things. Seven years' bad luck and all that. On a day like today, Chloe did not want to even *think* about the possibility.

Finally finding a space just off the main street near a recreational park by the lake, she removed her sunglasses and checked her reflection in the rear-view mirror, before applying a fresh coat of Mac 'Siss' lipstick.

Eventually pleased with what she saw, she got out and locked the jeep, but couldn't help checking her reflection once more in the driver's window.

Using her sunglasses to tuck her blonde bob behind her ears, she straightened her skirt and began walking purposefully down the street, smiling when a gang of teenagers loitering outside a café on the corner wolf-whistled as she passed them by.

Minutes later she pushed open the door of Amazing Days and marched directly to the sales counter.

"Chloe Fallon for Debbie, please. I spoke with her on the telephone yesterday," she announced without preamble.

The teenage sales assistant regarded her boredly.

"Cafe next door," the other girl replied. "On her lunch."

"I'm sure you can help me then," she continued impatiently. "I'm here to choose –"

"Hello there!" the aforementioned piped up from behind in the doorway, apparently back from her lunch break. The wedding designer smiled. "Sorry to keep you waiting, but I didn't think you'd be here until two."

Chloe said nothing. According to her watch it *was* two. Still, she supposed she'd better not be too uptight. "I'm just keen to get cracking," she said with as much cordiality as she could muster, while secretly hoping the place didn't apply this laissez-faire attitude to every aspect of their business.

"Well, I came up with a few options that should work. Come out back and I'll show you."

Chloe duly followed her to the rear of the store.

"You said on the phone that a friend recommended us?" the designer said.

"Alison Caffrey – well, she's Alison Kelly now," Chloe explained. "Everyone was raving about hers and when I began planning my wedding I asked her for your details."

"Ah yes, Alison," Debbie recalled. "She chose gold-inscribed linen, if I remember correctly. But you said you were looking for something a little less traditional?"

Something completely unlike Alison's actually. Chloe couldn't have people suggest that she was stealing her friend's idea. Not in a million years. These had better be good, and hopefully the drive down here to the back of beyond wouldn't be a complete waste of time.

"Take a look and see what you think," Debbie urged pleasantly. "Using the details you gave me on the phone I put together a few personalised samples."

Despite herself, Chloe gasped when she saw the assortment on the table.

"Wow, these are great," she exclaimed, examining a

white hammer-effect card with a cutesy flowerpot bride and groom graphic, tied with a scarlet ribbon – the colour of her bridesmaids' dresses.

Pretty but perhaps a little tacky though – she had been hoping for something a bit classier. Then another caught her eye: this one plain white with an embossed silver stained-glass-effect border and matching silver hearts in the centre.

She opened the card and felt her own heart leap with pride, as there inscribed in silver foil were the words she had been waiting for:

Mr John & Mrs Rita Fallon,

Request the pleasure of the company of......................

On the occasion of the marriage of their daughter
Chloe Maria,
to
Mr Daniel Ignatius Hunt

at St Anthony's Church,
Donnybrook,

On Friday, September 25th

and afterwards at the reception in
The Four Seasons Hotel,
Ballsbridge, Dublin.

"Oh, it's beautiful!" she exclaimed, putting a hand to her mouth.

She was getting married. She was *really* getting married. Chloe had been dreaming about her own wedding for most of her thirty years, yet she didn't think that it had really hit her, not until then – not until she'd seen the words written down.

Of course she'd done all the other stuff – reserved the dress, ordered the flowers, booked the hotel – but the dress was still just a sketch, it wasn't hers yet, and the flowers a 'concept' in the florist's artistic little head.

But here *now*, she was holding in her hand tangible evidence of her forthcoming wedding and she didn't think she had ever felt so emotional.

"Are you all right?" she heard Debbie ask kindly.

Chloe turned to her, blinking back tears.

"You know it's lovely to see a reaction like yours," the designer continued, when she didn't respond. "I've always thought that the wedding invite should be chosen with as much thought as the dress. After all, the invites herald the entire event, don't they? Your guests see those before they get to see the dress, the flowers and all the rest of it."

"No, I'm just being silly," Chloe brushed her off. She really shouldn't have let Debbie see her react like that. Now she would probably charge them a *fortune*.

"It's alright, pet," the designer said kindly. "You don't need to explain. Now do you fancy a cuppa while you finalise the one you want, or will I just leave you to it?"

"I think the design chose me," Chloe said, unable to let go of the silver-embossed card she grasped in her hand.

"You're sure? You don't need to OK it with Himself or anything?"

What? How dare she undermine her relationship. As if Chloe would have to 'OK' it with anyone.

"No, it's my decision and he'll be happy to go along with it. Anyway," she added dismissively, "you know what men are like."

"I do indeed," Debbie agreed, blithely unaware of her customer's affronted feelings, "but you'd be surprised. I had a couple in here last weekend and your man was calling all the shots - wouldn't let the poor girl-friend get a word in edgeways. I tell you, he was one of the fussiest divils I've ever come across, enquiring about the origins of the paper, and the environmental friendli-ness of the ink and all that palaver. And the same fella wearing a leather jacket? The misfortunate wife-to-be was mortified by the time they left."

So unprofessional. In Chloe's eyes, the customer was always right, and she wasn't too impressed to hear Debbie gossiping merrily about one client to another.

Ideally she would have preferred to employ a stationery designer from Dublin, but nothing in the city had come close to Amazing Days.

Idle talk was obviously the price you had to pay for dealing with a company in the sticks.

She chuckled inwardly. Dan would murder her if she said something like that in front of him. Her fiancé had been born and bred in the country and was proud of it.

Still, his culchie roots didn't show and that was the main thing.

Not that Mr & Mrs Hunt were farmers or anything like that – nothing of the sort. Although semi-retired, Dan's dad owned a construction company and Mrs Hunt had 'supported him' throughout his working years.

Something Chloe wouldn't mind doing for Dan once they were married. She hated her job as legal secretary to one of her dad's partners in his solicitor's practice. Although she supposed there were *some* perks. Like taking time off on a Friday afternoon to choose wedding invites ...

"Embossed Silver Hearts it is then," Debbie declared, writing the details in her order book, which Chloe noted seemed to be full of clients. The company had really created a name for itself, and it wasn't difficult to see why.

Would Amazing Days Design invites be two-a-penny by the time their wedding came around though, and would everyone poke fun at Chloe's lack of originality?

"The wedding is when – September?" the other woman said, a pen in her mouth. "And you said you wanted matching place-cards and evening invites too?"

Chloe nodded.

"OK," she said, studying the order book, "Should be good to go about the first week in June – how does that sound?"

"I'd prefer earlier, actually," Chloe said. That weeks away – how long did it take to run off a few invites for goodness sake?

Debbie looked apologetic. "The card you've chosen is one of our newer designs this year so I'm waiting on stock, and of course I'll need time to work on the inscriptions."

"Right." Well at least now she knew that her chosen design *would* be original.

"But I would always suggest that customers leave it as close as they can to the wedding itself before deciding on final particulars, just in case anything needs to be changed in the meantime."

Chloe couldn't help feeling affronted. "What would I need to change?"

Debbie spoke kindly. "I'm just speaking from experience, pet. You just never know. If someone is ill, or things don't go according to plan, or perhaps the date needs changing –"

'Pet' *my ass*..."Look, can we have them sooner or not? Or maybe I'll have to go elsewhere."

Debbie looked taken aback. "Sure ... I'll do my best."

"Fine. Give me a call when they're ready for collection."

With a curt goodbye, Chloe lowered her sunglasses and breezed out of the store – her sample invite clutched in her hand.

The stationery designer raised an eyebrow as the door shut behind her latest client with a flourish. A pure madam if ever she saw one.

And in this business, Debbie thought with a weary sigh, she had seen plenty.

TWO

NICOLA PETERS FINISHED GETTING DRESSED, tied her fair curls back in a messy knot and sat patiently in her chair. It was a mild summer day, but despite the temperature she couldn't help but shiver.

She heard a soft knock on the door. "You OK in there?"

"Sure, good to go," she called back, smiling.

He duly returned to the room and took a seat beside her. "So, I'm pleased to advise that you're in great shape."

She beamed. "Really?"

"Yes. Back-pain and tiredness are probably just down to stress and long hours at the desk but – "

"I had suspected as much," she interrupted, nodding, "but I thought better get checked out – just to be sure."

"Good call." The doctor glanced at her medical chart. "Now, blood pressure's dropped a little from your last reading – which is good news – though I still feel that you'd benefit from a lot more exercise ..."

Nicola looked down and grimaced. "Doc, you don't

have to tell *me* that. And at my age things can only get worse."

"Will you listen to yourself?" he chuckled. "I only wish I was still in my thirties. But for your own sake, definitely try to do something about the extra few pounds. A bit of shopping, out with the dog around the lake a few times – anything to get the blood moving. Though no bungie-jumping or any of that stuff if you can help it."

She laughed. "OK, promise I'll make more of an effort. Thanks Doctor."

She left the surgery and made her way back out to the car. It was quarter past eleven and she was due at work at twelve – not a lot of time to spare. The rumbling in her tummy reminded her that she'd skipped breakfast and she resolved to stop off somewhere on her way.

Traffic through Main Street was crazy as always. It was times like this that she really missed the bike. When she cycled, she used to zip around in no time – not to mention that all that pedalling was great for the figure too she mused, the doctor's advice still echoing in her brain.

Up ahead, she spied Ella's café on the corner. Perfect - she could pop in, grab a salad roll (and despite that advice, some of their famous chocolate Twix cake) and be in and out of there in no time.

Though the carpark nearby looked busy with no spaces close by the entrance. Nicola looked impatiently from left to right. She really didn't have the time to go searching for something further down and ... feckit, one of the parent and child ones would have to do – she wouldn't be more than a minute.

She made it back to the office just before twelve.

"Boss is out for lunch," the receptionist told her. "He said he'd see you later."

"Thanks, Sally. I'm going to grab a bite at my desk but if you need anything give me a shout."

A little while later, Nicola put her hands behind her head and yawned. Despite the sunshine earlier, the day had since turned wet and dreary – typical Irish summer – and she just wasn't in the mood for all this paperwork.

She couldn't wait until Motiv8 Leisure was doing well enough to employ an accountant full-time to look after this stuff.

Situated in the new business park just outside town, her boss Ken and his partners had spared no expense in setting up a state-of-the-art leisure club which they hoped would attract local residents as well as a growing commuter population. But initial registrations had been slow and their membership figures were well under target.

A Dublin native, Nicola had been surprised by the ambition of the place given its more rural Wicklow location. From the outside it looked nondescript, but once inside clients never failed to be impressed by the spacious and airy reception area decorated in soothing cream and purple. Huge banana plants, palms and ficus trees created a tropical and luxurious feel, as did the vivid modernist prints hanging on the cream-coloured walls.

A relaxation and meditation room was situated just off the main reception, and the glass-fronted gym helped staff to keep an eye on any overenthusiastic fitness fanatics.

A twenty-metre, mosaic-tiled swimming-pool and jacuzzi had been installed plus the obligatory steam room and sauna. But the most popular and most utilised area by far was the alternative therapies area. Nicola's first mission had been to employ a qualified aromatherapist, but her coup de maitre had been her insistence on a Hydrotherapy Unit – having experienced first-hand the benefits of such treatment while in London.

Luckily, Ken didn't object to her ambitious managerial plans, and had given her loose rein. Though he wouldn't budge on staff numbers, so instead of using her sales abilities and promotional aptitude to recruit more members, Nicola had been forced to look after the more mundane, everyday administration too.

"Just until we find our feet," he had said, when she'd complained about her growing pile of paperwork for the umpteenth time.

She moved across to the window and adjusted the lateral blinds to let some much-needed light into the room. Then stared idly at the lake in the distance for a few moments, until the telephone startled her out of her reverie.

The receptionist sounded out of breath with excitement.

"You will *never* guess who's on the line. One of the features editors from *Mode* magazine."

Nicola smiled. Irish features and fashion magazine, *Mode* had recently launched amid much hype and furore. Star-struck Sally had obviously been lapping up the coverage.

"Well if she's enquiring about membership, just send her the welcome pack and –"

"No, they want to do a feature - on us!"

"On the club?"

"Yes. Her name is Fidelma and she's on line two. Will you take it?"

"Of course." Nicola was intrigued.

The features writer was polite and charming and explained that the magazine would be running an extensive Health and Leisure supplement in a forthcoming issue. Would Motiv8 like to participate? They really would be mad to miss this type of exposure at such a competitive advertising rate ... blah-de-blah, blah.

Nicola rolled her eyes. Quit the sales jingle and cut to the bottom line. When the woman eventually quoted a rate, she discovered that it really *was* too good an opportunity to pass up.

"We'd love to do it," she told her warmly.

The exposure would mean fantastic publicity, which would hopefully translate into a rush for membership. Which in turn might mean an actual pat on the back from the boss.

When Ken – her manager from a previous job in another leisure facility – had contacted her a year ago and offered her an executive post in his new centre she didn't have to think twice. She'd worked with him in Metamorph, one of Dublin's most popular fitness centres and knew it would be a good move. He knew the business inside out and it had been his dream to set up shop in his beloved hometown.

But it had been a difficult first year.

The *Mode* features writer was still yammering. "I'm just getting participants finalised for now, and we'll also need some background info. So could I contact you again at a later date to arrange an interview? And just so we won't take up too much of your time, we should probably do the photoshoot then too."

"Sure, just give me plenty of notice, things can get a little hectic around here," Nicola said, grimacing at the notion of the photoshoot.

She was just about to try Ken's office extension to let him know about the feature, when he appeared in the doorway.

"All these half-days just aren't good enough," he said without preamble.

"Well, I'm sorry, but I recall telling you that I had an important appointment this morning."

"That's not the point, Ms Peters. We need you here – I need you here."

"Oh, really? I thought you were more than capable of running things when I'm not around, *Mr* Harris."

"Well, you thought wrong." She grinned as he came round her desk and lightly planted a kiss on her forehead. "I can't cope without you."

"Saddo."

"So how did it go?" he asked, crouching down alongside her.

"Grand."

Ken's eyes widened. "Just grand? Did you tell him about the tiredness?"

She shrugged. "He reckons it's nothing to worry about, but my blood pressure is still too high and I need to get more exercise."

"Didn't I tell you should give the swimming a go? Oh, and now that I think of it, the Wheelchair Association were enquiring about the Hydrotherapy Unit. Can you contact them about it? Organise some kind of a discount, maybe?"

"Sounds promising," she said, straight back in business-mode. "I'll give them a buzz later."

"And I wondered what your thoughts might be on a Mother and Baby swimming morning."

She grimaced. "Not so sure, if we're aiming for upmarket clientele ..." Some members brought their toddlers along to the swimming-pool and it was mayhem.

"Well we have to do something, Nikki. The numbers just aren't coming through."

Lately, he was looking jaded and more than a little dishevelled. His dark hair, normally closely cropped, was beginning to curl just above his ears and his chocolate-brown eyes – arguably his best feature – were today devoid of their trademark sparkle.

The partners were probably giving him grief, she thought, though Ken would never admit that.

"I might have just the thing," she said, hoping to put his mind at ease by outlining the upcoming advertising feature.

"I knew I hired you for more than your looks."

"Ha."

When she and Ken first got together, she wasn't sure whether she should continue working at the club. She was only a few months into her manager's job here when they'd begun seeing one another.

Living close by, she was able to spend lots of time on site, especially in the early days, and while she had always thought him a bit of a workaholic, as the months passed she began to view her old colleague in a brand-new light.

Soon, Nicola had inadvertently fallen in love, and when he eventually admitted he felt the same way, they had never looked back. He was everything she had ever wanted in a guy: honest, decent, and an open book.

What you saw was what you got.

"Oh and another thing," he said. "Laura was looking for you earlier. She sounded kind of harassed, actually – all the wedding palaver must be getting to her."

Her closest friend was getting married soon.

"I'd better buzz her back then," Nicola mumbled, grateful for the excuse to avoid her paperwork.

Ken gave her another quick peck on the forehead. "Are you sure you don't want me to call over later?"

"Nah, you enjoy your golf in peace – I'm baby-sitting. Anyway," she added, grinning mischievously, "I could do with a night off – you can be a bit of a handful sometimes."

"I'll remember that," he teased, his brown eyes twinkling, "next time you get a hankering for Ben & Jerry's and old muggins here has to drive halfway across the county to get it for you."

She winked. "At least you're good for something."

He was no sooner out the door than her extension buzzed again and this time it was Laura.

"Any chance I could pop down tonight?" her friend asked.

"Of course you can ... no wait – I'm baby-sitting and I told Kerry that I'd take her to the cinema. So unless you want to come along –"

"Nah, I'll leave you to it," Laura said quickly. "I'm not really in the mood for an all-singing, all-dancing Disney extravaganza."

"What's wrong?" She remembered what Ken had said about Laura sounding harassed.

Her friend grunted. "It's this blasted wedding – my mother is really getting on my nerves. *Now* she's not happy with the photographer because he's" – she affected a sing-song tone – "'supposed to be a bit of letch'. I went to school with Kieran Molloy and he's as gay as Christmas. As far as I'm concerned he can letch all he wants."

Nicola smiled but she could understand her friend's frustration. Laura and her partner Neil had got engaged at Christmas and promptly set the wedding date for the coming September.

They wanted a simple no-frills, fuss-free event, something Maureen Fanning couldn't tolerate. Not when she'd been dreaming about orchestrating her eldest daughter's Big Day for most of her life.

But there was a reason for the couple's no-fuss approach. Neil's mother had recently discovered a tumour and was about to undergo treatment. He was keen for his mum to have something to concentrate on other than her illness and wanted the wedding to happen sooner – just in case.

"You could always elope to Vegas and get married yourselves, just the two of you," said Nicola. *Like I did*, she added silently.

"Are you mad? My mother would have a heart attack. She's bad enough as it is."

Nicola frowned. It wasn't like Laura to be so down in the dumps.

"Hey, don't let her get to you. As long as you and Neil are happy with the wedding stuff, what else matters?"

"Yes, but you know my mother. And unfortunately Neil's no help." Her fiancé was as easygoing as they came and one of the few people who could handle Maureen without resorting to extreme violence. "To be honest, he's just too busy with the agency. At this very moment he's off on some fact-finding trip to Mauritius – lucky git."

Neil was a partner in his family's travel agency, and the business was currently attempting to break into the more exclusive faraway shores market.

"Anyway, the wedding isn't the real reason I wanted to talk to you," Laura added cryptically.

"Oh? I'm intrigued."

"Well if I can't see you tonight, I'm afraid you'll just have to wait." There was a smile in her voice.

"That's not fair. What's going on, Laura?"

"Nope – I'd prefer to tell you face to face."

"Ah, now I'm dying to know." She thought quickly.

"OK – why don't you pop down tomorrow night? Helen's over anyway, so the more the merrier."

The three had been friends for years but lately hadn't had many opportunities to get together.

But Laura hesitated. "Unless you'd prefer to leave it for another night – just the two of us?"

"No, it's grand. I'll bring a bottle."

"Do. We'll have a bit of chat, get the latest on Helen's new man and oh – I'll be able to show you *my* new wheels."

"Another new man? Where does she get the energy? No, don't answer that. And what did you get this time – some souped up Ferrari-type yoke?"

"I *wish*. Better go – I've another call coming in. See you tomorrow round eight?"

"Great, looking forward to it," Laura rang off, already sounding in much better form.

Nicola hit the other line. Was she *ever* going to get anything done today?

THREE

DECISIONS, decisions...

Helen Jackson held one black and one silver bag against her plum satin sheath dress. She adjusted the plunging neckline to ensure it didn't expose *quite* so much of her chest. She didn't want Richard gaping at her cleavage all night – or did she?

She smiled at her reflection.

Tonight was definitely the night. They'd been seeing one another for a while now, and she was certain that it was time to take their relationship to the next level. The thought of it made her more nervous than she'd normally allow herself to be.

Probably down to the fact that she liked him a lot – actually, *more* than a lot – and definitely *much* more than any of the others she'd been out with recently.

Richard was intelligent, good-humoured and *very* sexy. She worked as business consultant manager for XL Business Software and had met him after his recruitment company had sought their advice.

Throughout their first meeting, she'd been as she always was with a client – brisk, professional but unashamedly flirtatious. As she'd so often told her sales staff, feminism didn't earn anyone enough bonuses to keep them in two-bedroom seafront apartments on Dublin's Southside.

But Helen didn't have to force herself all that much to flirt with Richard. Shortly after their first meeting and a few equally coquettish phone consultations, the company had upgraded their office network and he'd asked her out.

Maybe finally she would have someone to take the empty chair at get-togethers. Her friends all sat across from their respective partners, as did colleagues, whereas Helen always got stuck with the empty chair. In fairness, she and the chair were way beyond first-name terms and over the last few years had become best buddies.

Deciding that with this dress the silver bag looked infinitely more glamorous than the black one, Helen rummaged through her wardrobe, and emerged with a pair of spaghetti-strap mules that were ridiculously high-heeled.

She ran a brush through her freshly blow-dried locks, and checked her watch. It was almost seven, and she was meeting Richard in town at half past. She'd better get a move on – who knew how long it would take to nab a taxi on a Friday night.

Helen picked up her bag and jacket, tottered downstairs and slammed the front door behind her – the impact shuddering through the large, empty apartment.

· · ·

"You look amazing," Richard smiled appreciatively as she wobbled unsteadily to where he stood waiting outside the restaurant. Those heels certainly hadn't been designed with the city's unevenly cobbled footpaths in mind, she thought following him inside, but worth the discomfort.

"What time are we eating?" she asked, glancing around the packed restaurant.

Richard raised an eyebrow. "Hopefully soon. I haven't eaten anything since midday."

Helen's gaze raked over the menu, but she found that she was so anxious she could barely see what was written on it.

She watched him out of the corner of her eye. He was studying the wine list intently – probably trying to decide between his personal favourites. It was a little scary actually: they had only been together for a short time, yet she could read him like *Cosmo*.

It had been the same with her previous guy, Jamie, who was as transparent as you could get. Too transparent, probably. Jamie had been so open that he'd one day informed Helen that he felt tied down and was taking off to South Africa to 'find himself'.

That was almost four years ago and since then he'd – handily enough for him – found someone else too.

OK, she decided, seeing Richard close the wine list, if he orders Australian it's a good omen and South African is *definitely* a bad one.

"Ready to order?" the waitress asked pleasantly.

"Yes, thanks. Helen?" Ever the gentleman, Richard

waited while she deliberated. She eventually decided on lamb and he ordered fillet steak.

"Wine?"

She smiled at Richard. "Better let the sommelier decide," she said, conscious that he considered himself a bit of an expert.

Pick the Australian.

Richard waved the menu away and smiled at the waitress. "Thanks, but I think I'll just throw caution to the wind tonight. Can you recommend anything?"

The girl paused for a moment. "Well, considering your choice of main course, I'd suggest the South African Guardian Peak. It's one of the most popular cabernets on our list, and the perfect accompaniment to red meat dishes – lamb in particular," she added, smiling at Helen.

Damn.

Richard beamed at her. "Perfect, thank you."

The waitress collected their menus and left the table, Helen berating herself for being so foolish as to think that the bloody wine she and Richard were having for their meal should affect their relationship. She'd really have to try and stop with all this signs and omens nonsense.

Another butterfly (always a latecomer) rose up in her stomach.

"So what have you been up to this week?" Richard reached across the table and took her hand in his.

"Not much. Got the Carver Property and Tip-Top Distribution contracts finalised and countersigned yesterday." She feigned a shrug, and hid a smile. "Quiet week, really."

Richard gave a disbelieving guffaw. "Bloody hell, you're something else, do you know that?"

She had told him previously that XL had been chasing both contracts for some time, and there was a real danger that one in particular would opt for a rival.

At the very last minute and following an especially persuasive meeting with Helen, the CEO changed his mind and signed a five-year contract with XL. Which meant that she could look forward to what could only be described as an obese bonus cheque at the end of the month. She filled him in on the story while they made inroads on their starters.

"Wow," Richard smiled and clinked her glass, "I think I'll keep you. The ultimate career woman, huh?"

The little voice inside her brain was deafening. *Go for it.*

She took a deep breath. *Relax,* said the voice. *You two get on well together and he really likes you. What difference could it make?*

She gulped a mouthful of wine, and set her glass back down on the table.

"Richard?" she asked softly and the words were out before she could stop herself. "How do you feel about children?"

Damn, the voice berated her. *It wasn't supposed to come out so quickly – you were supposed to ease it into the conversation. Typical you and your size four-an'-a-halves.*

Richard looked as though she'd just asked him to eat a bull's testicle. "Children?" he repeated warily. "Where did that come from?"

"I mean, do you like them?" She tried to lighten the tone. "Or by any chance do you have some of your own or ... or would you *like* some of your own?"

Oh crap, this was getting worse by the minute.

Richard now looked like he'd been presented with an entire plate of bulls' testicles.

"Helen, what are you talking about? You know that I've never been married ..." Before she could reply, his face changed. "Hang on a second ... are you up the duff?" he snarled. "Because if you think you can trap me into something ... I don't know what the hell *you've* been doing but, for the record, we haven't even shagged –"

"Forget it." She reached for her bag, red-faced. How dare he? If he'd behave like this over the mere mention of kids, how would he behave when he knew the truth?

What had happened to the perfect gentleman?

Richard softened when he saw her expression. "I'm sorry, I didn't mean for it to come out like that ... it's just I know *I* couldn't have –"

"It's not what you think – I'm not pregnant," she interjected hotly. "Not any longer, anyway."

He looked at her perplexed.

"I have a daughter. Since you and I were getting to know one another better and becoming – *I* thought – more serious, I felt that you should know."

"Helen ... I ... I'm sorry ..." His voice trailed off, but by his expression, she knew all there was to know.

They were finished. The usual story.

At that moment, the waitress appeared with their main course.

"I should go," Helen stood up.

"No, stay – please. Tell me about your – your kid." The way he said it, it was as though Helen had just told him she'd a severe case of leprosy.

"No, I think I *will* go, actually. Thanks anyway – for dinner."

He nodded. "You're welcome." Suddenly he was being as formal as he'd been that first day in her office. "I'll phone you?" he added, almost automatically and Helen knew, untruthfully.

"Sure."

Her feet must have been feeling sorry for her, because Helen didn't feel them once as she walked dazedly towards the taxi rank. She tried to bite back tears of frustration as she got into the cab she'd hailed with surprising ease. Then again, it was only nine o'clock. No one out enjoying themselves on a Friday night came home early.

No-one but sad, lonely spinsters like Helen.

FOUR

"THAT'S IT?" Nicola asked, surprised.

The following evening, she and Helen were sharing a bottle of wine in her living-room – three-year-old Kerry on the carpet in front of them tickling Nicola's dog. "You're not seeing him again?"

Helen shrugged nonchalantly.

"But why? I mean I thought you really liked Richard?"

"I did at first, but as time went by I realised that we weren't ... suited."

"Oh."

"Come on, Kerry, time for bed," she announced – conveniently changing the subject.

The little girl looked up disappointed, as did Barney the Labrador who was enjoying the attention.

Nicola was amazed. She'd baby-sat a number of times while Helen went out with this guy. Now her friend had casually announced that she wouldn't be seeing him anymore. It was weird the way she could go off a guy for no particular reason.

But she knew by Helen's tone (and the swiftness with which she swept her daughter off to the spare bedroom) that she wasn't prepared to discuss it any further.

Shortly after, Barney jumped up and raced eagerly towards the front door, a sure sign that another visitor was imminent.

Laura stood in the doorway, anxiously brushing her dark hair away from her pretty face and looking a little ill at ease. Then again, Laura nearly always looked ill at ease.

Barney, who adored her, jumped up and almost knocked her to the ground.

"Hey, relax boy," she laughed easily, bending down and ruffling his ears.

"You're early," Nicola ushered her inside. "Helen's already here but Kerry's just gone to bed, so we have to be quiet for a bit."

Barney jumped up and promptly closed the front door behind them with both paws.

Laura looked at him, her eyes widening. "Wow, I sometimes forget just how clever he can be," she chuckled.

"Good fella," Nicola patted him on the head and Barney followed them into the living room, tongue out and long tail wagging excitedly.

"Hi, Helen," Laura greeted. "How are things?"

"Hey." Helen barely looked away from the television.

"*Right*," Nicola sang, trying to lighten the tone, "Sit down there and I'll get you a glass."

"I'll get it." Helen got up and went out to the kitchen.

Laura looked at Nicola. "What's eating her?"

"Don't ask. She's barely said two words since she and Kerry arrived. Poor thing – she seemed to sense that Mummy wasn't in the best of form and kept offering her M&Ms."

"Man trouble?"

"Undoubtedly." Nicola rolled her eyes.

"Oh, wonder should I wait for another time then ..." Laura looked thoughtful.

"Another time for what?" Helen came back into the room with a freshly uncorked bottle and a third wineglass.

Laura sat and began nervously caressing Barney's silky coat. "Well, as I was telling Nicola on the phone yesterday ... I have a bit of news."

"Don't tell me ... you're pregnant."

Nicola watched Laura carefully. She had suspected the same thing.

"No, nothing like that." Her friend swallowed hard. "It's just ... well, yesterday afternoon ... I handed in my resignation."

Laura had sounded strange on the phone, but Nicola hadn't expected this. "You never said anything about another job – what's going on?"

"I'm thinking of starting my own business," her friend said timidly. "Well not thinking actually, I've already *decided* to start my own business."

"Doing what?"

"Designing and selling my jewellery."

"What? That's fantastic news!" Nicola was thrilled for her. "And about time too."

Laura had studied at Art College, but when a job didn't materialise after her diploma, for financial reasons (or more likely, because of her lack of self-confidence) she had taken a succession of office jobs rather than continue with her life-long passion for design. Lately though, she'd resumed her interest and had taken to creating distinctive and elaborate one-off pieces of contemporary jewellery for herself, family and friends.

Nicola had no doubts that she was favourably equipped to do well with her designs. She adored the glass-beaded and liquid silver bracelet Laura had gifted for her birthday a few months earlier. It was so 'her' and exactly what she would have chosen. She remembered being completely taken aback when Laura had admitted that she designed the piece herself.

"I've been doing a few bits and pieces at home," she had said shyly. "Neil sourced the materials."

Since meeting her fiancé, Laura had become a different girl. Neil brought out the very best in her and had obviously provided sufficient encouragement to give her the confidence to offer her designs for sale.

"You don't think I'm mad? For giving up my job and everything?" Laura bit her lip and looked warily at Helen, who was busily lighting a cigarette.

"Don't be silly," Nicola answered, when Helen didn't respond. "It's a fantastic idea. These days everyone wants something different and original – something they can show off."

"You really think so?"

"Absolutely. It's terrific news," Nicola reached across and gave her a hug. "Is Neil thrilled you're finally going for it?"

Laura nodded. "Well, yes, he's very much behind me on it and so supportive."

Of course Neil would be supportive of Laura's dreams, Nicola thought. He absolutely adored her, notwithstanding the fact that he knew first hand what it was like to be self-employed, working as he did in the family travel agency.

"I'd been working up to resigning for months and now – well, now I'm free to work on pursuing my dream!" She grinned excitedly. "Oh, I'm so pleased you're behind me on this. I wasn't sure what kind of a reaction I'd get. I haven't told that many people."

"Well, anyone who sees your jewellery will know as well as I do that you can make a real go of this."

Laura nodded seriously. "I've already begun the groundwork. The bank has agreed to finance a bit, and Neil and I are going to use some of our savings too. I've registered with the Crafts Council and the Enterprise Board – they've seen my designs and believe it or not, sound really positive, so maybe I might get some kind of a grant, I'm not sure yet ..."

Her pretty face glowed with enthusiasm and her dark eyes shone with passion. Nicola was delighted for her; she obviously wanted to make a real go of this, and her designs were excellent. Given time, this business could definitely take off.

She just wished Helen would say something.

Apparently oblivious, Laura outlined the remainder of her plans. "The Craft Council has already given me lots of help getting started with the accounting and the paperwork, so I hope to be open for business *well* before the wedding. I'll have a couple of months to find my feet, and then we'll do a full-on promotional drive before Christmas. With all that and hopefully a bit of word of mouth, I'll get the name out and about in no time." She grinned happily.

"Well, I'll be telling everyone all about you," Nicola squeezed her friend's hand. "Oh, I'm so proud of you. And speaking of proud – what did your mother say? She must be over the moon about it." Still, she inwardly urged Helen to say something – *anything.*

Laura shook her head. "I haven't told the folks about it yet – they'll just worry about my resigning with the wedding coming up. Anyway, I wanted to get everything up and running first."

"They'll be thrilled, Laura. Who wouldn't? Imagine their own flesh and blood – an entrepreneur."

Laura smiled bashfully, then drained her glass and stood up. "Back in a minute, nature calls."

When she was safely out of earshot, Nicola looked at Helen. "Why on earth didn't you say something? Didn't you see her trying to gauge your reaction?"

Helen frowned and exhaled a cloud of cigarette smoke. "I didn't say anything because I think she's stone mad. What does someone like Laura know about running a business?"

Nicola wished that Helen could see past their friend's timidity, and in this case realise that Laura was incredibly brave. But conversely she seemed to have a knack for making her feel inferior.

The two had been friends since childhood, but Helen had always been confident and independent, Laura the shy awkward one in her shadow.

For her part, Nicola had met Helen many years ago when she had been going out briefly with her older brother. The two had hit it off immediately and had stayed friends long after that relationship ended. She had since come to know Laura through Helen and discovered that you couldn't find a more loyal or generous person. More often than once and especially in recent years, Laura had been her rock.

Now she was prepared to return the favour, and give her every ounce of support and encouragement possible. It was the very least her friend deserved.

"Well, can't you just *pretend* that you're happy, then – for her sake? She's really excited about this."

"Maybe, but you and I know that Laura doesn't have the killer instinct."

Nicola made a face. "Killer instinct? Like you, you mean? Come on, give the girl a break."

"Seriously, Nic, she's too emotional, too *nice* to survive in the cut and thrust of the business world. It's dog eat dog out there, you know that."

"Sssh, she's coming back," Nicola whispered, hearing footsteps.

Laura rejoined them on the sofa, still full of obvious excitement.

"So what do *you* think?" she asked directly, her face eager.

Helen stubbed out her cigarette. "Are you absolutely sure that you've thought this through properly?" she said, and Nicola's heart sank even lower than Laura's expression. "I mean, realistically will it pay your mortgage?"

Laura looked away. "I not going into this blind," she said quietly. "Neil and I have discussed it. We have some savings to use as working capital and he's sure that we can make it work. I told you that I signed up with the Crafts Council and they think –"

"I'm sorry but I've never heard of anyone making much selling handmade trinkets – not someone like yourself anyway."

"Helen!" Nicola was shocked at her bluntness.

Laura looked duly wounded.

"Ah look, I'm not being nasty – you know exactly what I mean." She turned to Laura. "In business, you need a thick skin and an ability to hustle and, Laura, you're not like that."

"I'm sure she'll learn," Nicola said pointedly.

Helen took the hint and her tone softened. "Hey, all I'm saying is that it won't be easy. I'm sure the wedding's already drained a lot of your savings?"

Laura nodded.

"And what about the mortgage? How will the two of you cope on just one salary from now on? Laura, are you absolutely certain that you've thought it through?"

"Of course I have. Believe me, I've thought of little else for the past year and a half," Laura answered hoarsely. "I've done the market research, I've got a business plan and Neil thinks ... he thinks it's a great idea, that there's a market, that I would be *good* at it."

"Well, what is your target market then?"

"Sorry?"

Helen sat forward. "Your target market – will you sell directly to the general public, or are you hoping to be stocked by gift stores, accessory stores, etc? Wholesale or retail?"

"Well, both, I think."

"You *think*? Laura, you should know."

"I *do* know – it's just, I need to find my feet to begin with and ..."

Her voice trailed off and Nicola knew that Helen's reaction was now making their friend doubt herself. What the *hell* was wrong with her? Obviously things hadn't gone well on her date last night but she didn't have to take it out on them.

With all that Laura was about to undertake, plus an upcoming wedding in the mix, if she couldn't rely on the support of her best friends, then who *could* she rely on?

FIVE

FRUSTRATED, Dan Hunt snatched up the telephone receiver.

"What?" he barked down the line at yet another anonymous office junior.

For feck's sake, he thought. What was the bloody point of bringing in these school-leavers over the summer? They weren't running a bloody crèche here.

"Um," He heard the girl swallow hard. "Mr Dooley from Dooley Interiors is on line two asking to speak to you."

Bloody Lorcan Dooley again. The same Lorcan Dooley that had been tormenting Dan for the past two weeks, because his office had somehow lost the majority of their staff Tax IDs, and couldn't he have a word in the Revenue's ear? As if the Revenue was a living breathing person, instead of a crowd of civil servants used to hearing the same tired excuses over and over again . . . ? Well, Lorcan Dooley could go jump if he thought that Dan was going to spend the next three hours on hold trying to sort it out. He could already feel a knot of tension form in his brain as he hit line two.

"Lorcan, how are you?" he greeted cordially, trying his best not to sound like he felt.

A long telephone conversation later, a highly pissed-off Dan hung up. He was just about to dial Revenue's number when his extension buzzed again.

"Yes?" he hissed through gritted teeth.

"That's a nice way to greet your fiancée ..."

Dan sighed. The last thing he needed was Chloe in one of her moods.

"Sorry, just having a bummer of a day. How are you?"

"Listen, I need a favour."

"Go on." He groaned inwardly, while kneading his aching brain. Couldn't *anyone* do anything for themselves these days?

"I know you're up to your eyes, but I just got a call from Debbie."

"Debbie?"

"About the wedding invites?" she exclaimed. "Dan, do you ever listen to a word I say?"

"Oh right, sorry. What about them?"

"Well they're *finally* ready and I though you could pop down to collect them since you're closer."

Dan groaned. "Do I have to, Chlo? I was really hoping to get in a round with John this evening. Can't you pick them up yourself – or we could go down together tomorrow?"

"I have a fitting for my wedding dress tomorrow, you

know that," Chloe was petulant, "and didn't I already tell you that I'm meeting Lynne for cocktails?"

"OK, OK," he conceded. Anything for a quiet life. "Where is the place, anyway?"

At five thirty, a weary Dan picked up his briefcase and trudged out of the office. The last thing he wanted to do on a Friday evening was battle the traffic to Wicklow and back. It would be a bloody nightmare. Still, he supposed he'd better do as he was told. He adored Chloe, but it really was amazing how preparations for a simple wedding could turn a normally reasonable woman into something resembling a rabid dog. And lately, as the big day drew ever closer, she was behaving like the pit-bull variety.

To Dan's surprise, the traffic on the motorway was light, apart from a few caravan-pulling jeeps, no doubt on their way to the coast for the weekend. Lucky bastards, he thought. He could do with a few days off. He had been working like crazy these last few months, and all Chloe's wedding preparations were driving him demented.

You'd swear they were the only ones who were ever going to get married, with all her fussing and footering about the flowers, the cake, the dress and these blasted invites. He supposed he should be a little more support-ive, and maybe a little more enthusiastic about it all, but it just didn't feel the same.

Not this time.

Stop it, he told himself. No point in thinking about the past now. And Chloe was a stunner and a half. Dan just wished she'd lay off on the wedding talk.

He found the Amazing Days store amongst all the small but well-appointed craft stores and local enterprises on Lakeview Main Street. Lots of thriving little businesses in this part of the world, he noted wondering if he should pass around a few cards and try and nab some more work for his accountancy firm.

"I'm here to collect wedding invites – Hunt is the name," he announced to the sales assistant, who looked no older than ten.

The girl's jaws stopped chewing for a second, as she regarded Dan with an interested look. He was used to the attention. Over six foot, and often told he resembled a young Mel Gibson, he knew women found him attractive, despite the fact that he was heading for thirty-five and beginning to develop a bit of a beer-gut - which Chloe had been nagging him about too.

"When's the weddin'?"

"Sorry?"

"The weddin'," the girl repeated wearily, "when is it?"

"Oh – September 15th," Dan answered, panicking as he realised he wasn't quite sure. "Sorry no, it's September 25th – yes, definitely 25th." He puffed out his chest in an attempt to appear more assertive.

"Well, there's no Hunt here for September," she said, fiddling with a strand of her hair.

"Well, try Fallon then – my fiancé may have given her maiden name."

"'K." The girl disappeared beneath the counter again and seconds later produced an ivory cardboard box.

"Thanks, my fiancee advised that she's already

paid?" Dan put the box under his arm, as the girl nodded mutely.

He unlocked his Saab and tossed the heavy box onto the passenger seat. It was well after six and the traffic out of town was bound to be mental. Maybe he should detour down to the local hotel for a pint until the traffic cleared. One wouldn't do him any harm, and he'd drink it slowly.

Better than having to sit in a two-mile-long tailback, and having nothing to entertain him but a bunch of over-priced wedding invites.

SIX

NICOLA WAS ENJOYING her Saturday off. She and Laura had spent most of the morning wandering around the shops and even though the day was cloudy, it was mild.

Now they were in Ella's cafe for lunch.

Laura looked enviously at Nicola's plate and grimaced towards her own salad. "I can't wait until *I* can get back to eating lasagne again," she said ruefully.

"Keep imagining how gorgeous you'll look in your wedding dress," Nicola teased, tucking shamelessly into her food. "So tell me, how are the business plans going? Any news from the Enterprise Board?"

Laura's eyes lit up instantly at this, and Nicola smiled.

"Not yet," she said ruefully, "and I think it'll be a long wait. Still, everything else is coming along very well. I'm going to use one of the downstairs bedrooms as a mini-office until Neil organises a proper workshop for me in the garage."

"So you're going to work from home until then?"

Laura nodded. "I've sent some press releases to the newspapers and magazines that might be interested so you'd never know . . ."

"And what about the website, did you get someone to organise that for you?"

"Neil's cousin. He's only fifteen but he's an absolute whiz-kid. You should see the logos and animations he's come up with. I'm sure he has a big future ahead of him in graphic design or something like that."

"The website will be a big help starting out, particularly if people can order from you directly. When you're settled there's a guy I know Conor Dempsey, who does all our brochures and signage stuff. Octagon design, they're just up the road. His assistant Cara is a dote."

Laura smiled. "You're really in with the local business crowd aren't you? Recommending them and Amazing Days too... you should be on commission."

Nicola shrugged. "It's good to support local business and is usually reciprocal; you'll find that out for yourself soon."

Her friend sat forward, her eyes shining with excitement. "I'm almost afraid to say it out loud in case I jinx it, or something. My very own business, imagine." She bit her lip. "Let's just hope I don't fall flat on my face."

"And what does it matter if you do?" Nicola replied reassuringly. "At least you're willing to make a go of it. There aren't many who have the courage, and that's an achievement in itself. Anyway, I can't see that happening. Your jewellery is great and it's a terrific idea. Ken was delighted when I told him."

"Was he?" Laura smiled bashfully.

"Yep. And he said to tell you that if you need any help with finding a decent accountant or anything, you should give him a shout."

"He's such a sweetheart. You're really very lucky."

Nicola grinned. "Anyway, you're not doing too badly yourself with your big wedding and your big business."

She gathered her things, and followed her friend out towards the busy main street.

They were in and out of Amazing Day Designs within minutes, Laura eagerly clutching the white cardboard box she'd picked up from a sulky counter assistant – the same one who had been blatantly eyeing Neil throughout their first visit to the store a few weeks earlier she told Nicola.

When they were back inside the car, she excitedly opened the box but as she did, Nicola saw her friend's expression wrinkle in confusion.

"Ah, these aren't ours," Laura said irritably. She pointed at the sticker on the lid. "Look, they're labelled *Fallon*."

"The kid obviously misheard your surname." Nicola reached for the door handle. "Come on, better go back." She was halfway out of the car but stopped when she saw her friend staring fixedly into the open box, her eyes wide with alarm.

"What's wrong?"

Laura looked up, her expression uneasy.

"The groom ..." she said quietly. "It has to be ... it's Dan – *your* Dan. Nicola . . . he's getting married."

SEVEN

"WHAT DO YOU MEAN, it was an 'easy mistake'? How could it be 'an easy mistake'? Don't tell me that eejit of a girl can't *read*?"

"Mr Hunt I believe that you were in somewhat of a hurry yesterday, and –"

"That's not the bloody point!" Dan was becoming more agitated by the second. "You gave me the wrong box and you gave *our* invites to somebody else."

That was the terrible part, he thought. It was bad enough finding out that he had taken the wrong box, but the fact that Laura Fanning - of all people - had his, well ... that was even worse.

He hadn't noticed anything himself, not giving the box a second glance at the time.

In fact, it was still in the car until Chloe returned home earlier. She'd stayed the previous night at her friend Lynne's after being out on the town.

She was in great form, today's dress fitting having apparently 'gone well'. Dan wondered how a simple fitting for a dress could go any other way but he didn't bother to ask. She would simply sigh, give him one of her withering looks and tell him that he didn't understand.

And she was right. Dan didn't understand, he *couldn't* understand what all the fuss was about. It was strange, but he couldn't quite get it into his head that he was actually marrying her, and that she was no longer just his girlfriend, but his *fiancée*.

It had all happened so quickly. They had only been together for a few months or so, before he'd begun falling over the numerous hints that Chloe dropped about marriage proposals and engagement rings.

Most of the other women in her circle of friends were married and he knew that she was determined not to be the one left behind. Dan didn't want to spend the rest of his life being single either, although it wasn't just that – he did love her. She was bright, gorgeous, great fun (when she wasn't organising weddings) and Dan had to admit that the two of them were well-matched.

But he just didn't feel the same enthusiasm about this wedding as she did. Still, he supposed it was because he had been through the whole thing already. Although last time, things had been very different.

Chalk and cheese.

Shortly after her return home, Chloe had let out a screech that Dan thought would not only awaken the dead but have them covering their ears in pain.

"*These aren't ours,*" she yelled, waving the box lid frantically above her head.

"What?" Dan didn't bother to look away from the newspaper. "Who else's would they be?"

Chloe's shrill tones pierced his eardrums. "Well, *unless* you've suddenly changed your name to Neil Connolly and you're marrying someone called ..." She read the invitation again, "Laura *Fanning*, without telling me."

It was only then that Dan looked up. "What did you say?" he asked, leaping from his armchair.

"I said, unless you've changed your name to –" Chloe broke off surprised, as he abruptly grabbed the invite and read it intently.

He couldn't believe it. Talk about a coincidence.

Laura and Neil were finally tying the knot.

He swallowed hard. Nicola would almost certainly be one of the bridesmaids. She and Laura had been close for years. Then a thought struck him and heart pounding, he checked the wedding date: September 26th. Only a day after his own.

What if ...?

He had driven the Saab back to Wicklow as if it was on fire, waving away Chloe's protestations.

"It can wait until Monday. I'll phone them now, give them a piece of my mind and make sure we get not only an apology, but a hefty discount."

But Dan had insisted. He wanted to make sure that Laura wouldn't find out about his wedding, not like that anyway.

And if Laura discovered he was getting married again, it wouldn't be long before Nicola knew. So he *had* to get it sorted.

But when Dan reached the store, he discovered his worst fears were realised. Laura had indeed picked up his and Chloe's invites in turn.

Now Debbie was soothing. "Mr Hunt, I appreciate your position – really I do. With the surnames being so similar, and the proximity of the dates –"

"Oh for goodness sake!" Dan interjected. "If you people can't be bothered to double check names and dates, considering the business you're in ..."

"I could offer you a small discount on the invoiced amount – "

"I don't want a discount! I want an explanation as to how this could have happened. Do you have any idea how much trouble this could cause? Any bloody idea?"

"Certainly a mistake has been made, Mr Hunt. But the other party identified the mix-up and returned the box right away. While your invites are here, they are still waiting."

Dan knew what she was trying to say – that Laura was the one who should be standing here ranting and raving about mistakes – but Debbie didn't understand, did she?

"Can you let me have a contact number for the other lady?" he asked. "It's important that I speak with her ... to explain."

"Mr Hunt, our client's details are private," Debbie stated firmly, "but I can assure you that I myself have explained the situation, and she's been quite lovely about it and –"

"Can you just give me the damn phone number?"

Debbie took a step back and he could tell by her demeanour that she was beginning to lose patience.

"No disrespect intended, Mr Hunt, but these things

happen," she said, folding her arms across her chest. "The other client was absolutely fine about it and there's been no harm done. Now, I'm very sorry, but there's little else I can do and –"

Dan didn't wait for her to finish; he just grabbed the correct invites, shook his head and marched out the door.

These things happen. No harm done.

Little did she know.

EIGHT

NICOLA WAS YAWNING as she approached the leisure centre.

She hated opening up, especially at this hour, and sure enough there were some early birds waiting in the doorway, ready and waiting to fit in a workout before heading off to a day's work.

Although she wouldn't admit it to Laura, Nicola had been sent into a tailspin by the news of Dan's impending second marriage.

At the time, she had read the invite word for word and dismissed it with a cursory wave of her arm.

"What he does these days is none of my business," she said airily, waiting in the car while Laura went to return the invites to Amazing Day Designs. According to her friend upon her empty-handed return, the wrong box had been given out a day earlier and hadn't yet been returned.

Nicola now wondered whether Dan was aware of

the mistake, and if he had seen Laura's invites. He would almost certainly recognise the names.

It was as if somebody somewhere wanted her to know, since he hadn't bothered telling her himself. She hadn't realised Dan was even *in* another relationship.

Then again she thought, checking the acidity level in the swimming-pool, why would he tell her?

They had been out of one another's lives for a long time now. Still, the divorce had only come through last year. Good old Dan hadn't wasted any time, had he?

Though, *she* could hardly talk. She and Ken got together even before the divorce was finalised, and Nicola hadn't exactly gone running to Dan about that, had she? Although, that was a bit different since they'd known one another from when she worked with Ken previously. It wasn't as if Nicola was going out on the town looking for someone.

She wondered idly what Mrs Hunt 2 was like. Judging by the plush hotel hosting the reception, her family must be worth a few bob. She was probably young, definitely younger than Dan, anyway. Nicola smiled as she adjusted the pool backwash. She was almost certainly blonde. Dan *always* had a thing for blondes.

So he was getting on with it. Should she be really be all that surprised? It's not as though she'd even thought about him since her return.

Not all that much, anyway.

After their official separation and her move to London, Nicola had instructed her solicitor to begin divorce proceedings and luckily Dan hadn't objected to the terms, nor her plans to sell their home and split the proceeds.

Now he was getting married again. Should she care? Should it bother her that he hadn't told her? Then again, how could he, even if he'd wanted to? She was the one who'd insisted he stay away.

Her thoughts were interrupted by a loud roar coming from the gym. Great, she thought with a groan, the first treadmill casualty of the day.

That same evening at dinner, Laura was outlining events to her fiancé who'd returned from a work trip abroad.

"It was awful, Neil, I didn't know what to say to her," she said, spooning mashed potatoes onto her plate. "At least if I had gone on my own, I would've seen the mistake and said nothing."

He gave her a shrewd glance. "You would have said nothing? I don't think so, love. You wouldn't be able to keep something like that from her."

"Maybe," she sighed deeply. "Still, she carried on as though it didn't affect her but surely she must have felt *something*."

Laura knew her friend well enough to suspect that the incident must have knocked her for six. And why wouldn't it? It had certainly given Laura a shock. Dan – getting married again? It just didn't seem real.

"Maybe it doesn't bother her," Neil said. "Dan's well out of her life now and good riddance."

"Have you seen him yourself, lately?" She knew that he and Neil had continued their drinking buddy friendship for a while after the separation, until awkwardness of the split had eventually got to them.

He laid down his knife and fork. "OK, I may as well admit it. I knew about the wedding."

"*What*?"

He shrugged. "I didn't say anything because it's not really any of my business."

"Neil!"

"Well, it isn't. Anyway, John O'Leary rang me up one day looking for a cheap holiday and we got talking."

Laura snorted. "Typical." Dan's partner in the accountancy practice was as tight as a duck's backside and would try anything for a freebie.

"We met for a pint, so naturally I asked how Dan was doing and he told me he was getting married to – his exact words – 'a cute little blonde with a body to die for'."

Laura made a face. "Sleazebag. What else did he say?"

"Dan and this other girl had been going out for a while, and apparently they got engaged shortly after the divorce came through."

"Rat."

"Oh come on, what was he supposed to do? Nicola wanted the divorce."

"Hold on a second," Laura interjected hotly. "What was *she* supposed to do? Stay married to him?"

Neil answered with his mouth full. "Depends on how you look at it, I suppose."

"Just don't."

"What?"

"Don't start taking his side again."

"Laura, don't you think that they both suffered enough? Doesn't he deserve some happiness too?"

"What do you mean 'too'?"

"Well, Nicola's fine now, isn't she? Everything's back on track, she has Ken and a grand life and she's doing fine." Neil shrugged and continued eating, his point made as far as he was concerned.

"Will you listen to yourself – sticking up for that – that ass! Nicola is our friend, for goodness sake."

"OK, OK, I'm sorry. It's just sometimes ..." he trailed off.

"What?"

"Ah look, let's not talk about it anymore, there's no point in our fighting about it, is there?"

"No, but I can't believe you didn't tell me he was getting married again."

"What was the point? They're divorced, they've both moved on – end of story."

End of story? For Nicola's sake, Laura hoped so.

NINE

"HEY, guess where I'm off to next weekend?"

On her way out the door, Helen turned and fixed Tom Russell with a look that almost cut him in half. "*Hay* is something you generally find under a horse, Tom."

He swallowed nervously and at this, she grinned. "Where *are* you off to then?"

He was relieved. Sometimes you just didn't know what way the wind blew with the boss. One minute she was all smiles and chat and the next she was cold as ice. He supposed that was why some of the others on their team were more than a little afraid of her, which in turn meant that they tended to perform well and Helen's monthly sales figures were better than most.

"Two tickets, Kop Stand, corner flag," he grinned.

"You're kidding "Pre-season game with Madrid?"

"The very one." Soccer was the one thing that got always Helen's motor running. Her eyes lit up in the same way most other women's did when they stumbled across a bargain in the sales.

"How did you manage that? Those tickets are almost impossible to get."

"Me and my mate are going over this weekend – but if you ever fancy going sometime ..."

She laughed. "I might hold you to that, Tom."

Helen turned out of the car park and drove towards her childminder's house. Tom's 'invitation' had reminded her of just how long it was since she'd been to a match. Four years at least. Her daughter's arrival had put paid to that, as with most things.

She and Jamie used to take at least two trips abroad a year – winter in the Canaries and then somewhere further afield – the Caribbean or Red Sea and one wonderful time in the Maldives.

But one fateful morning had changed all that; when Helen discovered the blue line on her pregnancy test.

Throughout their six-year relationship, she and Jamie had never spoken seriously about children. At their age, there was no need. They were too busy spending their healthy salaries on impulsive weekends away, romantic meals and nights out in the pub. Nobody in their circle of friends had even discussed children.

Not Helen, that was for sure.

It wasn't that she didn't *like* kids; yes, babies were cute and cuddly and all the rest of it, but they were also loud, demanding and had a tendency to projectile vomit three feet across a room. She and Jamie could start thinking about that kind of thing after they were married, long after. Luckily he felt the same way.

Yet a few months after she and Jamie bought the apartment together (and had spent one glorious week christening every piece of furniture, never mind every *room*), Helen began feeling different.

She felt light-headed and out of sorts and worse, Jamie pointed out that she'd put on weight. At work, she was disinterested, listless and couldn't make a sale to save her life.

"Maybe you're pregnant," Laura had offered artlessly and Helen nearly had a stroke.

As did Jamie, when she did a positive home-pregnancy test and soon after a doctor cheerfully confirmed that she was indeed pregnant.

"What the hell happened?" he accused hotly, as they left the surgery.

And that was the beginning of the end.

She'd briefly considered termination, but knew that she would never be able to go through with it. Anyway, maybe they might get used to the idea. Maybe it might be the best thing that ever happened to them. They might even end up getting married as a result.

Jamie however, had other ideas. There was no question of him getting used to the idea. Throughout her pregnancy he couldn't even look at Helen.

He began to go out in the evenings, leaving her alone in the apartment, and on the evening she rang him in the middle of a poker game to announce that her waters had broken, she knew by his face when he came home that he had begun to resent her.

It wasn't any better after Kerry was born. For the first six months of her daughter's existence, Helen recalled getting only a few hours 'real' sleep a night. By the seventh month and just when the baby had begun to sleep better, Jamie was gone.

"This isn't what I wanted for us," he said. "I feel tied down."

Kerry's arrival signalled the end of life as she knew it – the spontaneous nights out, the romantic evenings in, the much-anticipated holidays abroad. The only holidays Helen had to anticipate these days were in dull, grey Glengarrah, where she and Kerry would spend the odd weekend at her dad's farm. Her daughter loved the farm animals, and got a great kick out of collecting hens' eggs each morning with her grandfather.

Now she parked outside the childminder's house, Helen berated herself. She hated feeling down like this, but sometimes she just couldn't help it. Things got on top of her now and again. Things like her non-existent life.

"Hi Helen," Kerry's childminder stood at the door with her arms crossed. Jo was a rotund, earth-mother type who had been looking after Kerry for since Helen returned to work after maternity leave.

Uh-oh, she thought, realising instantly that Jo wanted to have 'a little chat'. She often wanted 'little chats'.

"Is something the matter?" she asked. "Where's Kerry?"

"No, nothing's wrong. She's in the garden playing with little Mark from next door." Jo stood back and ushered her into the hallway. "Look, tell me to mind my own business but ..." the childminder apologetically wrung her hands together, "it's been a couple of months now and there's been little improvement. If anything, she's getting worse."

"Jo, what more do you expect me to do?"

"Well I don't mean to sound forward but ..."

Perish the thought.

"Are you still doing those exercises with her?"

"I'm doing what I can, but I don't always have the time," Helen muttered. "By the time I get home, have dinner and clean up, the evenings just seem to disappear."

Jo looked troubled. "I really wouldn't say anything if I wasn't worried. Just keep on eye on her, OK?"

What kind of a mother does she think I am? Helen thought, her pulse quickening with annoyance.

"I will." She didn't have the energy to argue though. "Now, if she's ready ...?"

"Of course."

She followed Jo into the living-room, where Kerry sat playing happily on the ground with one of the neighbour's children. Immediately catching sight of Helen, she beamed.

"Mommy!"

"Hi, hon. Ready to go home?"

"Yep!" She nodded enthusiastically.

"OK, get your things and say goodbye to Mark and Jo."

Kerry looked from one to the other. "Bye, M-m-m-m-m ..." The little girl reddened and glanced at her mother, but Helen couldn't look her in the eye.

"Take a breath," she urged quietly.

"Bye, M-m-m ..."

Jo took her hand. "It's all right, pet, he knows you're going. We'll see you tomorrow, OK?"

Kerry nodded again but looked upset.

In the hallway, Helen caught Jo's 'I told you so' look, and it rattled her.

She was getting a little tired of the childminder's interference. Yes, her daughter was a slow developer, but what could Helen do? Didn't she do her best for Kerry, working all day every day to keep them going? They now lived in a much nicer apartment than the one she and Jamie had, she always got the best of clothes, the best of toys, the best of *everything*.

Hadn't Helen taken her to the speech therapist when Jo noticed her speech blockages a while back? Hadn't she bought her that talking-book software that the speech therapist recommended? The idea was that Kerry would improve her speech through looking at pictures onscreen, and listening to the correct pronunciations of the words. The software was for her computer. Her computer! How many three-and-a-half-year-olds had their own computer?

Even though Helen *had* noticed some issues with her daughter's speech, she wasn't overly concerned. Kerry wasn't even four, for goodness sake. The problem would undoubtedly sort itself out with age. What did Jo expect – that she be able to recite the entire works of Shakespeare?

She had been sure that Jo was overreacting, but to get

the childminder off her back she had agreed to take Kerry to a speech therapist recommended by her GP.

They had their first consultation a while back and the therapist had advocated that each day Helen allot a 'selective listening' period, a relaxed time allowing Kerry to chatter away at her own comfortable pace.

Selective listening? Where was she supposed to find time for that?

Their first consultation with Dr Davis had been over two hours long, the therapist almost immediately diagnosing Kerry with a 'moderate-to-severe disfluency'.

Well, which was it, Helen had thought at the time – moderate or severe?

Dr Davis had droned on about how she would have to take time out to spend some quality conversation time with Kerry, and help her develop 'healthy and appropriate communication attitudes'.

If there was one thing Helen abhorred, it was psychobabble. There was nothing wrong with Kerry that time couldn't cure. Admittedly, she was shy and nervous, and didn't nervous people always have trouble expressing themselves? Like Laura for instance.

"She doesn't stutter because she's nervous," Dr Davis had explained. "Rather she is nervous because she stutters. It's a vicious cycle. Even a child as young as Kerry will realise that she isn't speaking as well as everybody else, but what is most important is that she does not acquire a negative self-image, or be ashamed or embarrassed about it. If she feels badly about her speech, she is more likely to struggle in attempts to be fluent, and if this happens, the problem will almost certainly escalate. As a parent, Kerry will look to you for a reaction. If you show any signs of frustration, fear or annoyance when she struggles it won't be long before she begins to show similar reactions. So, as well as increasing Kerry's concerns about her speech, these reactions may also increase the severity of her stuttering. Your own approach, and indeed your childminder's approach towards stuttering, will play a critical role in the development of a healthy attitude."

"I'm really not sure that she has all that much of a problem," Helen said defensively. "I mean, she doesn't even stutter all the time." Rarely around me anyway, she thought.

"A person with epilepsy doesn't have seizures all the time either, Ms Jackson. Stuttering by definition is simply a breakdown in our inbuilt speaking mechanisms, and the system does not break down all of the time. However, I would caution against taking this problem lightly – intervention at an early age is crucial."

Crucial for your bank account maybe, she thought uncharitably. She shook her head. "I just don't know – perhaps we should just wait and see."

In Helen's opinion the whole thing had been an expensive waste of time.

Jo however, had thrown herself wholeheartedly into the program. She was careful never to react overtly to Kerry's repetitions and never interrupt or finish a sentence for her.

Helen still believed that dramatising and paying too much attention to the issue was merely contributing to it.

The way Jo went on, you'd swear Kerry's struggles were all Helen's fault.

She glanced in her rear-view mirror to where her daughter was sitting in silence.

"So what did you do at Jo's today?" she asked, then idly remembered Dr Davis mentioning something about trying not to ask questions that required a lengthy response.

"We made Wice Cwispie buns," Kerry answered without stumbling.

There, Helen thought, she *knew* Jo was overreacting.

"And did Mark help with the Rice Crispie buns?" she asked.

"Yep," Kerry said quickly, "buh–buh-buh-buh ... " She hesitated and caught her mother's eye in the rear-view mirror.

Unbeknownst to herself, Helen was frowning. "But what?" she finished.

"Sometimes the w-w-w-words get s-s-s-stuck in my mouth, Mommy," she said mournfully. "Jo says it's called b-b-b-bumpy talk."

"You're still learning, that's all."

Helen was livid. Jo had obviously been putting ideas in her daughter's head. Now *Kerry* believed she had some kind of problem.

She felt a familiar impatience rise up from the pit of her stomach. It was all right for Jo, she had a husband to share the domestics and cater for her every whim, with nothing to trouble her but what to watch on television every evening. She didn't have to face a mountain of washing and an untidy apartment. She didn't have to spend the next few hours working on a presentation for a client and then be expected to 'listen selectively' to a three-and-a-half-year-old.

Helen sighed. Everything seemed to be getting on top of her these days. She knew that she had been unfairly negative with Laura about her plans for her new business, and she was being especially impatient and impossible at work. She needed a break. Even a decent night out would do, but when was the last time she'd had one of those? As expected, the delectable Richard Moore hadn't been in contact. In the same way that all the promising men she had gone out with had never again been seen or heard from, once they learnt of Kerry's existence.

Helen let them into their apartment building, then checked the post-box in the hallway. There was only one envelope addressed to her and she recognised the hand-writing immediately. Great – Jamie's guilt money. At least that might help pay some of those speech-therapy bills.

She put the key in the door of their modern, lavish ground-floor suite. What was wrong with her lately? Why was she so down these days? But she didn't need to look very far for an answer.

She wanted – no, she *needed* someone – someone to share the gossip when she came home after a long hard day in the office, someone to get excited as she did over the football results. She needed intelligent, exciting conversation, something more stimulating than questions from a three-and-a-half-year-old. She needed someone to cuddle up to when she was feeling down, someone to share her problems and tell her that everything would be all right.

Someone who didn't leave a mess in the kitchen, and toys all over the living-room.

Helen just needed someone to love her, to fulfil her, to make her *happy*.

In the same way Jamie had before her daughter had come along and ruined everything.

TEN

"NEWS? WHAT KIND OF NEWS?"

At the other end of the line, Laura detected a note of apprehension in her mother's tone.

"Nothing bad, Mam. Look, I shouldn't have said anything. I'll wait until we get there and then I'll tell all, OK?"

Maureen Fanning's miffed tone was palpable. "Suit yourself. But don't be dilly-dallying on your way – the dinner will be on the table at seven and not a minute later."

Laura rang off, having assured her mother that they would make it their business to be at her parent's house by dinnertime. She went back into the living room, where Neil was enjoying a rare opportunity to flop in front of the television, Eamonn the cat in his lap.

"Well, did you tell her?"

"She seemed a bit preoccupied. I think I might leave it for a while – at least until after the wedding."

"Why do you keep putting off telling them, love?

They'll be thrilled. And you said yourself that you'll be meeting so many people at the wedding it would be a shame to waste the opportunity for a little self-promotion."

"I know, but –"

"But what?" Neil indicated the space beside him and when Laura sat down he put his arms around her. At this, the cat flashed him a dirty look. "Look, I know you're nervous. It's one thing to talk about it amongst ourselves, but quite another to tell the world about it, right?"

She nodded.

"But this is what being in business is all about, love. You have to let people know you exist, otherwise how will you sell anything?"

Laura grimaced. "I know, I'm being stupid. But I just hope that people won't think I'm making a big mistake."

"Who cares what people think? What is it to them? *You're* the one taking the chance, and you're the one doing all the work. Not to mention taking all the profits," he added with a grin. "Hold off telling the world until after the wedding if you'd prefer. But you need at least to tell your family. With the likes of your mother on the case, you'll get as much coverage as a billboard in Times Square."

She sat up, eyes shining. "I never thought of that."

Neil was right. She *had* been putting off telling her parents about the new venture because she thought that they would worry about them having only one source of income, what with the wedding and the new mortgage.

But she had forgotten how much her mother loved to boast to all and sundry in the village.

When Laura's younger married sister, Cathy had produced twin boys – the first Fanning grandchildren – Maureen had been ecstatic and there was no one in Glengarrah that didn't know all about it, from the weight of the babies to the number of stitches her misfortunate sister had needed afterwards.

Maureen would be in her element with the news that her older daughter was entering the business world. She could just imagine her mother after Mass on a Sunday.

"Laura? She's in Dublin now. Yes, getting married to a lovely respectable fellow. Oh, you didn't know she had her own business? Yes, doing very well, can hardly keep up with the demand. But sure, we always knew she'd make something of herself."

It would be nice to give her mother something to boast about – for once. Laura had never been particularly bright at school and her exam results (with the exception of Art, at which she excelled) were usually best kept hidden. In her mother's eyes, the Art & Design diploma she had taken had been a complete waste of time.

"You'll never find employment drawing pictures and making matchstick men," she had told Laura shortly after graduation."You should go back to the Tech for a year and do a secretarial course."

Although in fairness, the one-year computer course she had taken after her diploma had certainly proved itself useful in Laura's finding employment. She had never any problems in that regard. The words that kept cropping up in her references were 'dedicated, diligent and dependable', which in her opinion translated to 'dull, dull and dull'. She found no excitement, no challenge in drawing up reports and churning out figures on some pre-programmed software package.

Her hobby had been her only escape from her mind-numbing working week, and it wasn't until she had met Neil, who made her feel as though she could do *anything*, that Laura began to consider putting her God-given talents to good use.

She couldn't remember ever feeling so alive, so bliss-fully happy. For the first time ever, she felt as though she knew exactly where she was going with the rest of her life.

Neil was right. It would be brilliant seeing the pride in her parent's faces. Their daughter – a successful busi-nesswoman, a brave entrepreneur?

Of *course* they would be thrilled.

ELEVEN

"WHAT DO you mean you gave up your job? Why would you do a stupid thing like that?" Maureen trilled, shocked.

The dishes had just been cleared away in the Fanning household when Laura made her announcement.

She felt her heart pound. "It's not ... stupid, Mam. I haven't been happy with what I've been doing for a long time now, you know that."

"Sure none of us are happy with what we're doing, but don't we have to put up with it?" Now Maureen began to sweep the floor. "Do you think that *I* was happy stuck here day after day cleaning up after you lot for most of my life? I had no choice."

"But that's it, I do *have* a choice. And I've decided ..." she looked at Neil and he gave her a supportive wink, "I've decided to go into business on my own – selling my jewellery."

Her mother gave a curt laugh and Laura felt her insides tighten.

"You mean the bits and pieces of plastic that you're always messing around with? Why would anyone be interested in the likes of those?"

"Because she's talented." By his tone, Laura knew that Neil was annoyed.

"But it's only a hobby," Maureen continued as if she hadn't heard him. "Your 'jewellery' is grand for the likes of us, but you don't seriously expect other people to pay good money for that stuff, do you?"

Laura felt the blood pulse through her veins and two spots of pink appeared on her cheeks as she raised her voice.

"That stuff was all right for you and your cronies down at the flower club when any of their daughters were getting married, or going to a debs, weren't they?"

Taken aback by her daughter's uncharacteristic outburst, Maureen pursed her lips and continued sweeping.

Laura felt as she always did when her mother tried this tactic –like an absolute heel. "I'm sorry – I didn't mean to shout, but this is really important and it's a big step. I had hoped you'd be happy for me."

"And what are you going to do – set up a stall above in Moore Street, or something?"

She bit her tongue. "No, Mam, it'll be a real business."

"I see." Maureen paused and put a hand on her hip. "But this family ... we're just ordinary working people,

Laura. We're not the types to be setting up businesses."
At this, she glanced slyly across at Neil.

"With all due respect, if you feel that way, then you
really don't know your daughter. She's worked hands-on
in retail for years, and knows as much about business as
any college graduate. Not to mention the fact that she's
damn good at what she does."

Maureen's head snapped up Neil's tone and at the
mention of what she considered a swear word.

"But giving up your job – now of all times, with the
wedding and everything," her dad said quietly.

Laura couldn't read Joe's expression, so she wasn't
sure whether or not her father agreed with Maureen.

"You should see some of the designs she's come up
with," Neil offered, hoping to turn the tide. "People are
raving about them already."

"Oh, for goodness sake," Maureen said tightly.
"People rave about my sponge cakes, but you don't see
me going off pretending to be the next Nigella, do you?"

Laura tried to bite back the tears she knew were
threatening.

"I think you're running away with yourself. And as
your mother, it's my responsibility to make sure that you
don't do anything stupid or fall flat on your face. Setting
up your own business, indeed."

The others were silent, and for a long moment the air
was thick with tension.

Eventually Maureen spoke again. "And what about
Miss Jackson – I suppose she's all for it, of course?" she
asked with heavy sarcasm.

"Helen is very supportive, yes." She wasn't about to

give her mother ammunition by admitting that in the beginning Helen had been far from enthusiastic.

"Well, isn't well for her to be supportive of some?" Maureen said. "And her poor father living all on his own above on the farm. He hasn't seen sight nor sound of her in months, he says." She had never made any secret of her dislike of Laura's childhood friend.

"Helen's very busy at work, Mam, she doesn't always have the time."

"And I suppose there's still no sign of the child's father?" Single motherhood was another cause of Maureen's sanctimonious ire.

"No, Mam, he abandoned them, remember?" For some reason Laura always felt obliged to stand up for Helen. Not that her friend would need anyone to fight her corner; Helen being well used to (and more than able for) the judgmental residents of their home town.

She sniffed. "No surprise he wouldn't marry her. That one was always too big for her own boots."

Out of the corner of her eye, Laura saw Neil shake his head. Maureen's narrow-minded attitude was often a source of entertainment to him, but it annoyed her no end that her mother couldn't even be the tiniest bit gracious about anyone that did their own thing.

"Helen works very hard to bring up her daughter."

"Sure don't we all, Laura? But it doesn't necessarily guarantee anything, does it?"

Laura tried to convince herself that her mother didn't mean anything by that last comment, that she was still talking about Helen and not about her. But why did it feel like that? Why did she feel that she had once again disappointed her, that no matter what she did she would always disappoint her?

Couldn't Maureen see how much this meant to her? Couldn't she understand how much Laura wanted this, how much she had always wanted it? It wasn't success as such, Laura thought – that wasn't it – it was just finally *doing* something with your life, doing something worthwhile, in essence following a dream. Didn't that matter at all?

"I'm not surprised the young one has problems," Maureen continued, apparently determined to continue bad-mouthing Helen.

"Kerry's stutter has nothing to do with Helen," Laura said wearily. "It's just one of those things."

"One of those things? I don't think so. Didn't she cut the young one's hair long before the child had said a single word?"

"What?"

"Sure every fool from here to Timbucktoo will tell you that that's why people stutter," Maureen announced. "You're not supposed to cut a child's hair before they say their first words."

"Right," Neil said, biting back a smile. Maureen had an old wives' tale for everything.

"Well, Helen's trying speech therapy now, so ..."

"Therapy, indeed. In my day, they used to belt the child across the mouth with a dish-cloth, but sure you if you did that now, you'd be up in court for child abuse," she said, her expression perfectly serious.

"And rightly so!" Laura was outraged.

"I'm only telling you what worked in my day. It was

either that, or walk around with a few marbles in the bottom of your mouth."

Neil sniggered and Laura gave him a reproachful look. She knew he found it hilarious that the 'In My Day' speeches were still alive and well. Coming from a more well-to-do background, he never failed to find amusement in Maureen's colloquialisms.

"Mam, those are just old wives' tales."

"Ah, your mother's not too far wrong, to be fair," Joe piped up from the corner. "Old wives' tales are superstitions and different versions are found in every culture."

Her father's long-standing subscription to *Reader's Digest* ensured that he could always be relied upon for little pieces of (factual) trivia. Joe would read anything – newspapers, magazines, even the back of a milk carton, if he was stuck.

"I suppose you got that from a book," Maureen sniffed, as if reading books was on a par with being drunken and disorderly on Glengarrah Main St, neither of which (as far as Laura knew anyway) she had ever done in her life. "Well, *I* don't need books to tell me things that are just common sense."

Laura hated the way her mother dismissed him. It had always been the same, as though she felt threatened by anyone claiming to know that little bit more about a topic than she.

Then Maureen turned to look at her. "So, about this – this *business,* then. What will it be called?"

Laura reddened. This was the bit she had been dreading. "Actually ... um ... I've decided to call it Laura

Connolly Designs." For a long moment, she couldn't meet her mother's eyes.

"Really? And who is Laura Connolly when she's at home?"

"I'll be changing my surname after the wedding, so I couldn't really use Fanning . . ." Her voice trailed off.

"I see."

Her expression telling Laura all she needed to know, Maureen turned to the sink and busied herself noisily with the washing-up.

Discussion over.

TWELVE

A FROWN SULLIED Chloe's usually attractive features as she studied Dan in the mirror. He was acting very strangely these days.

And worse, he hadn't yet said a thing about her outfit.

"Well? What do you think?" she demanded.

"What do I think of what?"

"My dress. You haven't even mentioned it." She turned back to the mirror and continued to apply her make-up.

"Nice." He was noncommittal.

She spun around. "What is *wrong* with you lately? You've been going around in a daze. What do you mean by just 'nice'?"

Dan ran a hand through his hair. "Look just because I don't worship at your feet every time you ask me how you look, doesn't mean you look bad. You look nice .... fine, what more do you want?"

"'*Fine*'" Chloe repeated, putting a hand on her hip. "I look 'fine', do I?"

"Yes," Dan said through gritted teeth.

"You wouldn't give a damn if I went out tonight wearing a pair of your pyjamas, would you? You wouldn't even notice."

Stung, she turned her back to him.

Dan *always* commented on her appearance whenever they were getting ready to go out somewhere. He loved it when she dressed up and she loved the way his compliments made her feel sexy, and nine times out of ten they both ended up horny and indulged in some pretty great bedroom action before going out at all.

But lately, he seemed to have lost interest – in sex and more worryingly, in *her*.

"Chloe, please don't start." He slumped back down on the bed and began to knead his forehead.

"Don't start what? Seriously, Dan, what the hell is wrong with you? You're away with the fairies these days, I can hardly get a word out of you." When he didn't answer she continued. "Can't you tell me what's bothering you? Is it work?"

It had better be something like that, she thought. It had better *not* be something else.

Like an affair.

But where would Dan get the time to have an affair? And why? Chloe turned back to study her expression in the mirror. She hadn't put on any weight and her breasts were small, but full and definitely still in their rightful place – unlike some others she could mention.

At the last dress fitting she had been shocked, but

more than a teeny bit gratified to discover that Lynne's boobs had very definitely headed south. *Her* skin was fresh and clear and she had even upped her sun-bed sessions lately in order to ensure she had a radiant glow for the wedding photographs. She was always up for sex, admittedly a lot more than Dan these days, so it couldn't be that. His sex drive had dwindled a bit, but probably because he was that bit older.

Chloe grimaced. Nah, he wouldn't cheat on *her*.

"So?" she turned her attention back to her fiancé. "Is it work?"

Dan gave a low groan. "Please, I'm just in bad form. You know I don't particularly want to go to this bloody party, and yet you expect me to be jumping up and down like a child on a promise to McDonald's."

She shrugged. "I don't know why you're so against it. I thought you got on well with Mick. I know Louise can be a bit of a pain but ..."

"It's not that – I'm just really not in the mood. Work is manic and ..."

Good, it was definitely work then. Relieved, Chloe turned her attention back to the mirror, and began to tease her blonde hair into face-framing flicks.

She had seen that very look on Cameron Diaz in a magazine the other day, and was certain that it would look great on her. Cameron always looked so stylish.

In fact, Chloe thought, standing back to take another look at her profile, she didn't look too unlike the actress herself in this get-up. She wondered if anyone else would notice the resemblance.

Oh, stuff Dan, she thought, dismissing her worries.

Just because he was in one of his moods didn't mean that *she* couldn't enjoy herself tonight.

He'd soon get over it.

Dan looked in the direction of Chloe's preening, but stared right through her.

He should call Laura.

It was his own fault. He should have at least tried to contact Nicola by now. But what would he say?

Maybe she wouldn't give a stuff about his new fiancée and his new life. And who could blame her?

Then a thought occurred to him. Maybe Laura didn't even read the invites. Maybe she just glanced at them, realised that they weren't hers and brought them straight back to the shop. So, maybe he was worrying for nothing.

And if Laura had read the invites, maybe she didn't recognise his name? Still Dan knew that if Laura read the name, Daniel *Ignatius* Hunt, of course she would recognise it.

Hadn't Nicola made great fun of it during their own wedding vows, ensuring the minister pronounced if fully and clearly, knowing that it would mortify him?

He smiled at the memory. That had been a good day. Definitely one of the very best of his life. So relaxed, so easygoing, exactly the way it should be. No great pomp or ceremony or any bullshit, just Nicola and him, pledging their love in front of a few close friends.

Not like this up and coming charade, whereby at Chloe's insistence he would have to wear that ridiculous top and tails get-up, all trussed up like a circus performer.

Why did some women go all mental over this stuff? All about performance, and exhibition, and 'look at me' bollocks. He loved Chloe, but there were times when her obsession with impressing people got to him big-time.

These days Dan couldn't really give a damn about what anyone thought of him, because worrying about that stuff in the past had been his own undoing.

THIRTEEN

NICOLA WAS DISCUSSING the following week's staffing arrangements with the assistant manager, when the *Mode* magazine team approached reception.

"Fidelma Corrigan looking for Nicola, please," the woman announced bossily.

"I'm Nicola – good to meet you." She moved out from behind the desk and extended a hand to the journalist.

"Oh, I thought ..." Fidelma seemed lost for words. "Sorry," she said, recovering herself, "I was expecting someone ... someone ... older."

"That makes two of us then," Nicola said, smiling brightly.

"And this is Sean, our photographer. If we could maybe start with a photograph of you here at reception ..."

It soon became evident that the features writer was a bossy little madam, and Nicola didn't appreciate being ordered about. It had already been a long day and she just wasn't up to it, having had a night of broken sleep while wandering in and out of vivid, lucid, dreams – worryingly, she thought, about Dan.

"Can you turn your head slightly to the left – no, to your other left, that's it – perfect. Now if your receptionist could again just move out of the way ... great."

She knew that Sally was disappointed that she wouldn't be featuring in the article. Fidelma informed her that they wanted only Nicola for the photographs, and could the receptionist stop 'popping up and grinning in the background'.

When the shoot was over, she led the journalist back to her office.

"So how long has the centre been in business?" Fidelma asked.

"Well, after a very encouraging first year, we're now well into our second year," Nicola replied confidently. She wasn't going to admit that their first accounting year had been a lesson in mathematics. Ken had been expecting losses but none quite so heavy as they had experienced. The pressure was on to ensure numbers improved beyond expectations, and hopefully this article would help do just that.

"I understand you also worked in the industry abroad, before taking up the position here?"

"Yes, in the UK. I spent a couple of years there and found Hydrotherapy highly beneficial to clients and of course a huge selling point for any leisure club." Nicola was anxious to veer the interview more towards the business, rather than the personal side of things. "Ken and I decided that such a treatment would go down well here with a burgeoning population of city commuter residents, and Motiv8 now offers the most diverse range of alternative therapies outside Dublin."

Fidelma nodded. "You and Ken Harris, you two go back quite a bit."

"Yes, years ago we worked together in a different centre in the city," Nicola was a little taken aback. The reporter had obviously done her homework, because not many people were aware of their previous association.

She didn't want to be drawn on their present association either and quietly resolved to deflect any personal questions.

After a while, Fidelma leaned forward in her seat, her eyes cat-like. "I have to ask ... isn't it unusual for someone like yourself to be involved in this industry?"

"What do you mean?"

"Well, you know ..." Her voice trailed off, as she looked Nicola up and down. "You normally wouldn't expect someone ...."

She waited, saying nothing.

"Well," Now the other woman looked uncomfortable. "Someone who isn't that I suppose ... well, you know ... active?"

Nicola bristled. She was sick to the teeth of people like Miss Fake-Tanned-Stick-Insect looking down their skinny little noses at her. Why did people think they could make instant deductions about others based simply on appearance?

She crossed her arms and took a deep breath.

"Fidelma, if you're trying to point out that I hardly teach aerobics classes or that I wouldn't be much good on a treadmill, let me assure you that it doesn't stop me from doing my job and doing it well."

The other woman at least had the good grace to look embarrassed. "Sorry, I didn't mean any offence, I just thought ..."

There was no point in blowing what would be a good publicity for Motiv8, by getting into a snit. "It's not a problem. But I'd prefer if you'd concentrate on the centre. You're not doing a feature on *me* after all."

"Sure." Fidelma duly backed off and at last began asking some useful questions about the facilities

"Well, thank you for your time," the journalist said eventually. "The article will appear in our next issue and I'll get the office to forward a copy."

"Can't wait."

Not long after her departure, Ken popped his head around the door. "Nic, sorry to do this to you, but is there any chance you can cover at reception ..." Then he paused, studying her. "What's up?" he asked, coming into the room and closing the door. "Didn't the interview go well?"

She shook her head, amazed that he could read her so well. "It was fine, but ... ah, don't mind me, I'm just a little out of sorts today."

She still hadn't told him anything about the Dan thing and the longer it went on, the harder it was to broach the subject. She didn't want Ken to think she was hiding stuff from him and she wasn't *really*, it was just ...

"Will this help?" He had come round to her side of the desk and was now gently massaging her shoulders.

"Mmmm ... that feels great," she said, closing her

eyes. She should tell him – it was only fair. She and Ken shared everything and he knew better than anyone what she had gone through to get where she was now. He understood how hard she'd taken the split. So surely he would understand that things felt a little ... strange now too?

"Ken –"

Just then, the intercom buzzed and Sally's voice blared over it. "Sorry to rush you, but Ken said he'd ask if you could cover – "

"I'm just on my way down." She reached for his hand and kissed it softly. "Duty calls."

"Sorry to do this to you. I know you have a lot on your plate at the moment ... "

A lot on her plate? Did he know?

"...but I'm looking into taking on additional staff, and that will free you up a little." He smiled, obviously thinking she was down because of pressure at work.

"Hey, it's fine, I don't mind covering, you know that. Listen, why don't you come over to my place this evening – I'll cook." Ken adored her cooking.

He walked with her to the door. "Sounds great but I'm playing squash with Charlie tonight," he said regretfully.

"Oh, I'd forgotten about that."

"I'll hold you to it, though – see you later." He grinned and headed back towards his office, leaving her unsure whether to feel relieved or annoyed that the opportunity to talk had gone amiss.

On her way down in the elevator to free Sally up for

a fitness assessment, Nicola tried to remember the last time *she* had carried out one of those.

Most leisure staff hated doing it and she was no exception. Nicola smiled. There was one particular time though, when she hadn't minded at all.

It was exactly how she had met her ex husband.

FOURTEEN

HELEN SAT BACK on the bed and rested her daughter's head against her chest as she turned the page.

"Then Snow White opened her eyes and looked into seven expectant little faces."

Kerry sat up, her eyes open wide. "Oh! W-w-w-was Snow White ... scaid, Mommy?"

"Why would she be scared, honey? The seven dwarves are Snow White's friends – you know that."

"S-s-seven dwawves her fwends?" When she could, Kerry often avoided using verbs.

As much as she hated to admit it and despite her hopes that pre-school would improve things, Helen had lately begun to accept that Jo and Dr Davis might have been correct in their earlier diagnosis of Kerry's speech disfluency.

The problem had aired itself again recently, when she had got a call from Kerry's pre-school teacher, concerned about her apparent lack of communication skills.

As a result, Helen was now trying to look past her own denials in order to seriously consider Jo's concerns. Yes, the childminder could be an interfering old so-and-so but at the end of the day, she did have Kerry's welfare at heart.

Helen had to admit that it wasn't good that she was still mispronouncing her consonants or using single words instead of sentences. The speech therapist has suggested she spend more relaxed time with Kerry and recommended Helen read out loud to her each night – the slower rate of speech useful in helping her become familiar with the correct pronunciation of words. Helen had done this ever since, even when sometimes all she wanted to do was flop in front of the telly.

"It's friends, Kerry, not *fwends*," she corrected. "Now say it again."

Kerry repeated it to her mother, concentrating hard. "F-f-fwends."

"No, no, listen to how I say it."

The little girl screwed up her face and tried again, but still couldn't pronounce the word properly.

Too late Helen remembered to do as the speech therapist advised and tried to hide her frustration so that her daughter wouldn't feel under pressure or self-conscious. Kerry shook her head. "I g-g-go sleep now, Mommy," she said quietly.

"OK, hon." Helen kissed her softly on the forehead, sensing that she might have been too hard on her. She was tired, and her speech was always worse when she was tired or upset.

She plugged in the nightlight, and was about to leave

the room when Kerry sat up again, as if remembering something. She looked at Helen and pointed nervously towards her wardrobe. "Mommy, monstaw."

Helen opened the wardrobe, having been through this many times before. "Kerry, there's no monster in there. Look, he wouldn't fit in with all your toys. Anyway, what about the sign?" She pointed towards a sign hanging on the back of the bedroom door, one Laura had bought Kerry a while back to help curb her fears. It read: *No Monsters Allowed*.

Kerry looked from Helen to the sign, the wardrobe and then back again to Helen. She grinned and lay back down, snuggling under the covers.

"N-n-night, night," she said.

"Night, honey."

Helen shut the bedroom door behind her. She couldn't understand how she could be such a nervous child, sometimes. She had heard the fairytale many times before, yet she always worried that the dwarfs would hurt Snow White. In the same way she worried about monsters in her wardrobe, and that Helen would somehow forget to pick her up from the childminder every day.

If anything, she was becoming clingier as she got older. Worrying too that she still hadn't settled in at the pre-school. Helen had also gathered from the teacher there that Kerry was shy around the other children and found it difficult to make friends. It was still early days but ...

She shook her head, knowing that if anything she seemed to crave solitude. She loved the interactive books

Nicola had bought her for her last birthday, and spent hours just sitting and looking at the pictures or playing with her dolls and animals. Helen often heard her in her room trying to pronounce the words out loud when she thought no one could hear.

Hopefully, with the combination of her exercises at home, and the help of the teacher and therapist, they would see a real improvement in Kerry's speech soon. Helen certainly hoped so; she would be starting proper school in September and the teachers there certainly wouldn't have time to give her any extra attention.

Still, there was little else Helen could do. She was trying everything, had painstakingly gone through the exercises the speech therapist had recommended and was insisting that Kerry practise her pronunciation, particularly with her R's and Th's.

Anyway, she thought, returning quietly to the living-room, she'd better do some exercises of her own before she ended up letting herself go altogether.

And letting herself go was not an option.

Exercising always gave her plenty of adrenalin, and tonight, Helen thought wryly, she would certainly need that.

She warmed up, did a couple of stretches and then did her usual fifty tummy crunches and hip-and-thigh bends. She missed her old gym sessions – these days she was lucky if she got there even once a month. And worryingly, she thought, it was beginning to show.

Having finished her exercising, Helen poured herself a glass of Ballygowan, put a CD on low volume, and sat on the sofa to catch a breather. For a quiet few moments, she sat back and listened to the soothing tones of David Gray tempting her to sail away.

She stared at the phone. Should she do it? She'd been so determined earlier, but now she wasn't so sure. Blast it, he who hesitates and all that ...

Helen dialled the number from memory and despite herself, felt her heartbeat quicken as she waited for a reply.

"Hello?"

"Hi, Richard?" she greeted, using her huskiest voice, the one she used on all the male clients at work.

"Yes, it is. Who's calling please?"

It sounded as though she had caught him at a bad time. "It's Helen."

A slight pause at the other end. "I'm sorry, who?"

Helen thought she would die of mortification. Despite all the time they'd spent together, Richard Moore didn't recognise her – or even worse, didn't remember her.

"Helen... Jackson."

Another pause. "Oh, hi ... I ... um ... I didn't recognise your voice."

"So I gather," she said coquettishly. "So tell me, how are you doing, how's business?"

"Is this a business call?" Richard said, in a tone that suggested he wanted her to get to the point.

She suddenly felt very silly. She had been working up to this for a while now, had thought that maybe with a little time Richard might come round. They'd got on so well and he had never made any secret of his interest in her ...

"No," Helen said quietly. "No, it's not. I just thought you might like to ..."

Go on, her inner voice told her, *might as well be hung for a sheep as a lamb.*

"I thought you might like to meet up some time, you know for a drink, or something."

Another, longer pause. "Helen, I'm sorry, but I really don't think there's any point. I mean you're a fantastic person but –"

"Just because I'm a mum doesn't mean that anything has to change between us, does it? It's not like I expect you to ..." Helen knew she sounded desperate, but she just couldn't help herself. She *was* desperate.

"I'm sorry," Richard said again. "I just don't think it would work. It was great fun but ..." he hesitated. "Look, the whole kids thing just isn't my scene, but thanks anyway." With that, he disconnected.

Helen stared at the receiver, mortified. Was this what she had been reduced to? One of those clingy, cringeworthy, desperate women she had always detested?

She clenched her fists in frustration. What was *wrong* with her? When was the last time she had to beg a man for a date? How the hell had she ended up like this?

But of course, there was only one answer to that.

Wasn't she entitled to a life of her own too? Yes, she was a mother but did that mean that she had to sacrifice everything that was important to her, everything that made her happy?

Helen face crumpled. The very fact that she felt this way made her feel worse. The guilt was sometimes crucifying. Here she was, pathetic and embittered on the sofa, while her poor child was sleeping innocently in the next room. It wasn't Kerry's fault heaven help her, that her mother just wasn't maternal.

She couldn't help it. The feeling had just ... never come. Exceptional, overpowering, unconditional love that all the magazines and the baby books were so sure existed. Yes, she loved Kerry, in the same way that you might love your baby sister, but a mother's love? Helen didn't understand it.

After the difficulties she'd endured throughout her pregnancy and with Kerry's initial poor health as a baby, Helen had been expecting – had been *waiting* for the big flash, the big realisation – the so-called burst of maternal love.

At first she had thought it was because she was still pining for Jamie, and thus projecting her own misery. And at the time, she hadn't been able to discuss it with anyone. Her own mother had died when Helen was in her early teens, but the two of them had a relatively normal mother/daughter relationship, so no amateur psychology clues there.

She had lost contact with most of her and Jamie's circle after the birth, and especially during Kerry's illness. Laura had been great of course, calling to see her, helping in any way she could, but that was Laura – Miss Reliable.

Nicola had sensed something once, a long time ago, when Helen was feeling particularly sorry for herself, but she hadn't pursued it.

"It takes time," she had said. "You've had some huge

upheavals in your life – the pregnancy and the end of a relationship. You just need time to get back on track. Then everything will fall into place."

Helen had been almost ashamed at the time, because back then Nicola was dealing with a huge upheaval of her own and coping admirably.

So, she had said nothing and just waited. Waited for it to happen, waited for things to 'fall into place'.

But by the time Kerry's first birthday came around, Helen had decided that maybe she just wasn't like that. Maybe she just wasn't the maternal type.

Surely she couldn't be the *only* mother out there who felt this way? Weren't all people different in the way they felt - in the way they loved? Wasn't it possible that some women just weren't made that way?

To her surprise, she felt warm tears streak across her face. Why couldn't she just be normal?

But what was normal?

Of course she loved Kerry. But Helen was torn between what she felt and what she *should* feel – what magazines and TV and society in general insisted all women should feel.

And it just wasn't there.

FIFTEEN

TANGERINE PRALINE, or Irish Mist Truffle – which to choose? The luscious selection of Elysium chocolates, the scent of which wafted heavily throughout the air, was almost sinful.

Laura eventually made her choice, and along with cup of steaming hot chocolate, she nabbed an empty table at the buzzy new city cafe. She took a sip of her beverage, and shivered deliciously as the decadent, mouth-watering aroma filled her nostrils.

Nicola would murder her for choosing somewhere like this as a meeting-place. The three had arranged to meet up for pre-wedding shopping but the girls were so far running late.

As bridesmaid, Nicola didn't need anything other than shoes, but Helen needed a hat, dress, handbag– the works.

Laura had also asked Helen to be her bridesmaid but she'd refused, offering Kerry instead as flower girl. She obviously had her own reasons and Laura didn't mind all that much, but it would have been nice to have her two best friends by her side on the day.

"Hey, what are you dreaming about?"

She looked up to see Helen, Kerry and a smiling Nicola approach their table. She had a bundle of magazines under her arm.

"Page 22," Nicola said with a grin, tossing a copy of *Mode* magazine on the table, "and *now* I know what they mean about the camera adding ten pounds. I look like a whale in that pic." She gave a sideways glance. "And a place like this *isn't* going to help. Oh, is that a Tangerine Praline – thanks." She winked and popped one of Laura's chocolates into her mouth.

"Hi, Auntie Law-law," Kerry grinned, her wide brown eyes twinkling with fun. Her blonde curls were tied back in a high ponytail and she looked the epitome of cute, dressed as she was in pink dungarees and a tiny denim jacket. Laura grinned back.

She studied her friend enviously. And how did Helen manage to look so amazing all the time too? Today, she had tied her blonde hair in a casual knot and wore a caramel belted leather jacket, figure-hugging skirt and highly fashionable, but dangerously high-heeled suede boots. Laura wouldn't be able to walk ten yards in those, and she definitely wouldn't get very far before people started pointing and laughing at her tree-trunk thighs. But on Helen's slender frame and long legs, the outfit was stunning.

She felt as she always did in her friend's presence: dowdy and inconsequential.

She lifted Kerry up onto her lap. "Hey darling. Were you and Mummy shopping today?"

Kerry nodded, looking happily at her mother.

"And what did you buy?"

The child paused and took a deep breath. "B-b-b-b ..." Kerry screwed up her face and Laura's heart went out to her. "Baawbeee!" she finished delightedly.

"A new Barbie," Helen clarified sardonically, "to go with the other two hundred she has at home."

Laura looked at her and wondered, not for the first time, why Helen was so hard on her. When Kerry eventually got her words out, she looked immediately to her mother for approval – which was rarely forthcoming.

Helen removed her jacket and went to order coffee, while Laura and Nicola pored over the long-awaited Motiv8 feature.

"Well, what do you think?" her friend asked with a broad grin, leaving no one in any doubts about her own opinion on the article.

"I think it's fantastic," Laura said. "You look wonderful in the photograph and this will be terrific publicity for the centre."

Nicola gleefully rubbed both hands together. "I know. It worked out a lot better than I expected and luckily they didn't use any full-length photos. I told you what that journalist said, didn't I?"

Laura nodded. She knew that some people could just be thoughtless, but others downright ignorant. Nicola was fantastic at her job - at *everything* - and no one had any right to make her feel bad about herself.

"I hate that photo of me in the office, but the one of reception looks great, doesn't it?"

Laura smiled. For all her talk about the feature being more hassle than it was worth, she could see that Nicola was pleased with the way it had turned out. Things were going very well for her now – so much so that despite the initial surprise of Dan's new marriage, she had taken the news in her stride. She was obviously long past letting her ex get to her and rightly so.

"I'm just so glad it's over and done with," Nicola said, referring to the article. "I have to admit, I was a bit apprehensive, but I think it's worked out well. Now I can concentrate on getting the client numbers up, and that should certainly help."

Helen reappeared, laden down with a tray. "As soon as they read this, people will be clambering for membership. You and Ken will be fighting them off. Speaking of which, how *is* the gorgeous Mr Harris these days?"

Nicola beamed. "Great, he was asking about the two of you, actually – and Neil of course. We'll have to organise a night out together soon."

Laura smiled. Ken was a dote and so perfect for Nicola. It was funny, she thought, remembering – for ages before they got together, *Helen* had had her eye on him. But apparently he had no interest, despite Nicola's best attempts to set them up. It was a terrible thing to be thinking, but she felt mildly gratified that not *every* guy fell under Helen's spell.

"So where will we go first today? Stephen's Green Centre maybe?"

Nicola made a face. "Too many escalators."

"OK I suppose we'll just hop in and out of the shops on Grafton St then. Laura, what do you need to get?"

"Nothing really. I just thought I'd tag along with you two, and maybe check out some of the competition in the accessories stores."

"Good idea." Helen took the milk jug out of Kerry's reach. "While you're at it, you should pitch your stuff to some of the craft shops or the tourist shops."

Laura's heart raced. She didn't think she was ready for that just yet.

"Nervous about the wedding?" Nicola asked, obviously sensing her reticence. "Only weeks now till D-Day."

"Stop it, it's ages away still. And no, I'm not feeling the tiniest bit nervous. I love Neil and I can't wait to marry him."

"Good for you."

"I've always thought that whole wedding nerves palaver was a bit silly," Helen said airily. "If you don't know by now, you never will. Kerry, will you *please* leave it alone." She snatched the milk jug out of the little girl's grasp.

"I thought *I* knew," Nicola said softly, "but I was wrong."

Sorry," Helen said quickly, wiping Kerry's wet hands with a tissue. "I didn't mean ... I just didn't think."

"You made the right decision in the end – don't forget that," Laura added, seeing Nicola's troubled expression, and wondering if she might have been wrong in her earlier assessment.

"Did I?" she replied, with a watery smile. "I can't

help wondering that maybe we both should have paid more attention to our wedding vows."

"Nicola . . ."

"I know, I know, it was a long time ago." She smiled but her eyes told a different story. "Sorry, Laura, I hope I'm not putting you off altogether."

"Of course not." She patted her hand. "I know how hard it was for you and Dan and - "

"For Dan?" Helen exclaimed, outraged. She had always thought there was nothing wrong with Nicola's ex that couldn't be fixed with a brick to the head.

"Ah forget it," Nicola said lightly. "Old ground."

"So how are the plans for LCD going?" Helen briskly changed the subject. "Did that computer whizz work out?"

Laura nodded. Despite her initial misgivings, her friend had been terrific in helping her source a reliable CAD software developer. While pencil drawings would suffice for the moment, she eventually hoped to use 3D technology for her more ambitious designs.

"So all systems go for the big launch?"

"Well, there's no launch as such. I'll be open for business next week, and everything is pretty much in place." Laura beamed. "My parents are coming over tonight to see my workshop."

"Great, I must pop over myself. For goodness sake Kerry, can you not sit still for *one second*?" Helen snapped.

"Relax, she's fine," Nicola soothed, stroking the little girl's silky blonde curls.

"She's *not* fine. Kerry, sit *down*," Helen uttered with

such emphasis that people at the surrounding tables turned to see what the ruckus was about. Then she stood up, flustered. "Look, you two go ahead, and I'll organise to come out some other time."

"Helen, don't be silly, she's no trouble." Laura was taken aback. "She's just excited to see us, that's all."

"I'm s-s-s-solly, Mummy." Kerry's bottom lip began to stick out, genuinely contrite. "I w-w-w-wanna go w-w-w-with you and – "

"Forget it, missy. I told you that we had a lot to do today for Auntie Laura's wedding, and that you had to be a good girl, but did you listen? No."

Laura gave Nicola a look of mild shock. Helen was often strict, but this was going overboard.

"I'm sorry," she said to Laura. "I'll buzz you later. Maybe then we can talk in peace." Helen fixed a by-then tearful Kerry into her buggy and lobbing her bag over her shoulder, walked resolutely out of the café, leaving Nicola and Laura looking at one another in discomfort.

"I don't know what's got into her lately," said Nicola, "but whatever it is, she shouldn't take it out on Kerry."

Laura didn't want to criticise. "In fairness, I'm sure it's difficult on her own. There's no one to consult with and no one else to share the load."

"Still, Helen has it easier than most. She has her own apartment, an excellent salary, a reliable childminder and no shortage of friends who are only too willing to help out if needed."

"Yes, but it's very easy for us to talk," she said, imagining how lonely it must be. "You said a while ago she was seeing someone?"

Nicola shook her head. "She told me that he was good fun, but in the end they weren't suited. Ah, she's just too damned fussy."

"Do you think that's it?"

"Of course. Think about it – of all the guys she's been out with since Jamie, every single one of them had some kind of fault. Either he was too young, too old, too short, too tall, too bald, too hairy ..."

"Maybe you're right. It'll take something special to satisfy our Helen."

"Jimmy Choo possibly?" Nicola grinned and drained her coffee cup.

Laura sat forward, her mind on something else. "Hey, you haven't really said anything, so I don't know if you want to talk about it but ..."

"The Dan thing?"

"Yes. Are you OK about that?"

Nicola shrugged and looked into her coffee cup. "Maybe I'm stupid, but I think he could have told me. I'm probably expecting too much, we both know what he's like and we are divorced after all. But I know that if *I* was the one moving on ..."

"I get that," Laura said, "but is the fact that he's getting *married* again bothering you?"

"Difficult one. Since Ken and I got together, I haven't given Dan a second thought. I mean, why would I? Ken's wonderful and everything's great between us but ..." She trailed off. "Dunno, I suppose all of this has thrown me off kilter a bit."

"What does Ken think?"

She grimaced. "I haven't told him yet."

"Nic ..."

"I know I should have said something, but then again, is it such a big deal? What's done is done. I'm getting on with my life, Dan's getting on with his and good luck to him."

"You're sure?"

"Yes," Nicola laughed, ending the discussion. "Now come on, we're getting nothing done nattering away like this."

Laura reached for her coat. "Let's head down to Brown Thomas accessories department. Give me an idea of what I'm up against."

"Sure," Nicola followed her to the door, but moved so quickly she bumped hard against a nearby table. She looked in dismay at the two women seated, one of whom was mopping up spilt cappuccino. "Oh, I'm so sorry," she gasped. "Let me get you another one."

"It's no problem," the woman replied, uncomfortably. "It had gone cold anyway."

Nicola looked apologetically from the woman to her companion and suddenly her features broke into a wide smile.

"Carolyn?" she gasped. "It *is* you – isn't it?"

"Hello," said the other woman. "I didn't realise ... I hardly recognised you."

"Yeah, bit of a change since the last time we met," Nicola said laughing. "But how are you?"

"Fine, fine. This is Alma McGuinness. Alma – Nicola Hunt."

"Well, it's Nicola Peters now." She smiled and shook

hands with the other woman, who warmly returned the greeting.

"Oh, I'm sorry, I'd almost forgotten you and Dan were ..."

"No worries at all. How's John?"

"He's fine."

"Tell him I said hello."

"I will."

There was a short pause; an *awkward* pause Laura felt, but Nicola didn't seem to notice.

"Carolyn, I must go - my friend is waiting, but we should meet for coffee soon?"

"Yes. Good seeing you again."

The two made their way back out onto the street.

"Carolyn O'Leary," Nicola said, shaking her head from side to side. "I haven't seen her in years."

"That's who she is – I couldn't place her." The wife of Dan's business partner, Laura recalled.

"She looks fantastic as usual. She must have got some shock when she saw me." Nicola chuckled self-consciously. "We really must arrange to meet up soon. I could do with a night out and Carolyn was always great for a giggle."

SIXTEEN

LATER THAT EVENING, Maureen Fanning was shuffling around Laura's workshop, her mouth set in a firm, thin line.

She had asked her mam and dad to visit in the hope that they would notice the professional set-up, and perhaps realise that she was truly serious about this – that it wasn't just some frivolous notion. She had spent most of the previous weekend making a selection of pendants, necklaces and earrings and laid them out in full view, hoping her parents would be impressed.

If it wasn't for Neil, Laura wasn't sure if she would have the confidence to continue with her plans. He and Nicola had been so supportive and enthusiastic about the idea that maybe they had instilled a backbone in Laura that she didn't really possess. Maybe her mother was right. Maybe she was mad to take a chance.

Yet, something else was telling her that she should go for it. Neil's cousin had done a fantastic job with the website and used 'every trick in the book' to ensure the site was well placed in the search engines. She never tired of logging on and putting test orders through.

But while sometimes her excitement soared, there were times when her confidence dived sharper than a kite without a breeze.

Now was one of those times.

"Looks like you've flittered away more money on this than your own wedding," Maureen said, her caustic tone cutting to the quick. Obviously alluding to fact that Laura and Neil were only having a small wedding.

"Mam, I know you'd like all the relations to be there, but you know we just want a quiet family occasion," she said patiently.

"But do you not realise that I'll get the brunt of it?" her mother continued her complaint, and much to Laura's disappointment ignored her displays and returned to the kitchen.

She couldn't understand how her mother failed to see that her siblings were a bunch of freeloading users. If any of them needed a loan (or more often a handout never to be repaid), Maureen was the first one they turned to. If they needed a lift to or from the town, she would hop in the car without complaint and take them where they wanted to go. She never got anything in return, but for some reason was afraid of her life to risk upsetting her family.

"Listen, love," Joe spoke in a conciliatory tone, "why don't we give you a few quid to put towards the day? Maybe then you might be able to stretch to a few extra relations."

Laura was resolute. "I'm sorry, Dad, but Neil and I

have made our decision. The others can come to the afters. I'm sorry but that's the way it has to be."

There was silence in the small kitchen for a few moments, and Laura soon began to feel Maureen's disapproval eat into her conscience. She wished Neil was here – he'd think of something to say that would bring the discussion to a close. As it was, Laura didn't even want to talk about the wedding. She wanted her parents to say something, at least make some remark about the business.

"So what did you think of the workshop, Dad?" she asked eventually. "Neil did a good job of the spare room, didn't he?"

"Laura, would you ... ah ... would you not forget about this notion of yours, and just go back to work?"

She spun around in surprise, her heart constricting with disappointment. "Is that what you think this is?"

Whatever about her mother, she had always thought that her father – her dad who knew how much she loved to sit and draw quietly when all her friends were out playing on the streets, who loved arts and crafts and used to jump at the chance at making home-made cards and decorations every Christmas – would be supportive.

"You're father's right." Maureen smiled across at her husband. "I don't know what kind of ideas Neil's been putting in your head, but I think it's about time somebody put you straight."

Joe's tone softened when he saw his daughter's pained expression. "Look, pet, would you not try this part-time first and see how it goes? You don't want to be putting yourself and Neil under pressure."

"You don't understand, Dad," Laura's voice was

barely a whisper. "This is something I've wanted to do for most of my life. And it's not all about money, it's about being *happy.*"

"It is all about money when you buy a house in an uppity spot like this." Maureen wrinkled her nose. "Honestly, I saluted one of your neighbours on the way in earlier, and she looked at me as if I was a bit of dirt. Well, I'll tell you, Laura, that wouldn't happen down our way – down home we all know where we come from, and none of us think we're something we're not."

"Mam, it's the city – people don't live in one another's pockets here. The neighbour wasn't snubbing you – she just didn't know you. She doesn't even know *me,* for Christ's sake."

Maureen pursed her lips. "No need to used the Lord's name in vain," she said looking away piously, and Laura knew she had already lost the battle. Her parents weren't here to see her or the work she had done for the business, they were here to try and talk her out of it.

And of course, to talk her into inviting more relations to the wedding.

Laura felt disappointed, manipulated, and very alone.

SEVENTEEN

"OH, it was just amazing, Lynne. Like paradise in your mouth. And I could feel the pounds creeping on as I swallowed it down. Oh, I *know* I'm not, but I still *have* to be careful ... I don't want to look like a giant snowball on the day."

Hearing Dan come in, Chloe sat up. "I have to go, Dan's here and he'll be dying to know how I got on. Talk soon!"

She hung up and turned to face her fiancé. "I picked out the most amazing cake – it was just unbelievable ..."

She stopped short when she saw his face. "What is it? Dan, you look awful."

"I feel awful," he said, laying his briefcase on the floor and flopping down on the sofa. "I've just spent two hours in bloody bumper-to-bumper traffic, and my head feels as though a kanga hammer has been doing overtime in my brain."

Chloe bristled. "I take it that dinner is off, then."

"What dinner?"

"Dan, we *agreed*..." Try as she might, she couldn't keep the whinge out of her tone. He was *always* tired these days. "Food tasting for the wedding."

"Ah, Chloe, we can do it another night, can't we? I'm just not able for it right now, sorry." He loosened his tie, and ran a hand through his hair.

"Right."

"Ah hell – I come home after a humdinger of a day, I've got a splitting headache, and now you expect me to get all trussed up and go gallivanting with you?"

"Gallivanting? Dan, this is our wedding – doesn't that mean anything to you?"

She had been *so* looking forward to this. Being fussed over in a fancy hotel, discussing the wedding preparations ... it would be better than sex. Almost.

But now Dan had to go and ruin it.

"Of course it means something. But if I had known how much hassle all this was going to be, I don't know if I –" He broke off.

"You don't know what, Dan?"

"Look, I said I'm sorry. What more can I do?"

"First of all, you could try showing just a modicum of interest in what is supposed to be the most important day of our lives."

"Chloe –"

"But of course, I forgot," she continued, putting a hand on her hip, "I forgot that's all old news to you, isn't it?"

"For goodness sake, calm down."

"Calm down? Calm *down*?" She blinked. "Do you think I don't notice? That I don't see how disinterested you are? Well, remember something, Dan, *you* were the one who proposed to me. You were the one that wanted to get married, to make it official. And up until a few weeks ago, everything was fine." She stepped back, shaking her head from side to side, as he moved to comfort her. "I don't know what the hell is going on with you lately. Have you met someone else, is that it? Well, if that's the case, you can go jump –"

"Chloe, stop, please, it's nothing like that."

"Nothing like that ... then there *is* something."

With a sigh, slumped back down on the sofa. "You're right, there *has* been something on my mind lately, but it's not what you think. I mean, I haven't met anyone else."

"What, then?"

"It's my ex."

Chloe felt her stomach constrict as she sat down beside him. She didn't know much about Dan's first marriage, other than the fact that he and his ex-wife had parted on unpleasant terms. Dan was loathe to talk about it, but reading between the lines she suspected that the ex-wife had been a bit of a wagon. Had Nicola tried to contact him since? Was she still in love with Dan, or trying to get money out of him even?

"What about her?"

"Remember the mix-up with our wedding invites that time?"

Chloe nodded, frowning.

"Well, the ones we got by mistake were Nicola's best friend's."

She rolled her eyes. Great. So much for Amazing

Day Designs being original. She tried to recall the name. "Fanning?"

"Laura, yes."

"And?"

"And because they mistakenly got *our*s, there is a very good chance that Nicola – or at least Laura – knows about our wedding"

Chloe shrugged. "And why is that a problem?"

Dan began to knead his temples with one hand. "I haven't told Nicola that I was getting married again. And I didn't want her to find out like that, or worse think that I was trying to keep it a secret."

Chloe was confused. "So what? What does it matter?"

"I'm not sure it does," he answered softly. "I just didn't want her to be hurt by it, that's all."

"But you two are divorced and she could even have remarried herself ...."

"She's not married," he said quietly.

"How do you know that?"

Had Dan been keeping tabs on his ex?

"Because believe it or not, I came across an article about her in one of your magazines. She's back from England and she's running a leisure centre." Chloe saw him smile almost as if he was ... *proud* of her.

He shuffled through some newspapers on the coffee table and finding a copy of *Mode*, opened the page and pointed at a small headshot.

"*This* is Nicola?" Chloe repeated, staring at the photograph. Somehow, she had always imagined Dan's ex as that bit more glamorous. The fact that she was an overweight plain-Jane was rather gratifying. "But what has any of this got to do with you now?"

He looked strained. "I know it's hard for you to understand ...."

"You're right," Chloe said, seizing the opportunity to find out what this was all about. "So maybe you'd like to explain it to me."

He wouldn't meet her eyes. "Nicola and I ... we ... we just couldn't make it work. I've never liked to talk about it because ... well, I suppose I blame myself."

Chloe wasn't sure she liked where this was going. Of course she was curious, but she didn't want Dan thinking about it too hard either.

She tried to move the subject along. "So if you're that bothered, why don't you just set the record straight?"

"What do you mean?"

"Well, her number is plastered all over that article – they must be desperate for business – why don't you give her a call?"

"You wouldn't mind?"

"Nope, go right ahead."

"OK, then – I think I will," He looked relieved but she thought, a little nervous.

Him and his bloody principles. Sometimes Chloe's fiancé was far too considerate for his own good.

While he showered and changed, she studied the photograph in more detail. Clearly Nicola was nothing to worry about; dumpy and decidedly *un*glamorous – she was the *last* person you'd want promoting a fitness centre.

Yet despite what she'd said to Dan just now she was

curious. He was always so reticent to talk about his ex and what went down between them.

So maybe Chloe should do a little digging of her own.

Just in case.

EIGHTEEN

LAURA COULD BARELY CONTAIN her excitement. As of today, Laura Connolly Design was open for business, and now she was officially proprietor of her own company.

She looked around her small garage workshop with immense satisfaction. The logo was simple lilac and silver wording on a white background, and inside the jewellery would be presented on white satin.

Helen had suggested an official LCD opening to gain some publicity, but Laura wanted to leave such an outward proclamation until closer to Christmas, when buying gifts would be foremost in people's minds.

For the moment, she was quite happy to start slow, build up a decent catalogue and hope that her profile would be raised by satisfied customers spreading the word.

She picked up her own personal favourite, one of the very first pieces she had designed since going out on her own.

Going out on her own... She still couldn't believe it. This bracelet had taken her ages to make – the fine silver metal chain being almost impossible to thread. She had strung shimmering crystal aurora beads on the chain and covered the metal clasp with blindingly bright aurora rhinestones.

She was definitely going to experiment with her own wedding jewellery too, and come up with something fabulous, something her bridesmaids would treasure for years to come.

Laura was so engrossed in the work that she almost didn't hear the doorbell ring.

A deliveryman stood at the door, holding the most amazing and unusual flower arrangement. Earlier, Helen had sent a gift basket of handmade chocolates, Nicola had sent her a Good Luck helium balloon, and Neil's mother, despite the fact that she was in hospital having chemo, had sent a magnum of champagne.

These were from Neil.

'Congratulations, LC,
Guess who has designs on your heart?'

As she read the card attached, Laura tried to hold back the tears. He was being so wonderful; *people* were being so wonderful, her parents excepted.

And as long as she such great support, surely everything would be all right.

·   ·   ·

Helen checked her watch. She was sitting in the bar of the Stillorgan Park Hotel and her client was late.

Forty minutes late. If there was one thing she hated, it was professional discourtesy.

As if on cue her mobile rang.

"Helen?" The woman sounded rushed and harassed. "Miriam Casey here – I know this is last minute, but could we possibly postpone today?"

Helen bristled. She had been up all night working on a presentation for *Mizz* Casey and now the wagon was cancelling?

"I'm so sorry, it's just that one of the kids has taken ill, and I really can't leave him. Tell you what, why don't you stay for lunch and bill it to the company? Please," she insisted, when Helen hesitated, "it's the very least I can do."

It looked as though she wasn't the only woman struggling to hold a career and motherhood together.

Noticing a decidedly attractive guy staring at her from the bar, Helen dropped the frown, composed her features and automatically assumed her sexiest pose.

"Call me when you want to reschedule," she said shortly, putting her phone back on the countertop.

Great. So much for rushing around like a madwoman, trying to get a full day's work into one morning. Despite the offer she didn't fancy eating on her own. She debated just going back to the office, but it was such a gorgeous day outside ...

Helen paused. She *could* just collect Kerry from pre-school and go home early, but there was hardly much point in doing that when the childminder was probably already on the way.

And she realised, as she saw the attractive guy now giving her a full-on come hither stare, for the first time in as long as she could remember she had an afternoon to herself.

Maybe she should head out to Laura's and see how she was getting on in her first day in business or – even better – pop down and visit Nicola in the leisure centre, maybe stay for a massage or a long soak in the spa.

Grafton St. was also there to be conquered, and how better to spend an idle afternoon than shopping? She still needed to get an outfit for Laura's wedding, a racy little Julien McDonald or Jenny Packham number, something to get them all talking.

Helen checked her watch. She could be in town by three, and still have plenty of time before she needed to pick up Kerry from Jo's at five.

"So, are you waiting for someone, or is this just my lucky day?"

It was a line if ever there was one, but Helen didn't mind. The way he was looking at her sent an involuntary shiver of excitement down her spine. The dark, downy hairs sneaking over his sleeve sent her imagination sprinting, and suddenly she began to imagine running her fingers along his chest. She let the sensations work their way from her mind down along the rest of her body.

Man, it had been ages ...

"So what'll it be?"

"Sorry?"

"Well, are you going to join me for a drink, or do you have somewhere else to go?"

Helen smiled and sexily crossed her legs once more.

NINETEEN

IT DIDN'T MATTER that she didn't know this guy, or anything about him – all that mattered was that Helen was more turned on than she had ever been in her entire life.

She clung to his damp body like her life depended on it.

After what seemed like hours, he collapsed heavily on the pillow beside her, hair on his forehead damp with sweat and his tanned skin glistening in the afternoon light.

He turned to look at her, his pupils still dilated with lust.

"So, what was your name again?"

She kicked him in the leg. "Names were about as far as we *did* get before … this," she smiled slyly.

"Well *this* as you call it, this was bloody fantastic."

She shrugged. "If you say so."

"What?" His eyes widened. "You're kidding me, right?"

There was a slight twang in his voice that Helen hadn't noticed until now. She laughed. "Of course it was fantastic."

"So now we should at least get to know one another better, don't you think?" He began running a finger along her ribcage and she felt herself respond almost instantly to his touch.

"Y ...es."

"So, tell me all about yourself," He traced his tongue around one of her nipples.

Her breathing began to quicken once more. "Well, I work in sales and ..."

"No," he whispered, putting a finger to her lips. "*Tell* me about yourself – for instance ... tell me how you're feeling now, how this feels." He moved his hands lower along her body and she struggled to speak.

Afterwards, they once again lay together in, Helen thought, a very comfortable silence.

"So, what about you then?" she asked eventually.

He sat up. "What about me?"

"Well, I'm guessing you're in business too – "

"Pensions," he interjected.

"Pensions?"

"And investments," he finished. "Not what you imagined, huh?"

"No, not exactly." She had figured a partner in some high-powered corporation, not quite a lowly salesman.

"So what do you think?" he asked with a daring smile.

"About what?" Helen felt a tingle of anticipation.

She knew where this was going. He wanted to see her again.

"About dinner on Saturday night?"

"I'd love to," she said coyly, pulling him closer, "but I think I need to get you know a little better first."

TWENTY

"HELLO NIC."

It was as though she could feel every cell in her body constrict with tension but amazingly, her voice when she spoke sounded casual, almost ordinary.

"Dan – it's been a while."

He cleared his throat again. "Um, welcome back ... I mean, I didn't realise you were back and ..."

Welcome back?

"What do you want?" she asked, sitting forward in her seat.

He hesitated. "I just wondered if maybe we could meet up – for coffee, or something."

Silence.

"Please, Nicola. I'd really like to talk to you."

She wanted to see him too but she didn't know if she could stand it. How could she look into those eyes again, those ice-blue eyes that would remind her of everything they used to have? But she was fine now, she had Ken and she loved him and ...

"I'm not sure, things are busy here at the moment."

"Yes, I'm pleased for you." She knew by the sound of his voice that he was smiling. Then he sighed. "Nic, I don't know if Laura told you ..."

"About the wedding? Yes, she did." She wasn't going to tell him that she had actually seen his wedding invites.

"I'm sorry you had to find out like that. I would have told you, but I didn't know how to reach you. I hope that – "

"It's not a problem," she interjected breezily. "If it's the reason you're phoning or concerned about my feelings, then don't be. We're divorced now, remember?"

Good old Dan and his guilt. Not that his guilt had stopped him before.

"I know, but I just thought – "

"Sorry, but I really have to go," she interjected quickly. "All the best with the wedding and I hope you'll be very happy."

"Do you really mean that, Nic?" he asked, his voice soft and hopeful.

She felt her heart sink. *Did* she mean it? But surely she *should* be happy for him – happy that he had found someone else to love, as she had with Ken.

Had she moved on, really? Sure, everything was going fantastically for her now and she had absolutely no regrets about coming home, or about the divorce. And of course, falling in love again was the best thing that could possibly have happened.

Yet, news of Dan seemed to have stirred up old feelings – feelings Nicola thought she had successfully buried a long time ago.

Why, out of all people, did Laura's wedding invites have to get mixed up with her ex-husband's?

Maybe she needed to purge. Maybe, if she met with Dan now and didn't feel anything, she would be free to move on for good.

So maybe that's what she should do.

"You're right, we should meet up for coffee, sometime. I'd love to hear all about the new Mrs Hunt." She injected some warmth into her voice.

"That would be really great, Nic. I'd love to see you." He sounded pleased, but also a little surprised.

"Well, I'll give you a call."

"You still have my office number?"

"I think so." The number of Hunt of O'Leary Chartered Accountants was etched somewhere in her brain, even after all this time.

"OK, well, nice to talk to you again, Nic. Oh, by the way, I saw that magazine article. You look great."

"Oh." Nicola was surprised by this. "Thank you."

She replaced the receiver and stared unseeingly at the phone for what seemed like ages, trying to decide whether or not she had made the right decision.

TWENTY-ONE

DAN'S BUSINESS partner answered on the second ring.

"O'Leary Hunt – John speaking."

"Hi, it's Chloe – Dan's Chloe," she clarified.

"Babe, how are you?" John spoke as if they were old friends. They weren't that close – in fact she could count on one hand the number of times she had met the guy. "Sorry Dan's in a meeting at the moment, I'll get him to phone you back?"

She cleared her throat. "Um, I'd like to talk to you, actually, if you have a minute."

"Oh. Fire away."

She could almost picture his bemused expression and decided to get right to the point. "You knew Dan's ex-wife, didn't you?"

"Nicola? Of course. I hear she's living down the sticks these days. Why are you asking me?"

Chloe's stomach tightened. Dan must have told John

that Nicola was back from London. She began to feel even more uneasy.

"I just wondered what she was like, that's all." She tried to sound offhand but despite herself her hands shook a little. "I mean, of course Dan told me a watered-down version of it, but I'm kinda curious about the reason they split up."

"Getting cold feet eh?" He guffawed. "Not to worry pet, that's perfectly normal. And if you ask me *that* marriage was doomed from the very beginning," John said in a tone that suggested he wasn't all that enamoured of Nicola. "They were having problems since day one, considering the parents weren't mad on her, as I'm sure Dan told you."

"Um, yes." Chloe couldn't admit that she hadn't a clue. Dan was right about John enjoying idle gossip. Better to let him warm to his subject. So Dan's folks didn't care for Nicola?

"Of course, I felt bad for her and all the rest of it, but ... to be honest, we didn't exactly gel from the get-go."

"Oh?" She was surprised by the admission. The guy loved to give the impression that he was everyone's best friend, a 'sound man'.

"Yeah. She and Carolyn got on well, but at the beginning when we set up the partnership, she got this notion that Dan was the one doing all the work." Chloe sensed him shrug. "Wasn't my fault that her husband stayed working late. Maybe if he had someone a bit more relaxing to go home to he wouldn't need to," he added bitterly. "It's a pity, I suppose, and they were a great couple, but you need a very strong marriage to survive these things."

What things?

"John –"

"Want to see how you measure up, eh? Well, I can tell you that Nicola was a looker in her day but now ... well, god love her I don't think there's any comparison."

"Thanks, John." Chloe was gratified by this much at least. She knew what Nicola was like these days of course, but she idly wondered whether Dan had any old photographs of her stashed away. "It's just he doesn't talk about all that very much, and I wondered what she was like."

"Ah, you've nothing to worry about, babe," John said condescendingly. "Dan's well over her by now."

Over her? Chloe didn't like the sound of that. Plus it could only mean one thing, that Nicola was the one who'd ended the marriage.

Was Dan over her?

Or had her reappearance sparked something in her fiancé other than guilt? She thought about how distracted and impatient he had been over the last while.

Was Chloe a fool after all to suggest that he contact his ex?

"Listen, I really should go, I have a three o'clock I need to prepare for and –"

"OK, thanks John – listen, you won't mention this to Dan, maybe?"

He laughed. "Are you mad? He's still so touchy about all that, I wouldn't dare risk it."

Chloe hung up, her unease multiplying with each

passing minute. This hadn't exactly assuaged her curiosity; if anything, it had made it worse.

The wedding was only weeks away, and she was damned if she was going to let Dan's ex get in the way of her Big Day.

She still didn't understand the reason for the break-up, but now, Chloe was determined to find out.

TWENTY-TWO

HELEN STOOD ALMOST TRANSFIXED outside Brown Thomas.

That dress. Well, if you could call it a dress, she thought. It was Issey Miyake, daringly short – black and silver-embroidered at the bust. Demure, but very sexy and would look just amazing with her newly bought, silver strappy heels.

Not quite right for a wedding, but Paul would absolutely love her in it and probably she thought with a grin, love her even more *out* of it.

Lately, she couldn't keep the smile from her face. They'd met a number of times since that glorious afternoon and the sex was becoming more intense each time.

It was crazy, they hardly knew one another, and yet it was as though they were in perfect sexual synch. Twice they had planned to meet for lunch, and twice they had ended up at his place, unable to even *think* about food.

And earlier he had rung Helen at work and asked her

to meet him for 'lunch' tomorrow. She didn't know why he even bothered pretending.

"Afterwards, we could try your place for a change of scenery," he had said, in a tone that had her already shifting in her seat.

But Helen wasn't prepared to bring him to hers yet. She needed to see whether she and Paul were as well matched personally as they were physically.

Not to mention the tricky subject of Kerry.

She gave a quick glance at her watch. Six twenty. It was late-night shopping and Jo had agreed to keep Kerry until seven, to give her a chance to pick up something for Laura's wedding.

She'd go in, try on the dress and maybe have a quick run-around. She'd be a little late collecting her daughter, but Helen *had* to have that dress. Yes, it was expensive, but sometimes a girl just had to treat herself, didn't she?

By the time she left the store, she had picked up a cute handbag, another pair of Jimmy Choos (but these would go with just *everything*), and possibly the entire Agent Provocatuer Spring/Summer Collection.

And because she would now almost certainly be late collecting Kerry, she had raced downstairs to the make-up department, and chosen a little bottle of perfume for Jo.

There was something terribly indulgent about buying anything Gucci, she thought, handing over her credit card and idly wondering if maybe she should get a bottle for herself while she was at it. No, she decided firmly, enough was enough. Although she could do with some new make-up and Ruby & Millie did some amazing lipsticks ...

When Helen reached Jo's house, it was after eight.

"I'm so sorry," she started with the explanations as soon as she got out of the car. The front door was open and as she approached, Helen knew by Jo's expression that the childminder was pissed off. "The traffic was crazy and – "

"Helen...." she interjected angrily. "I told you that Pete and I were going out for our anniversary dinner tonight. The only reason I agreed to keep Kerry late was because you swore you'd be back by seven *and* you told me you were desperate."

Helen stopped short. She had never even heard Jo raise her voice, let alone bite her head off.

"Sorry," she began, "it's not as though I was late on purpose. The traffic was mental and there was no way I could have got here by seven." She looked behind Jo in the hallway. Where was Kerry? At this stage, she just wanted to just grab her daughter and run. "Oh, and I got you a present," she added, quickly holding out the tiny Brown Thomas bag.

"Really?" Jo drawled, completely ignoring Helen's peace offering. "The traffic was mental, was it? So how come my husband who works on the Northside left the office at *six,* and was home ages ago?"

Helen cringed inwardly. Damn – she'd forgotten all about Pete.

"I promise I'll make it up to you, OK?" she began quietly. Maybe honesty was the best policy here. "I was right in the centre of town and it was very busy, and I just didn't notice the time going and – "

Jo's eyes narrowed. "*You didn't notice the time going.* In other words, you just didn't bother your backside until you were good and ready."

"No, no, that's not it at all."

"It *is* it, Helen. It's *always* it with you. Honestly, only for the fact I adore that little girl, I would have told you exactly where to go a long time ago."

"Jo, I'm barely half an hour late – "

"Try an *hour* and a half, but that's not the point, is it? You're *always* late, Helen! You're *never* here at five, and then you flounce in, all excuses but no apology. Then in the mornings you call too early. Crikey, Helen, if you're not interrupting our dinner then you're interrupting our breakfast by dropping her off at all hours. But then again, we're lucky if you remember to collect her at all!"

Helen reddened. Jo was referring to that first afternoon she had met Paul.

She had been so dazed and euphoric after, that she had driven straight home in another world, forgetting to pick up Kerry. And of course at the time, Helen had to open her big mouth and jokingly admit to an unimpressed Jo that she *had* forgotten.

"That was one time and – "

"But it *shouldn't* happen at all," Jo lowered her voice, and glanced behind her in the hallway. "I asked Pete to keep Kerry occupied, because I didn't want her to hear any of this when and *if,* you arrived. She's upset enough as it is."

"Jo, that's not fair."

"Helen, of *course* it's not fair. It's not fair to that poor little sweetheart in there who absolutely adores you. Do you realise Kerry spends most of the day telling us, in her own sweet way, what Mummy does and what Mummy says. But we can see the worry in her eyes when five o'clock comes around and Mummy's not here yet. Your daughter is as good as gold, and she worships you, but you don't realise it. You don't realise what a blessing that child is and how any mother would be so proud to have her as their own."

There were tears in Jo's eyes, and Helen knew that she was getting maudlin over the child she herself had miscarried last year.

"I'm very sorry that you feel that way, Jo. However, you seem to have conveniently forgotten that I *pay* you for looking after my daughter – you're not doing me any favours. And I'm not stingy with Christmas presents or anything else. That is Gucci perfume." Helen crossed her arms across her chest. "Funnily enough, I thought you and I were friends. How was I supposed to know you were so resentful about minding her? You never said so."

"For goodness sake, Helen –"

She put up a hand to silence her. "We might as well have it out once and for all. As Kerry seems such a trial, then you won't mind my taking her off your hands altogether." That'd soften her cough for her, Helen thought, knowing that Jo and Pete weren't exactly rolling in it. They relied on her childminding to make ends meet.

"Fine. Because that's exactly what I came out here to tell you. I don't want to take Kerry anymore, and heaven knows it has nothing to do with the child. It's you, Helen.

It breaks my heart to see her struggling with her speech like she does, and I know damn well that your attitude isn't helping."

"How dare you? What the hell do you know about raising a child?" she said nastily. Jo winced, but Helen didn't back down. "Sitting on your backside every day watching the telly while your husband goes out to earn a crust. You know nothing about having to work long hours and your fingers to the bone."

Jo gave her a sceptical look. "Helen, you have a professional manicure twice a month, so fearful are you of messing up your nails. So don't play the martyr with me." She turned back inside. "I'm going to say goodbye to Kerry now, and it breaks my heart. If it were up to me, I'd probably put up with your carry-on just for the pleasure of spending time with that wonderful little girl. But Pete has put his foot down."

Helen was apoplectic. "I'd never have left either of you *near* her in the first place had I known you felt that way about me."

A grim-looking Pete appeared in the doorway. "I'd appreciate it if you didn't carry on like a fishwife on my doorstep."

"Oh, well, *excuse* me!" she stormed. "I'll wait in the car, and maybe when you and Mrs Sanctimonious are finished 'saying your goodbyes' you can send my daughter out."

Pete shook his head. "You know, I feel sorry for you," he called after her.

"Excuse me?"

"I feel sorry that you don't appreciate what a wonderful gift she is."

Helen rolled her eyes. "Spare me the sentimental shite," she said, getting into the front seat and slamming the driver door.

A few minutes later, a tearful Kerry joined her in the car. "J-J-J-Jo don't w-w-want to m-m-mind me anymore, Mommy," she said, her bottom lip curling.

Helen started the engine. "No, *Mommy* doesn't want Jo to mind you anymore, pet."

"Then w-w-who –" Kerry tried to take a breath, but was so upset she couldn't get the remainder of the sentence out.

But Helen knew exactly what she was trying to say.

"I don't know who'll mind you from now on, love," she answered grimly, thinking of her upcoming lunch with Paul, "but we'll have to find someone."

TWENTY-THREE

LAURA SOLDERED the last freshwater pearl onto a thin strand of wire. Then holding it carefully with a tweezers, she lifted one of the silver coated leaves she had painstakingly fashioned the week before, and positioned it at the base of what now was beginning to look like a tiara.

It was so delicate; she knew it wouldn't tolerate any abuse. She'd have to make sure the hairdresser was gentle with it on the day of the wedding.

Next, she would begin work on her own and the bridesmaid's neckpieces, as well as a smaller replica of her own tiara for Kerry. It was just as well that she had all this to do, she thought with a sigh, because there was precious little else.

Laura Connolly Jewellery Design hadn't taken off with quite the fanfare she'd hoped. Not that she *really* imagined everything would just fall into place, and that people would be clambering over themselves for her designs. It was just that she thought there might have been *some* interest.

She had invested a lot of time and money in the sample packs she sent to the jeweller's and gift stores, and had followed some of them up with timid phone calls, enquiring as to whether or not they were interested in stocking her. But the response so far had been dismal.

In fairness, Neil was great at keeping her spirits up.

"Now is the time to concentrate on fine-tuning your range, and getting stock built up to sell directly to suppliers. Who knows, when you *are* busy, you mightn't have any time to spend on actually making stuff."

In fairness, it wasn't all doom and gloom. The Crafts Council had promised to circulate her name throughout the trade, and of course there was always the Crafts Expo.

With renewed vigour, Laura set about finishing her wedding tiara and making a start on the jewellery for her bridesmaids.

She was so engrossed in her work that she almost didn't hear the phone ringing.

"Laura, where were you, I almost hung up." Helen sounded frantic.

"In the workshop – why, what's wrong?"

"I need to ask you a *huge* favour."

"Sure, what?"

"Is there any chance you can collect Kerry from play school today? She finishes at two. I'm really sorry to ring you like this, but I have meetings all afternoon. Please? You'd be doing me a massive favour."

Laura wouldn't dream of leaving Kerry stranded. She

wondered idly why Jo wasn't doing it though. Helen's childminder was normally so reliable.

"Laura?" Helen was waiting for her reply.

"Sorry, yes, yes, of course I'll do it – no problem."

"I owe you one, Laura, I really do. I'd go myself only – only we're hoping to nail down a big account here, and I really need the commission."

"Right. And do you want me to drop her over to the office to you or ...?"

There was a sharp intake of breath. "Is there any chance you could hold onto her? I'll call and collect her from your place after."

"Sure. See you later then. Good luck with the meetings."

"Yeah, thanks."

Laura hung up and went back into her workshop. Wasn't it really lucky that she worked for herself now and was able to get away when she felt like it?

Otherwise poor Helen would be really stuck.

Later that afternoon, just as Laura reached Kerry's play school, her business line began to ring.

After six rings the answering machine came on, and her voice filled the empty workshop.

"Hello, thank you for calling Laura Connolly Jewellery Design. We are unavailable to take your call just at the moment, but please leave your name and number, and we will call you back as soon as possible."

A short throat-clear after the beep. "Hello? Sorry, I'm on a mobile and it's a bad line. I saw your stuff online and

. . . ink it's great! My name is Ge ... lden and I wanted to speak to someone ... out the possibility of having an engagement ring commissioned. I was hoping for something really unusual. Something ... pecial and money's ... object. I'm planning to propose soon, so I'd really like to ... someone as soon as possible. My number is 086-2 ... 26 ... 68 ... Look forward to hearing from you!"

TWENTY-FOUR

AS SHE SAT in a quiet pub on the seafront, Nicola was staring out the window at a young couple pushing a buggy along the pier.

It was a spectacular summer afternoon. Seagulls soared above the water, occasionally dipping down towards the waves, and further out a flotilla of yachts passed slowly along the coast, obviously making the most of the settled weather.

It had been a long time since she'd been here.

When they lived in the area, she and Dan had spent many a Sunday afternoon walking lazily along the promenade with all the day-trippers, skateboarders and dogwalkers. He could never resist stopping off at a kiosk to buy one of those whipped ice-cream cones. And according to him, it was no good at all unless it was slathered in raspberry sauce.

"Hey." He appeared at her table as if from nowhere.

She felt her stomach spasm as she looked up into his face for the first time in over four years. He had aged.

His hair was cut in a short crop which emphasised his lined forehead, and he looked as though he could do with losing a few pounds. But he was still the same old Dan.

He was smiling, but looked uncertain. "I was almost afraid to disturb you. You looked like you were miles away."

She gestured to the seat across from her. "Can I get you a coffee or something?" It sounded strange, like she didn't recognise her own voice.

"One on the way – thanks." He pulled a chair forward, and rested an arm on the table. "Thanks for agreeing to meet me, Nic. You look ... terrific. How have you been?"

She wished he wouldn't call her 'Nic'. It was way too familiar.

"I'm very well thanks – you?"

"Not too bad."

He cleared his throat, and she sensed that he was struggling to say more, to move the conversation forward, yet didn't quite know how.

There was a long tension-filled pause.

"So how did things go in London?" he asked eventually.

Nicola studied the bubbles on her cappuccino. "Not too bad. I'm still the same old me." She forced a smile. "I'm sorry, I suppose I should have told you I was back."

"It's fine. No more than I deserved." He gave her a sad look. "It was a shock getting those divorce papers out of the blue like that though."

"There was nothing else I could have done." Her

mouth tightened. "I didn't want to see, or even speak to you back then."

"I know." Another pause. "Did you get ... I mean did your aunt pass on my letter?"

Of course she had passed it on. Nicola could still recite every word, every sentence.

"Yes she did, thank you." Then she smiled. "Look, let's not talk about old times, Dan." While she still felt unsure why she'd come, she was certain she didn't want to rake up the past. What was the point?

All that time in London, she had thought about him, wondered how it would feel, how *she* would feel when she saw him again.

But in truth, now Nicola felt nothing other than ... nostalgia. It was liberating.

He gave a rueful smile. "Fair enough. So how long have you been back?"

"A year or so. Ken asked me to manage his new place."

"Really – and how *is* good old Ken these days?" His voice was hard.

Nicola put down her cup, and reached for her handbag. "This was a mistake."

His face fell. "Hey, I'm sorry, I couldn't help it. I know I have no right to – "

"I didn't agree to see you so that we could take up where we left off. If we're trying to be someway civil it would be better if we didn't drag up the past – *any* of it."

"I'm sorry," he repeated. "It just popped out."

She nodded and tried to relax a little. She didn't want this meeting to blow up into a big waste of time. It had taken a lot to come here and she had felt guilty enough about it in the first place.

She'd told Ken about Dan's call and he hadn't been as understanding as she'd hoped.

"What the hell does *he* want?" he'd snarled.

"To talk, I suppose."

"But why now?"

"What do you mean?"

"Well, why didn't he want to *talk* in the first place? Why didn't he want to *talk* before you two separated? But no, he couldn't do that, could he? He had to wait until you were back on your feet and enjoying life again, before bursting back onto the scene."

"That isn't it." Nicola was taken aback. He'd never thought much of Dan but she hadn't expected him to be so bitter. "He's not 'back on the scene' as you put it. He's actually getting married again."

"Oh? And who's the next poor misfortunate?"

"Ken."

"What? What do you expect me to say – that I hope the asshole has a nice life?"

"What's really going on here? Why are you so annoyed?"

"I'm annoyed because it took you long enough to get over the bastard and now you seem quite happy to invite him back into your life without a second thought."

"Without a second thought? Of course I've thought about it. I've done nothing but think about it since ..." she trailed off, realising she had revealed more than intended.

Ken immediately picked up on this. "Since what?"

She sighed. "I knew Dan was getting married again before he told me himself." She explained about the mix-up with the wedding invites.

"So he probably had no intention of telling you at all, and yet he snaps his fingers and you come running?"

"Hey I'm not running anywhere," she retorted, eyes flashing.

His jaw worked. "I just don't understand why you feel the need to meet with him. Surely a phone call is enough."

"It's not that I need to – I *want* to."

He looked at her. "Why? Do you still have feelings for him? Because if you do, then you really need to think hard about what you're doing with *me*. I love you and I know how hard things were back then. I don't want you to have to go through it all again."

"I know that. But this isn't going to affect what you and I have now. He's moved on, and I've moved on too. That's all there is to it."

Ken gave her a watery smile, but she knew he was still unsure – and definitely unhappy – about this meeting.

Now she looked across at Dan. "I suppose I might as well tell you – Ken and I are together now."

"Together – as in *together*?"

"You look surprised." No, Nicola thought, he looked *shocked*.

"Not as such. I mean, I just didn't expect that you – "

"That I would find someone else? Why not?" She chuckled inwardly at his discomfort.

"No, it's not that. I mean ... of course I knew you'd

find someone else," he said, flustered. "I just didn't expect it to be bloody Harris, that's all."

That had certainly pulled the rug out from under him.

"So what about you?" she asked, changing the subject. "How are the wedding plans coming along?"

He shot her a wary look, as if he hadn't expected her to be so casual. "Ah, it's all busy, busy, busy. A bit too much fuss for my liking, to be honest."

"Is she much younger – your fiancée?"

"Chloe? Not too much – almost thirty."

"Chloe – nice name."

"Yes."

"So how long have you two been ...?"

"Together? Not that long," Dan said quickly.

"Oh, a short engagement then."

"Yes, Chloe was keen to tie the knot." He shrugged and trailed off as a waiter approached with his coffee and they were both silent until he had retreated.

Dan breathed out. "Nic, I just want to say how sorry I am that you found out second-hand. I would have told you myself, but I had no idea you were back."

"It was partly my own fault for recommending the stationery place to Laura in the first place. Though I couldn't have known... " Her voice trailed off and she changed the subject. "Anyway, how are things with you now? The practice going well? How is John these days – and Carolyn?"

"John's fine, but he and Carolyn are separated now."

"Oh." Nicola was surprised. She had sensed that

Carolyn was a little distant with her that time in town with Laura. Now she knew why.

"I thought they'd make it but you just never know, do you?"

She could feel the weight of his gaze on her face.

"No, you never know." She looked out towards the water.

There was yet another short strained silence.

"And what about Laura and Neil?" he asked smiling. "Finally."

"Yes."

"I'm pleased for them."

"Well, she deserves it and Neil is a good guy."

"Unlike some we could mention?"

She giggled, knowing exactly what he meant. Before she and Dan were married, and long before her friend had even met Neil, Laura had been going out with a pompous know-it-all called James whom they all hated.

Dan had managed to get on with him for appearances' sake, but Nicola and indeed Helen, had disliked him passionately.

"You and Helen gave that guy such a hard time," Dan said with a groan. "Remember the time we went to that restaurant, that Thai one –"

She chuckled. "And yer man rambling on and on about the menu, pretending to be some kind of connoisseur because he had a flight stopover in Bangkok once."

Dan guffawed at the memory too. "And then he got in a big sulk with Jamie for snickering. How is Jamie? Ah, he was a gas man altogether. I haven't seen him in yonks."

"Neither has Helen, sadly."

"What? What happened? I thought those two were together for life."

"A lot's changed since. Helen has a daughter now, Kerry – she's a beautiful little thing, the spit of her mother."

"She met someone else?"

Nicola made a face. Trust Dan to assume that *Helen* was the problematic one.

"No, Kerry is Jamie's. But the pregnancy was unplanned and they went through a tough time. Jamie took off to South Africa after deciding he wasn't able to face up to his responsibilities. He left her on her own, apparently not caring whether she sank or swam."

"Well," Dan said pausing carefully, "maybe he was just overwhelmed and wasn't quite sure what was best."

"And what about her? She didn't have much of a choice, did she? What was *she* supposed to do?"

"Give him some time to get to grips with it, maybe?"

He looked her straight in the eye then, and they both knew that neither was talking about Jamie.

She looked away, and said nothing.

The two eventually talked some more about mutual friends, carefully skirting around their own situation, before eventually they ran out of inconsequential subject matter.

"So tell me more about Chloe." Nicola was pleased she could speak about the other woman so easily.

He looked unsure. "Chloe? Well, she works as a legal secretary at her dad's firm."

"Her dad's a solicitor?"

"Yes."

"Oh, your mother must be pleased then." Nicola couldn't keep the bitterness out of her voice.

"Actually, she doesn't know her all that well."

"I see." She waited for Dan to elaborate on this but he didn't. Instead he reached into his pocket and from his wallet produced a photograph of a stunning blonde.

Wow. Nicola studied the picture for a long moment.

"She's gorgeous."

Dan laughed. "And doesn't she just know it."

Was she nuts? Here she was sitting with Dan joking with him about his new wife-to-be. Was that progress, or just downright stupidity?

Just then, his mobile shrilled.

"Hello?" He looked at Nicola, and when he heard the voice on the other end his expression became guarded and his eyes lowered. "Hi."

Discerning it was Chloe, she looked away. *Speak of the devil...*

"No, I wasn't at the office. I'm ... meeting a client."

She marvelled at easily he could lie – still.

"No, hold on, Chlo ... just slow down a minute ... I don't understand ... what kind of problem?" From what Nicola could make out, the other woman seemed frantic.

"*What?*" Now Dan was agitated. "You've got to be kidding me. OK, OK ... just give me a half an hour or so and I'll meet you there." He hung up and then looked at her, his expression weary. "I'm so sorry about this, Nic, but I really have to go."

"Trouble in paradise?"

He rolled his eyes.

"Oh dear."

"I'm sorry to rush off – "

"Not a problem." Nicola put her empty mug on the table. "Dan, it was nice seeing you again."

He hesitated for a second, then looked directly at her. "Nic, I really am sorry." The way he said it, she knew he wasn't just talking about having to leave.

She managed a tiny smile. "We'll talk again sometime."

"It was really good seeing you again."

"You too," Nicola said quietly, as she watched the man who had once been the love of her life rush away to meet another woman.

TWENTY-FIVE

NICOLA HAD SUSPECTED from the very beginning that Shannon Fogarty had set her sights on her husband.

The other woman and Dan had worked at the same accountancy practice well before Nicola came on the scene, or before Dan and John went into partnership.

The trio were close friends at the time and Shannon made no secret of her dislike of Dan's new girlfriend.

He had invited her to a company dinner and John's wife had tipped her off about Shannon beforehand. Nicola had always liked Carolyn, and the two women clicked immediately upon their first meeting. She was chatty, bubbly and well able to handle John.

"Pure wagon," she said referring to Shannon. "Very possessive of her 'boys'. The first time I met her I didn't know what I had done to offend."

Nicola grimaced. "Great. We've only being going out a few weeks, I don't know half the people there and already one of them hates me."

"Ah, something tells me you'll be more than a match

for our Ms Fogarty. And I for one can't wait for the sparks to fly."

By the time they reached the restaurant, Nicola and Carolyn were a little on the late side. John was already seated, but the chair beside him was empty so Nicola deduced that Dan must be either at the bar, or in the bathroom.

"Hey everyone," Carolyn beamed. "Nice to see you all again. This is Nicola – the main reason Dan's been going around with that big fat grin on his face lately."

She knew instantly that the tall, redhead looking daggers at them was the famous Shannon. Talk about winding the woman up.

While Dan's colleagues she didn't already know shook hands and introduced themselves, Shannon sat button-lipped and completely ignored her.

"Hey, all," Dan appeared at the table and put a protective hand on Nicola's back. "Sorry ... I was caught talking ..." Then he stood back. "Wow, you look amazing."

She was wearing a white silk dress with tiny gold butterflies running diagonally across the bias-cut skirt. The neckline plunged to a sharp 'v' emphasising her deep cleavage and the white looked stunning against her colouring.

"I know, I'd kill for a figure like that."Carolyn, who was the epitome of glamour and also dressed to the nines, gave her an almost imperceptible wink.

Shannon peered across the table. "I must be mixing you up with someone else. You're not the ... aerobics girl, are you?"

Nicola clicked her tongue. "Not exactly. I'm a fitness instructor - we do a lot more than just aerobics."

"Oh?" You just seem *very* different from Dan's usual type."

Not long after, she and Dan flew to Vegas for a spur of the moment wedding (much to his parents' disapproval) and by the time they'd moved to their new place in Bray, she'd almost forgotten about Shannon. Dan and John had been making plans to set up a partnership and go out on their own.

But a couple of months in, the other woman began phoning the apartment at all hours, whining and crying over guys, wanting Dan to comfort her.

"She's getting desperate," Carolyn said, when Nicola mentioned it. "She knows that he's leaving the firm, and pulling out all the stops."

"But he's also married. Shouldn't *that* scupper her?"

She held her counsel for as long as she could until one evening Shannon appeared at her front door looking for her husband.

"He's still at work," Nicola said from the doorway.

The younger woman looked pointedly at her watch, feigning surprise. "You mean he's not here?" He left the office early this afternoon. I wonder what he's up to?"

Still she refused to rise to the bait. And all too soon she and Dan had a different kind of distraction.

Nicola still remembered his nervousness while waiting for the little line to change colour.

"I feel like Homer Simpson," he'd said. "Purple means 'doh!', red means 'wohoo!'."

She was so fraught with anticipation that she was

unable to answer. When finally that line began to change colour, and continued to darken, Dan picked her up and spun her around the room.

"Wohoo! Woohoo!"

She was laughing through her tears as he laid her on the bed and they made love, exhilarated by the fact that an extra link was soon to be added to their bond.

Nicola couldn't remember ever feeling so elated. Just when she thought things couldn't get any better, she was about to become a mother.

She tried to get her head around it, tried to abandon herself to the pure unadulterated elation she felt; yet deep down inside she couldn't help feeling afraid.

Afraid that all of this might soon come crashing down on top of her.

What had she done to deserve such happiness?

TWENTY-SIX

KEN WHO HAD a key to Nicola's house, was waiting for her when she returned that evening.

As she pulled into the driveway, she saw him and Barney standing together in the doorway – the Labrador's tail wagging so hard she thought there was a danger it might fall off.

"Well, how did it go?" he asked when they were inside, his expression completely unreadable.

Nicola grimaced and rubbed the dog's glossy coat. "The only word I can think of at the moment is – strange."

"Strange?"

"Yes. I don't know what I'd expected exactly, but he's still the same old Dan."

"But how did it *go*?" he repeated. "I mean, what did you two talk about?"

Nicola sat back in her chair. "Seeing him face to face after all this time felt odd obviously, and it was tense at the beginning. Still after a while, I think we both began to relax. I'd imagine it was weird for him too."

Ken's facial muscles twitched slightly, but he said nothing.

"But it wasn't that big of a deal. I mean, what could we say to one another? So much time's passed and – "

"Surely he must have at least asked how you were? Didn't he say *anything*?"

She grimaced. "Well, we didn't get much of a chance to talk, actually. The ice had been broken, we were laughing over something stupid and then, the fiancée rang."

"Oh. And did she know he was meeting you?"

"I don't think so – he rushed off shortly afterwards. But he showed me a photograph of her."

"He *what*?"

She grinned. "Yep, blonde, petite, gorgeous - your typical trade-in model."

"I can't believe he actually showed you a picture of his new fiancée." Ken gave her a sideways glance. "And ... did that bother you?"

"No, it didn't actually." There was a slight pause and then she smiled. "I'm really glad you're here."

He finally sat down beside her. "I wasn't sure whether or not you wanted me here, considering. And I didn't know if you wanted some time alone after –"

"Of course I want you here." Nicola looked at him. "Like I told you before, my seeing Dan was never going to change anything." She sat forward. "Actually, I think today brought it all home to me."

"What do you mean?"

Her eyes were shining. "You might think this is silly – but when I pulled up in the car just now and saw you and Barney together in the doorway, I felt like ... I don't know ... like I'd come home, or something."

Ken was smiling. "Are you *sure* you're all right? Nothing happened to you on the way back – like a blow to the head, or anything?"

"Ha! Here I am, trying to be nice to you ..."

"No, seriously, go on."

"Well, on my way here, I couldn't help going back over it all, and I came to the conclusion ..." she paused, and blushed a little, "Or should I say I suppose I've always known that if it had been *you* – if you had been my husband back then, things would have turned out differently." She felt him squeeze her hand. "And then turning into the driveway tonight and seeing you two standing together like that, I felt a kind of –" she searched for the right word, "clarity, I suppose. Like this was exactly where I belonged – with you."

"So, that's it then?" he asked softly. "There's nothing left between you now – no unfinished business?"

Nicola reached for his hand. "That's it," she said decisively.

TWENTY-SEVEN

WAS THERE ANYTHING MORE MORTIFYING than having to postpone your own wedding? Chloe didn't think so.

It had been so *embarrassing* having to ring everyone on the guest list, explaining that the wedding was off until next year. She could almost sense the sniggers behind the masked sympathy.

She'd *never* get over this.

With barely a month to go until the big day, Chloe had called the hotel to confirm the arrangements for September 25th.

She should have guessed that something was wrong when the receptionist sounded confused and then nervous, quickly promising that she would 'check the arrangements and have someone phone back'.

Minutes later, the hotel manager phoned and in smooth tones informed Chloe that yes indeed there *was* a wedding booked for September 25th – in another name.

"I've examined our records and it appears that the Fallon/Hunt wedding is scheduled for September 25th *next* year." He spoke slowly, as if Chloe was some kind of simpleton.

"No, no, that must be a mistake," she argued, her heart racing madly. "Our date was confirmed ages ago. I signed the forms myself."

There was a slight shuffle at the other end. "I'm sorry, Ms Fallon, but this is the information I have. As I said, we already have another wedding for September 25th this year."

"Well, we'll see about that," she said resolutely, before hanging up.

That evening, after finally managing to trace Dan, the two of them called to the hotel to personally examine the booking form. To Chloe's absolute horror, she discovered that next year's date had indeed been inputted – and she had signed it.

"I don't believe it," she said tearfully, putting a hand to her mouth. "How could I not have noticed the error? When I phoned initially, enquiring about 25th September, they told me it was free."

Then she recalled a recent conversation with the hotel about the flowers. There had been some confusion as to whether the 25th was Thursday, or Friday. She also remembered that the receptionist sounded a little bit strange on the phone. Probably wondering why anyone would be making arrangements for flowers a whole year in advance, Chloe thought glumly.

Damn... She should have realised then that something was up. Now some other couple would be celebrating their big day there on *her* day.

"Isn't there anything you can do?" Dan urged, frowning. "Maybe accomodate us in a conference room, or something?"

Chloe cut in before the manager could answer. "I'm not holding my wedding reception – the most important day of my life – in some dingy conference room, Dan. No way. We'll have the banquet hall or nothing. That's the reason I chose this bloody hotel in the first place."

The hotel manager intervened. "Unfortunately all our facilities are fully booked in any case. If you'd like to wait until next year– "

"We *can't!*" Chloe said, gritting her teeth. "Everything's arranged, the flowers, the cake, the invites ..." At this, she broke off, remembering the day she went to choose those blasted invites – the same day she broke that car wing-mirror on the street.

That was it ... she decided. All of this was her punishment – her seven years' bad luck. First the mix-up with the invites, then the reappearance of Dan's ex – and now *this*!

"Maybe we could try elsewhere –"

"But where?" She *couldn't* give up on this hotel, not when it was to be the piece de résistance. She wasn't going to end up in some kip on her wedding day. No bloody way.

The hotel manager cleared his throat. "I'm sorry, but we're completely booked up til the end of January next year."

Chloe's mind began to race. *A winter wedding ...*

OK, she might have to rethink the dress, and instead of a veil possibly go for one of those Snow Queen cape-type things, but that wouldn't be a problem. The flower arrangements would have to change of course; orchids would die a quick death in January, but just imagine a wintery bouquet with berries, ivy and frosted apples ...

"January would be perfect," she trilled.

"Chloe, hold on a second." Dan pulled her to one side, out of the manager's earshot. "We should discuss this."

"What's to discuss?"

She was having visions of a snow-decked church as background to her wedding photos. And if there was no snow, Chloe was sure they could organise some fake stuff for the photographs.

Oh, it would be gorgeous.

And much more unique than any old run-of-the-mill, summer wedding. OK, it was disappointing to have wait that bit longer, but at least she wouldn't have to spend her wedding night in some grotty hotel elsewhere.

Now Chloe looked over at Dan, who was busily engrossed in his newspaper. Even though he was as disappointed as she had been with the delay, she still got the feeling that his mind was continually elsewhere.

"Dan?"

"Hmm?" he answered idly.

"Remember you were thinking about getting in touch with your ex..."

He stiffened, and instantly she knew that he had already done so. Why hadn't he said anything?

"I spoke to her," he said. "She's fine about it."

Chloe was miffed. Well, why *shouldn't* she be fine about it?

"Did her friend – you know, the one with our invites, did she tell her about us?"

He nodded. "Yep, but she wished us well. I showed her a photograph of you and she thought you looked gorg – "

"*What*?" Chloe interjected, before he could finish the sentence. "You mean you met with her – face to face?"

Dan reddened, and she knew that he had let that last bit slip. He hadn't planned on telling her about his little rendezvous with the ex at all. Instantly, she felt her hackles rise.

"Yes, I was going to tell you – "

"Well, why didn't you then?"

"Because I knew you'd react like this – that's why." His eyes flashed with annoyance.

"Yes, but you said you'd *phone* her. You certainly didn't tell me you'd be having a cosy meet-up."

"Chloe, can you please just give it a rest – *for once*." Dan stood up, infuriated.

"For once? What the hell is that supposed to mean? Anyway, what do you expect me to think?"

"There's nothing *to* think. All I was trying to do give was treat my wife – my ex-wife – with the respect she deserves."

"What's that supposed to ... where are you going?" Her tone dropped a level, seeing him head for the door.

"Out," he said. "Where I don't have to listen to *this*."

With that, he grabbed his jacket, walked out the door and slammed it loudly behind him.

Chloe stared after him, her thoughts running a race alongside her heartbeat. She sank down in her seat, and with more than a little trepidation, recalled Dan's words.

The respect she deserves...

What the hell did *that* mean?

TWENTY-EIGHT

DAN DROVE FURIOUSLY DOWN the dual carriageway.

Damn. Why had he let that slip? Chloe would never shut up about it now and bloody hell she was a nightmare once she had something to complain about.

So unlike Nicola really, he thought, turning onto the coast road. In fact, the two of them couldn't have been more different. Nic had always been pragmatic and level-headed (most of the time), whereas Chloe would fly off the handle at nothing.

Not that Nicola would hide from confrontation, he thought with a wry smile. Quite the opposite.

But his ex didn't get her knickers in a twist over things like ... well, like the *colour* of her knickers, and whether or not you could see it through her trousers, or if it went with this dress, or those boots or....

Dan found himself tuning out during Chloe rants about her clothes, her shoes, and lately, about this bloody wedding.

He was sorry in a way that it had had to be delayed, because now he'd have to put up with even more planning – not just the Perfect Wedding – but the Perfect *Winter* Wedding.

She was already talking about dressing the men up in some kind of Russian-themed get-up, complete with furry hats and high leather boots. His father would certainly love that.

He knew that most women went a little bit batty over their Big Day, but was only realising now how lucky he had been the first time round. Wedding trivia had never bothered Nicola, and she was delighted with their cosy, intimate affair in Vegas.

He stopped in the carpark overlooking Sandymount Strand.

Despite himself, he was thinking about Nicola a lot these days. He was getting married in a few months, for goodness sake. But yet since meeting her face to face, he just couldn't stop thinking about her.

She had been so calm and so *together*. He had expected the worst – anger, admonishment, bitterness – *something*. But she seemed fine; she seemed strong, calm and ... happy.

She looked beautiful too, he thought wistfully. No amount of physical change could dampen that spirited, determined glint in her eye, the very thing that had attracted him to her in the first place.

Yes, she had always been the strong, forceful one in their marriage, always able to handle anything that was thrown at her, never letting anything faze her.

Dan looked out to sea.

Except for that one time.

They were almost a year married.

Nicola was struggling, and he didn't know how to help her. It was like as if he didn't know who she was anymore. What had happened to his wonderful, sunny, carefree wife?

Well, of course he knew what had happened. It had been a tragedy and a disappointment for them both. But however much they wanted that baby, and however much it hurt, there was absolutely nothing they could do to bring it back.

There was no reason, no explanation, it just happened.

"Time will heal," they all said, doctors, nurses, Laura, her mother.

So each day Dan would come home from work, hoping for some improvement, some tiny glimpse of the old Nicola but she'd still be sitting listlessly in front of the TV.

Dan knew she was grieving but he also thought she blamed him. He should have looked after her better, or should have at least realised that something was wrong.

Eventually as the days went by, she seemed to at least come out from under her blanket of fog, went back to work and about her day to day business just as before.

Except she wasn't the same Nicola. She was this faraway, preoccupied Nicola, and Dan didn't recognise her anymore. He couldn't remember the last time they had had a conversation that lasted longer than two sentences, and it was never about anything other than trivialities. She got on with her life as though he didn't exist.

It hurt. Desperately. He was losing her, and he didn't know how to prevent it. After a while, it became almost impossible to stay in the same room with her grief and unable to share, talk, or laugh like they once did.

So Dan found that he began to avoid spending time with her. It started out subconsciously; he would stay late at work. And he told John that yes, of course they could take on more clients, even though the practice had already been more successful than either had anticipated and their respective offices already overburdened.

Eventually it was easier that way. Dan could live with himself. He could live with himself because he didn't have to see the pain and disappointment in his wife's eyes every time he looked at her, and he thought that maybe if he stayed away long enough, then one day the old Nicola would return.

One evening in particular, he was sitting in his office staring at the computer screen, and thinking about all that he was about to lose, or worse, about what had already been lost.

"Dan?"

Shannon popped her head around the door of his office. "What are you still doing here?"

"Feck, you scared the living daylights out of me. I didn't think there was anybody else here. I'm working on – on the P35 for Manning Packaging." John had recently taken on their old colleague as PA, in the hope that she could help them deal with the workload. He picked up the first company file that came to hand.

"At this time of evening?" she frowned. "Dan, don't you think you should be heading home?"

"I just have a few small things to finish up, then I'll go. What about you? It's not like you to be working late either."

"I wasn't, actually. I left earlier but I forgot my mobile, so I came back to get it." She gave him a mischievous look. "I'm expecting an important call."

Dan grinned back. "Oh? Do I know about this one?" Shannon always had some man on the go.

"He's new on the scene," she said coquettishly. "Nice, seems like my type."

"Nice? That definitely doesn't sound like your type." He laughed for what seemed like the first time in ages.

"Oh we'll see how it goes, anyway." She moved back towards the doorway, then paused. "Hey, is everything OK?"

He stiffened. "Why wouldn't it be?"

"I hope you don't mind me saying so, but you look awful."

"Thanks a million."

"No, I don't mean ..." She floundered. "Look, I just wondered how things were going – at home, I mean. You haven't said much and well, we haven't really had a chance to talk about it."

Shannon knew about the miscarriage, everyone did. Should he confide in her his fears about Nicola?

He needed to confide in someone, but it almost felt like a betrayal. Especially as they had never seemed to get on all that well and as a result Dan had consciously cooled his friendship.

Yet he and Shannon were still friends and had always been close. He threw down his pen. Feck it, he needed to talk to someone, otherwise he'd crack up.

"Things are a little … delicate," he offered eventually.

"It's understandable, you know. I'm sure losing a baby wasn't easy for her."

"It wasn't easy for me either, but nobody seems to even consider that."

Shannon looked at him. "Look, let's go next door for one, and we can have a good old chinwag."

"Are you sure? Don't you have somewhere else to be?"

She shook her head. "Not really. If lover-boy rings, I can talk to him from there. Go on, get your things."

As he shut down his computer and collected his briefcase, Dan realised he was feeling better already. As he followed Shannon out and locked the office door behind them, she flashed him an inviting smile.

A cosy pub, a decent pint of plain and a good listener; sure what more would you want…

TWENTY-NINE

AT THE TIME, Nicola didn't think she could cope, let alone be expected to help Dan through it, when she couldn't even help herself.

It was as though a dark cloud had descended on their marriage since ... since she lost the baby.

She remembered what the doctor had told her afterwards.

"You're young, leave it a few months and then you can start trying for another one," he had said after performing a D&C. She had wanted to kill him then. She had wanted to catch him and strangle him and make him feel some of what she was feeling.

Try for another one? How could he even suggest that? She and Dan had been so happy, so thrilled about it all. She should have known, though. She should have known that it was bad luck going into MotherCare picking out bits and pieces 'for the baby'.

What baby? Now those purchases were locked away

up in the dark attic, never to see the light of day. Much like Nicola's feelings.

Would she ever be able to look into his eyes again without seeing blame and sorrow reflected in them?

Because she knew Dan blamed her. She knew that he thought she should have gone straight to hospital when the pain started, instead of ignoring them and hoping it would go away. But to be honest, she didn't really think that anything was wrong. How could she possibly have known?

The medication helped her get through it, helped her sleep at night and admittedly, sometimes during the day, thank goodness. And because of those pills, Nicola had been able to let it go, to come to terms with it all – eventually.

But Dan couldn't. Instead, he worked all hours of the day and often long into the evening.

"The practice is still in its infancy," he had said. "I need to put the hours in."

Yet the practice had been going great long before any of it had happened. Work had been important, sure, but never as important as their relationship had been. Dan didn't need to work late – at least not for the sake of the practice. He needed to work late because he couldn't face her.

She knew he was spending a lot more time with Shannon Fogarty these days too. She could smell Camel cigarettes on his clothes every time he walked into a room.

Maybe Shannon was helping him.

Work was her only refuge, and Nicola spent as much

time at the leisure centre as possible, albeit in a world of her own, until one day her manager challenged her bad humour and unhappy disposition.

"Nikki, what's wrong?" Ken asked, his face full of concern. He was the only one who ever called her Nikki and normally she hated it. This time though, it sounded comfortingly familiar. "I know you, and you haven't been the same since ... well you haven't been your usual bubbly self for a while."

"Sorry." She looked away.

"Hey, I didn't mean it like that," He put an arm around her and led her away from reception towards his office. It felt good – strong. When he let her go in order to close the door behind them, Nicola was sorry the contact was broken.

"Hey, I'm not having a go at you," he said, motioning her towards a seat. "So are you going tell me what the matter is?"

"It's Dan," she said flatly. "Our marriage is over."

"What? You can't be serious."

She nodded again. "He's having an affair." There – it was out. She had finally said it, finally admitted it out loud.

"What?" Ken exclaimed again. Without waiting for an answer he went on. "How do you know? Did you catch him, did he confess?"

She shook her head.

"Well, what then?"

"He doesn't have to confess. All the signs are there."

"What kind of signs?"

"You know, avoiding me, supposedly working late, all those things."

"Nikki," Ken walked around his desk and knelt beside her chair, "you and Dan have been through a lot lately."

Nicola looked at his kind face and noticed for the very first time how attractive he was. His eyes were like pools of melted chocolate. And his eyelashes were so long, feminine almost.

"Dan adores you, he wouldn't cheat on you."

"Don't be so sure."

"Tell me what happened to make you so sure."

"He's been out drinking late into the night with a colleague, his so-called friend. But she's been after him for years," she told Ken bitterly.

"So, why hasn't anything happened before now then?"

"Because ... because things were going so well between us, we loved one another, he didn't blame me."

"Blame you for what – the baby?" Ken put a hand on hers. "OK, I don't know Dan that well, but I do know that he loves you, everyone knows that. And nobody is to blame for what happened. It's just one of those things."

"He keeps avoiding me, he doesn't touch me. Ken, he can't even look at me. My husband hates me so much that he can't even look at me." The tears were flowing now, and he put an arm around her and held her close.

"I hate to see you like this," he said. "Look, go home early, get some rest and then talk to him – tonight. You two need to get some things out in the open."

"I can't."

"Of course you can. You and Dan are the happiest couple I have ever come across – and you guys are married," he added. "It's weird."

She nestled comfortably in the crook of his arm. It felt good. Good to be comforted, to be cherished. She and the rest of the staff at Metamorph had always joked that their hard-nosed manager was like the Tin-Man in *The Wizard of Oz* – no heart. But today she had discovered that beneath that tough, business-like exterior, Ken Harris's heart was not made of tin, but solid gold.

"I had no idea you were the sensitive, in-touch-with-your-feelings type," she said, beginning to feel better.

He looked at her. "You'd be surprised."

Nicola couldn't pinpoint why, but at that moment the atmosphere in the room transformed. All of a sudden, her nerve-endings were sharp as knives and her stomach began to tremble.

Ken was still holding her and when she looked up at him, she saw his expression had changed too. She watched the attractive curve of his mouth, the faint beginnings of dark stubble on his chin.

He had a very sexy mouth, dangerously sexy, even. At that very moment for some reason Nicola very badly wanted to feel that mouth on hers. She imagined him planting tiny kisses on her neck, then moving down towards her collarbone, then her breasts, then ...

Suddenly, she didn't have to imagine any more. Suddenly, Ken's mouth *was* on hers, kissing her, his tongue probing and teasing and then they were both standing, clinging to one another.

Neither of them heard the slight rap on the glass, nor the sound of the office door opening.

"Ken? Do you know where Nicola is supposed to be today? Oh!"

The voice brought her right back to reality and the two of them looked towards the doorway to see Lisa the gym attendant staring wide-eyed and embarrassed.

Followed by a white-faced, stunned, and utterly horrified Dan.

THIRTY

NOW, Nicola's extension buzzed startling her out of her reverie.

"What's going on, I phoned you ten minutes ago," Ken's exasperated tones drifted through the air.

Darn. She had completely forgotten.

She hurried to the elevator and was in his office within minutes.

"Sorry," she said with a mischievous smile, "I got waylaid by a client."

He grinned. That was normally the excuse they used on the other Motiv8 staff when they wanted to steal a moment together. They were either 'seeing a client' or 'phoning a client'.

Ken shuffled through a number of printouts on his desk, picked one up and without a word, handed it across the table to her.

Her heart thumped as began to read it. She was silent for a moment. Then her eyes widened and she looked up, delighted.

"I don't believe it," she exclaimed. "The figures are insane."

It was incredible. Membership uptake was always at its slowest throughout the mid-summer months. People out and about in the fine weather saw little need for pounding on a treadmill when they could enjoy the exercise much more in the park or on the beach.

But the report Nicola held for the summer read as well as the one for January.

"That article was an absolute godsend, Nikki," Ken smiled. "Those figures should carry us through for the rest of the year. The accountant will be happy, as will the partners so I'm confident of getting a capital top-up for next year. Should free us up to spend a bit more on this place. Well done." He winked at her. "I always knew you were the right person for this job, you know."

Initially, she had her reservations about coming back to Ireland and taking up Ken's job offer, unsure as to whether she would be able for it – unsure if coming back home was a good thing.

She had also been quite touchy, suspecting that Ken had suggested her for the job simply because he was feeling sorry for her.

But he had been insistent that she would be perfect for Motiv8 and he was right. She loved this place and within months had dispelled any of her own qualms about Ken's ulterior motives for offering her the manager's post.

She was good at this, and she knew it.

Soon she realised that he had offered her the job not just because he understood her need for independence and a chance to regain some normality – but also because he in was in love with her.

She hadn't known it at the time, hadn't even known it that day in his office when Dan walked in.

But when she eventually did find out, she didn't care about Ken's original intentions, because by then she had fallen in love with him too.

THIRTY-ONE

"GOOD AFTERNOON, LAURA CONNOLLY DESIGN," Laura closed her eyes in silent prayer. Please, please, let it be that man calling back – the one looking for the bespoke engagement ring.

Though weeks later it was unlikely.

That day, having returned from picking up Kerry, she had waited for him to call back. The disappointment had been unbearable as was the fact that there was no chance of piecing together his name or number.

Still, Helen had been so grateful that when she came to collect her daughter that evening she'd presented Laura with the most gorgeous bottle of designer perfume.

"Hello?" she repeated, when there was no reply.

A short pause at the other end. "Um, hello? Is that Laura?"

"Yes, it is."

"Laura, how are you, pet? Kathleen Brennan here."

"Oh, hello, Kathleen."

Kathleen Brennan from Glengarrah. Was it possible

– could it be that she was looking to order something? Her heart lifted. Perhaps her mother had been telling people about the business, after all. Why else would the village busybody be phoning?

"Well, it's like this, Laura," Kathleen began, as if reading her thoughts, "your mother told me all about how you're working for yourself these days."

Wow, Maureen really had come through for her, after all. But what would she be looking for; a brooch to wear to Mass on Sunday, or maybe a present for her husband? She could do a gorgeous set of cufflinks that would suit Con, something simple but elegant and he'd love ...

"And she told me that you might do me a turn and book tickets online..."

Laura bristled. This was the *second* time she'd played booking agent to someone from home. The other day, one of her sister's friends had asked if Laura would go online and arrange flights to London *and* a hotel. She didn't mind doing anyone a favour, but she was getting a little sick of being used as the village web café.

Yet she hadn't the heart to say no - in the same way she couldn't say no to Helen either, despite the risk of missing important business calls.

Since that first time, Laura had collected Kerry from play school three days out of five in the last few weeks, and again this afternoon.

Later that same evening, Helen duly breezed in - looking like someone who had just stepped out of *Cosmo*.

Laura thought she saw Neil throw her friend an

admiring glance, and felt immediately self-conscious in her supermarket-bought trousers and T-shirt.

OK, so working from home didn't require dressing to the nines and she wasn't exactly inspired to go through the entire make-up rigmarole either when the only living thing she came into contact with was Eamonn the cat - who couldn't care less whether Laura wore SuperCurl or Superglue on her eyelashes.

Still, she decided she should start making more of an effort to look the part of the professional career woman.

"Mommy!" Kerry brightened instantly. "Look what I d-d-did today." She handed Helen a drawing she had done earlier at preschool. "This is me, this is you and this is B-B-Baawney."

Helen took the drawing and smiled. "That's lovely, darling, aren't you a clever girl?"

Pleased, Kerry took her mother's hand. "When can we get a doggy like Baawney?"

Helen sighed, and made eyes at Laura. "Now pet, I know how much you love Barney, but I told you before that we're not getting a puppy. He looks after Auntie Nicola because she lives on her own, but you don't live on your own, do you?"

Kerry shook her head from side to side, her eyes filled with disappointment. "But Auntie Law-law has Eamonn, and s-s-she lives with Uncle Neil," she countered.

Helen paused, unsure how to answer, and Neil decided to help her out. "Yes, but that's because Auntie Laura is at home on her own all day, while I'm out at work."

Kerry pondered this. "Can I stay at home all d-d-day

while you work, Mommy? Then I could have a d-d-doggy to look after me."

"But wouldn't you miss pre-school?"

Kerry shook her head. "No, I h-h-hate pwe-school."

"This is the latest thing." Helen rolled her eyes.

"Why don't you like pre-school? Aren't there lots of nice boys and girls there for you to play with?" Neil probed.

Kerry shook her head from side to side, her eyes wide.

"No nice boys and girls – at all?" Laura asked

"No – don't like them."

"Don't mind her, she's been like this ever since she stopped going to Jo's."

Laura wasn't so sure. She'd collected Kerry from play school a lot and not once did she mention another child or playmate, which Laura thought was sad. She was a naturally shy child as a result of her stutter, and Laura wondered if maybe she was having problems making friends. But speaking of Jo ...?

"So have you found another childminder, yet?" she asked Helen.

"I know, I know, I'm sorry. But it's been so busy at work, I just haven't had a chance."

Laura instantly felt like a heel. Kerry was a dream to look after and it wasn't as though she was rushed off her feet here – she just hated being away from the office in the afternoons, especially since she missed that call.

Still, what else were friends for? Helen would do the same for her, if the situations were reversed.

"Listen, why don't you two stay for dinner?" she said, anxious to make amends.

"Oh, can we, Mommy?" Kerry looked delighted. "Auntie Law-law made sheep's pie!"

"Would you mind?" Helen looked uncertain.

"No, not at all. Come through to the kitchen, it's nearly ready."

"So how's business going?" Helen asked while they ate, taking tiny morsels from her overloaded plate.

Laura's insides tightened.

"Getting there," she answered, trying to sound more enthusiastic than she felt. "The website is working out well and I've had enquiries from all over."

"She'll be going international before we know it," Neil added proudly, shovelling a forkful of potato into his mouth.

"Any stockists yet?"

There had been a few, but they weren't ordering enough to make any kind of impact on her accounts. "The Crafts Council has my name on file and I'm sure it's only a matter of time ..."

Helen must have felt her reticence on the matter because she changed the subject soon after.

Laura's confidence was rapidly eroding with each passing day. It was as though her self-esteem, her entire self-worth were tied up in this business venture, and what had started out as a great business idea and a rush of excitement had now turned into something she was almost ashamed of.

What if she couldn't make this work? What if she had to admit defeat, and throw in the towel? Nicola would support her of course, but probably feel sorry for her. Helen would undoubtedly say, 'I told you so' and Laura didn't have to even wonder about her family – *they* would probably start celebrating on the streets.

But what about Neil? Loving, supportive, hard-working Neil? Would he begin to pity her, or even resent her if she packed this in?

Because the way she was feeling at the moment, Laura thought, watching Helen engage her fiancé in what must have been riveting conversation, she wasn't sure if she could keep this up for much longer.

THIRTY-TWO

WHEN SHE WAS ABSOLUTELY positive that Dan and John had left the building, Chloe entered the offices of O'Leary & Hunt, Chartered Accountants.

"Hello," she said to the young receptionist at the front desk who she knew had absolutely no idea that the blonde standing before her was her boss's fiancée. "I'm looking for …" she made a great show of studying the folder she carried, "for Dan Hunt, please."

"I'm sorry, but Mr Hunt is out of the office for the afternoon." The girl spoke as though she had rattled off that line many times before.

"Would Mr O'Leary be available, then?" Chloe asked, knowing full well what the answer would be.

"I'm afraid Mr O'Leary is also out for the afternoon."

"Oh, that's a shame."

"Did you have an appointment?"

"No, it's a spur-of-the-moment visit, actually. I'm here on behalf of a previous client. I'm her legal representative and was really hoping to speak to one of the partners about my client's affairs." She briefly flashed a business card.

"Well if you'd like to leave your name and number, I can get Mr Hunt to phone you …"

"No, I just popped in on the off-chance. I was really hoping to speak to someone, though." Chloe sighed dramatically but then her eyes widened, as if she had just thought of something. "Tell you what, maybe *you* could help me. You're Mr Hunt's personal assistant?"

The girl blushed, flattered. "No, I'm only a student on work-experience. Mr Hunt's PA is upstairs. Would you like to speak to her?"

Chloe pretended to study her folder again. That was *exactly* what she'd like.

She had spoken to Dan's PA on the phone a few times but they had never met. Luckily.

The woman wouldn't know Chloe from Adam, so hopefully by using the solicitor's ruse she might be able to glean the information she needed. Just a *teeny, tiny* white lie, but no harm done.

It was a brainwave really.

She looked up and smiled imploringly. "If you wouldn't mind, that'd be perfect."

"No problem." The receptionist dialled the extension and spoke pleasantly into the mouthpiece. "Shannon, are you free for a moment? There's someone at reception hoping to speak with you."

THIRTY-THREE

LAURA WAS sorry she had ever made a phone call to Maureen enquiring as to whether her sister had remembered the wedding-dress fitting this coming weekend.

"Honestly, Laura," Maureen sniffed. "I still can't understand why you had to go and get your dress made in Dublin. Plenty of seamstresses down this way too, you know. And poor oul' Cathy having to traipse all the way up there on the bus, every time you snap your fingers."

She took a deep breath, trying to calm herself. Lately everything her mother said – everything *anyone* said – was getting on her nerves.

She wasn't usually so touchy but of late found herself becoming oversensitive and irritable. "Mam it's the final fitting before the wedding," she said as calmly as she could muster. "Cathy knows that."

Maureen harrumphed. "Well, that's all very well, but I'm the one that's stuck looking after the twins while the two of you are living it up in Dublin."

"I have to go," Laura said now, through gritted teeth,

"there's another call coming in and it could be important."

She hoped it would be. She *needed* it to be.

"Too high-flying these days to have a decent conversation with your own mother?"

"I really have to go," she said, refusing to rise to the bait. "Tell Cathy I'll meet her outside Easons on Saturday morning."

"Make sure you don't leave her waiting too long ... with the way things are going in Dublin these days, you wouldn't know – she could get shot or anything –"

"Goodbye, Mam." Laura disconnected and briskly picked up the other line. "Good afternoon, Laura Connolly Design?"

"Hello, I'd like to speak to the owner or manager please?" a chirpy female voice asked.

"Speaking."

"Great. If I could just have a few minutes of your time, it won't take that long and if you could give me some information about the company I could design a sample business strategy and –"

Brilliant. Another telemarketer. "So sorry but I'm not interested," Laura began.

"Well, maybe we can arrange a more convenient time? I could perhaps call to the premises and explain exactly what we could do for your business. Say ten am, Monday?"

"No, I really don't think –"

"Ten it is then. Looking forward to it, Business Network Marketing can grow –"

"I said *no,*" Laura repeated, her hands shaking with

adrenaline. "I don't *want* a meeting and I don't *need* a constructive marketing solution – whatever that might be. I *told* you I wasn't interested!"

Her face hot and her heartbeat going a mile a minute, Laura hung up.

For a long moment, she stared at nothing in particular, trying to get a grip on herself. Why was it that everyone thought they could roll her over like a trained dog?

Only the other day, Helen had persuaded her to drop off something to a client in Dun Laoghaire. "There's no rush with it or anything. But seeing as it's on your way to the preschool ..."

It was nowhere *near* the preschool – in fact it was an extra forty minutes in traffic *out of the way* of the preschool.

At first she was happy to do Helen a turn but why couldn't her friend do the same? Why couldn't she see that Laura was working, that she was trying to get her business off the ground, and that being away from the office wasn't helping?

At least Kerry would be starting school soon, so hopefully she wouldn't need her anymore. But as far as she knew Helen hadn't found another childminder – as far as she knew she hadn't even looked.

Just then, the phone rang again and Laura snatched up the receiver, deciding that if this was Ms Telemarketer bothering her again, she was really going to give her a piece of her mind.

"Hello, is that the jewellery design place?"

"Yes, this is Laura Connolly – how can I help you?"

"Well," the caller began, "I know this might be a bit short notice, but my boyfriend and I are getting married and we were thinking of ... well, I was thinking of, getting our wedding rings specially designed. I have a few ideas in my head ..."

Laura was so excited she barely heard the rest of the sentence. A customer, a real live customer – and someone looking for a one-off commission too.

"So, I wondered if I could maybe call into your studio and show you what I have in mind?" the caller went on. "You're in Ballinteer, aren't you? I could call on my lunch break – around two if that suits? I'm so sorry for calling at such short notice but –"

"Of course, yes. That would be fine, absolutely fine," Laura replied and then her heart sank. She had to collect Kerry from play school at two though.

Oh, blast it, she had to be here for this. It was her first ever personal consultation for goodness sake!

No, Laura thought, her thoughts tripping over themselves as she tried to find a solution. She would ring Helen, explain the situation and her friend would have to make alternative arrangements. She knew Helen's work was important, but hers was too.

"Terrific! I sooo appreciate it," the caller sang, and Laura couldn't resist a smile.

This was a sale, it was definitely a sale. She could feel it in her bones.

Then she grimaced. Now, she had to tackle the rather unpleasant task of telling Helen she couldn't collect Kerry this afternoon. First she dialled Helen's mobile, and not getting any answer from that, tried her direct line at XL.

"Hi," her friend's sultry tones came through the mouthpiece and Laura idly wondered if sounding like an advertisement for one of these phone-sex lines was good for business. Maybe she should try it herself. It certainly seemed to work for Helen anyway. The woman could buy and sell anyone. She was about to speak, when the voice continued, "Please leave a message."

Damn. She couldn't just leave a message. What if Helen was in a meeting and didn't get out 'til after two? Poor Kerry would be in an awful state. No, she couldn't do that – she'd have to find some way of letting Helen know. She bit her lip and mulled over it. Then it hit her. She could ring XL reception find out where she was and if she was contactable or, alternatively, leave the message to pass on.

"Good morning, XL, Paula speaking."

"Hello, I was looking to speak to Helen please," Laura said pleasantly.

"I'm sorry, she isn't in today," the receptionist said, and Laura sat up in her chair.

"Isn't in? Isn't in the office, you mean?"

"No, she isn't in at all."

"She's out sick?" Laura said, more to herself than to the receptionist. But how did Helen get Kerry to the preschool this morning if she wasn't well ... wait, she thought, mind racing, *that* was even better because there was a chance that Kerry wasn't in either, so she wouldn't need to collect her...

But then why hadn't Helen let her know that?

"No, she took an annual leave day. I'm holding all calls 'til tomorrow, so if you'd like to leave your name and number –"

"What?" Laura gasped. "She knew she'd be off today?"

"I'm sure that someone else here can help you and –"

"It's fine, thank you," she said shortly.

What was going on? When Helen had called to pick up Kerry yesterday there was no mention of a day off or a 'personal matter'. If she had the day off, why didn't she tell her?

Laura stood up and, trying to clear her mind, began tidying her office space, hoping to make it look a little bit more presentable for her client's visit.

Then she stopped, remembering something Helen had said. "I might be a bit late collecting her tomorrow, if that's OK," she had said on her way out. "The boss scheduled something last-minute. I hope you don't mind," she added with her trademark winning smile.

What was Helen up to?

Two hours and umpteen phone-calls later to Helen's apartment, her mobile, the play school and back again to XL and still Laura was none the wiser.

The only thing she knew for sure was that yes, Kerry *was* in play school and she had no choice but to go and collect her now. She had been lucky in a sense that the school – now familiar with Laura – agreed to let her pick up Kerry an hour earlier, so at least she could be back in time for her consultation.

But she didn't feel right about doing that and it was

embarrassing having to ask. She shouldn't even have to –
Helen was the child's mother after all.

But she was nervous enough about this meeting
without having to worry about whether or not Kerry
would be OK by herself in the next room, or whether she
might come in and interrupt them, giving the client an
unprofessional first impression.

What should she do?

Later that evening, Helen sailed into the hallway in a
cloud of *J'Adore.*

"Where the hell were you today?" Laura snapped,
Kerry safely out of earshot in the kitchen with Neil.

"What? What do you mean where was I?" Helen
stopped short warily.

"Well, you weren't at work," she continued, "because
I tried to phone you earlier to tell you that something had
come up, and I wasn't available to be your gofer today."

"My gofer? Is this about collecting Kerry from play
school? I asked you yesterday and you said –"

"No, you *said* that you would be late collecting Kerry
today because you had some meeting, yet according to
the office you took a day off." Laura's voice shook and her
heart pounded. "Isn't it well for you to be able to take a
day off and leave the worry of looking after your child to
someone who actually *was* working today?"

In the end, the client was lovely and was so
impressed by Laura's designs that she signed up to
commission her wedding rings. She was more relieved
than anything else, her annoyance with Helen so great

that she wasn't even in the mindset to enjoy her small triumph.

"Hey I'm sorry, really I am but Paul and I had organised this trip and ..." Helen stopped short, and reddened.

"Paul? Who the hell is Paul?" Laura repeated frowning, although one look at Helen's face told her all she needed to know. Obviously some new Romeo she'd hooked up with. She didn't *believe* this...

"He lives in Cork and we haven't seen one another in a while. I just didn't think you'd mind. I wasn't that much later than usual so –"

"That's not the point though, is it? Weeks ago you asked me to do you a favour and because you're my friend and you were stuck, I obliged. But *I'm* working too, though you don't seem too concerned about that. If I was working in an office, would you expect me to take time off every day to collect Kerry?"

"Well no, but – "

"It's the same thing. But because you don't take me – or this business – seriously, don't think you can walk all over me, Helen. Now you're using me to hook up with some guy."

"Laura, that's not true," Helen said, putting a hand on her arm. "I promise I have been looking for another childminder, really I have. But it's difficult to get someone at this time of year ..." She trailed off, her shoulders slumped. "Look, I'm really, really, sorry," she continued, her voice barely a whisper. "I know I've been taking advantage, and I would have told you about Paul, it's just ..." She blushed slightly, "well, it's early days, and I didn't feel comfortable saying anything before now."

"But it's dangerous too though. Forget the fact that I couldn't contact you because it wasn't convenient – what if something had happened? What if little Kerry got sick or there was an accident or something?"

The entire afternoon Laura had been going over in her mind what she was going to say and how she was going to tell her to stick it, but now that Helen was here, looking truly apologetic and pouring her heart out, she just didn't have the resolve.

Sensing that she had calmed, Helen looked up at her, her beautiful eyes sorrowful. "I promise I will make it up to you, and I'll get moving on another childminder first thing. You know I really appreciate what you're doing, and I promise you won't have to mind her for much longer OK?"

Silence."Laura?" she urged. "I swear."

Eventually, Laura sighed again and nodded wearily.

But knowing Helen, she wasn't so sure.

THIRTY-FOUR

"NICE PLACE." Paul sat up, zipped up his jeans and glanced fleetingly around Helen's ground-floor apart-ment. "You're obviously very good at what you do."

From where she lay half-undressed on the ground, Helen gave him once of her most provocative smiles. "I thought you of all people already knew that?"

He laughed and kissed her again. "Come on, it'll be closing time soon."

Helen straightened her clothes and went to the bath-room to retouch her make-up and brush her hair.

"Come on, come on, you don't need that crap, you look gorgeous as you are," he called after her impatiently.

"I am not going out with bed-head," she retorted. "Even if it's only as far as the local."

She followed Paul out the door, and took one last look around the apartment to ensure that none of Kerry's toys – which had been deliberately hidden earlier – had managed to evade her.

All she needed now was some Tweenie doll sticking

its head out from one of the sofas. *That* would certainly make an impression.

Thank goodness Nicola had agreed to look after Kerry this evening. Helen had pleaded a work do, but Nicola was suspicious.

"OK, OK, I might as well tell you. I've met someone – someone new."

There must have been something in her tone because Nicola knew straight away that this guy wasn't quite 'new'.

"You dark horse," she said. "Why didn't you tell us?"

"There's nothing much to tell," Helen said, unwilling to elaborate. "Anyway can you baby-sit, or not? If not, I'll have to ask Laura, and I feel bad enough as it is, asking her to collect Kerry during the week."

And Helen did feel bad about it. But she just hadn't had the chance to find another childminder at such short notice. Anyway, Laura loved having her and Kerry loved being there – in fact, she couldn't think of a better person to take Kerry. And it wouldn't be for that much longer, what with her starting school soon.

"I'll take her on Friday night," Nicola said. "I won't be going anywhere anyway."

"Laura told me you met up with Dan recently. How did it go?"

"Not bad," Nicola said guardedly, and she knew that her friend didn't want to discuss it. She supposed she could understand why. She hadn't been terribly supportive of Nicola throughout the break-up – given everything that was going on with Jamie at the time.

To this day, Helen still felt guilty about that. She

must pop over and have a proper chat, but she was just so busy these days with work and Kerry and now ...

Things had begun to get serious between her and Paul lately, at least as serious as they could be with him away so often. His work meant that he was constantly on the road, and apparently his mother wasn't very well, so most weekends he travelled to Cork to spend time with her.

Aside from Paul's obvious sexual magnetism, it was this fact that particularly endeared him to her. Who would have thought that this sexy, macho man was nothing but a big softie? Travelling all that way each weekend just to be with his mother.

It wouldn't have been Helen, that was for sure, but then again her own mother was long gone, and she didn't have to worry about visiting her father, who tended to be much happier left to his own devices on the farm back home.

But because of this side to him, she was certain he would eventually take to Kerry. But when to tell him?

She had thought about that a lot lately, but as the weeks went by, it was getting harder and harder to broach the subject. What was she supposed to say? 'Oh, by the way, I nearly forgot – I have an almost four-year-old'?

No, she had to think a little more about it. After her experience with Richard, Helen had to bide her time, and wait for the right opportunity.

"So what are you up to tomorrow?" Paul asked her.

"Well, because I have the day to myself *for once*, I'm going shopping ..." She trailed off, realising what she had said. "I mean, I normally have a lot of work to do at home and this week I got it all finished early and – "

"You're really dedicated to your job, aren't you?" He didn't notice anything amiss, nor hear the fearful pounding of Helen's heartbeat.

"I need to get an outfit for a friend's wedding next month. I don't have much time so –"

"A wedding? I love weddings."

The way he said it, Helen knew he was angling for an invite. But how could she invite him when Kerry would be there as flower girl?

Oh how she'd love to bring him to Laura's wedding. It had been so long since she'd had a partner at a social event. For once, she wouldn't be on her own – and have someone other than Nicola and Ken to talk to at their table. Helen didn't really ... connect with Ken. He was nice enough but could be a little on the dull side...

She bit her lip, and grabbed a stool at the bar while Paul stood waiting to order drinks. Maybe she should just bite the bullet and tell him. Now that they were a couple, a real couple, well – she was almost obliged to, wasn't she? That was probably where she went wrong with Richard – she should have told him long before.

She chuckled inwardly, imagining herself arriving at Laura's wedding in Paul's sleek, black Audi. She'd emerge outside the church in a show-stopping outfit, something expensive, tight and probably indecently short (definitely something to scandalise the Holy Marys in Glengarrah). Then as the rest of the congregation stood back and stared, she would enter the church on the arm of the sexiest man this side of

Dublin. That might finally stop the ould biddies in the village rambling on and on about 'the poor child's father'.

She glanced idly round the darkened pub, trying to remember the last time she had been in here. Generally, she and Paul met for dinner or drinks in town. This was the first time they had gone out near her place and, after their little bonking session on the floor earlier, he'd stay with her tonight.

She was probably pushing her luck in asking Nicola to have Kerry stay over, but she adored Kerry and luckily enjoyed having her. It couldn't have worked out better really, Helen thought, smiling to herself. The pub was busy and judging by the banners and balloons hanging from the ceiling, a 50th birthday celebration was taking place. She looked across at the revellers who, surprisingly for that hour of night, included a few youngsters – probably grandchildren, she reasoned. The kids looked tired and sleepy.

"I think we should stay here at the bar," she said to Paul. "Looks dangerous down there." She chuckled, indicating the busy seating area where the birthday girl and her companions were now dancing around the tables.

Paul shook his head. "That's why I can't stand these local spots," he said "They're always filled with bloody kids."

She knew what he meant; sometimes big groups could be overbearing, but this lot weren't doing any harm. She felt a bit sorry for the kids actually, since it was late and the grown-ups looked like they were just getting started.

"I think they should be banned from pubs altogether." Paul took a sip of his drink. "No place for rug-rats."

Helen wondered whether he meant this out of concern for the kids, or concern for the drinkers?

"So you're not a big fan then?" she asked, trying to sound casual. "Of kids?"

Paul nearly spat out his Guinness. "No way," he said. "My sister has three and they're right little whingers, all moaning and groaning and crying. You're expected to feed, clean and clothe the little feckers day in, day out for the best part of eighteen years, and what do you get in return? Grief, that's what."

Helen's throat felt dry. She took a huge gulp from her glass. "Horses for courses, I'm sure," she said, rubbing her hand provocatively across his thigh. "Anyway, we won't stay long."

His earlier annoyance forgotten, Paul grabbed her hand and squeezed it. "Babe," he purred, "you're definitely my kind of woman."

THIRTY-FIVE

THE FOLLOWING SATURDAY MORNING, Laura and Nicola drove into town for the dress fitting, accompanied by an unusually sullen Kerry.

Apparently, Helen had gone out again with the famous Paul the night before and this time left her at Nicola's for the night. Obviously she was making this new guy her utmost priority.

"The poor child is being shunted from pillar to post," her friend said grumpily. "I've had her the last two weekends and I'd say poor Kerry is sick of it."

"She loves staying with you though."

"Maybe, but I'm sure she'd like to spend *some* time with Mummy at the weekends too – she hardly sees her during the week." Nicola sounded well and truly out of sorts. "I'm going to have to confront her about it soon," she added grimly. "It's not good for the poor kid."

Laura grimaced. Nicola or Helen disagreeing with *anyone* was not a pretty sight, let alone locking horns with one another. If they did so over Kerry's welfare, Laura wouldn't want to be within throwing distance.

"You're in very bad form today," she said. Despite her friend's insistence that meeting Dan was a good thing, Laura worried that she might have been deluding herself.

Nicola exhaled deeply. "Dan rang me at work yesterday, wanting to meet up again."

"Again – why?"

"Honestly? I think he just wants to remain friends. The thing is, I don't want it causing trouble between Ken and me. He was wary enough about it in the first place."

"You couldn't blame him though." Laura settled Kerry in the back seat of Nicola's Focus. "And I feel guilty. If it weren't for me and my invites –"

"But it wasn't your fault they got mixed up," Nicola said. "Anyway, he rang me as a result of the Motiv8 magazine feature. He would have found me either way." She checked her rear-view mirror. "We'd better get a move on – poor Cathy will have been kidnapped by the time we get there." She gave a broad grin, Laura having earlier relayed the conversation with her mother about 'poor Cathy' being left all alone in the Big Bad City. "Now, do you have the neckpieces with you, and the earrings?"

Eyes wide, Laura raced back to the workshop. She'd spent long enough working on the wedding jewellery to have it all ready for the final fitting – she'd have gone mad if she'd left everything behind.

A little later, they all stood before the mirror in full wedding regalia.

Kerry in her satin violet flower girl dress was leaping around in delight, proclaiming that she was a fairy princess. Laura's sister was studying her reflection and making a determined attempt to suck in her rounding stomach. The boned bodice sat awkwardly on her midriff and the crushed silk skirt strained across her hips.

Either Cathy didn't know, or hadn't bothered telling Laura that she was pregnant again. Though she didn't look at all happy about it to be fair.

Neither did Brid Cassidy. The bridal designer was today joined by an assistant named Amanda that Laura hadn't met before, and the other woman, noticing Cathy's expanding waistline, gave Laura a conspiratorial look.

She knew that Brid could be temperamental, and this new development was not going to go down well – at all.

"We need to put an extra panel in there," the designer concluded briskly to Cathy before turning to examine Laura. "What do you think? Are you happy with your dress?" She tugged gently at the straps. "I think maybe we could tighten these a tiny bit, just to lift you slightly at the bust and ..."

"It's perfect." She glanced across at Nicola who was studying her earnestly, a proud look on her face.

"It is. You look amazing Laura."

"So do you."

"Arrah, the rest of ye won't hold a candle to *me* on the day," her friend added with a wicked grin. "I'll be the talk of town."

Laura laughed though she understood Nicola well

enough to know that, despite the self-deprecation and offhand jokes, she was still a little self-conscious about going up the aisle.

Now Laura opened the box and took out the jewellery she had designed for her wedding party. "See how this looks with it."

The neckpiece was fashioned with silver so fine it looked like hand-spun thread. Each concentric circle was intertwined with amethysts, the stones accentuating the colour of the bridesmaid's dresses. There were earrings to match and the designs had a vague tribal-princess look – an effect that Laura had been trying to perfect for quite some time.

Brid and her assistant moved over to take a closer look.

"Wow," she gasped. "Where did you get these – they're fantastic."

Cathy looked across with interest, but her face fell when she realised. "I thought you'd buy us something," she said mournfully. "As a keepsake."

"But it *is* a keepsake!" Nicola gave her a look of astonishment. "Wow, this is gorgeous, Laura, just – incredible."

"You made these?" Brid looked up.

"Laura's a jewellery designer." Nicola said proudly. "Didn't she tell you?"

Laura reddened, unused to all this lavish praise. "I haven't been doing it for very long," she said apologetically.

"Amazing," Brid said, fastening the neckpiece on Laura, and standing back to admire the effect. "All this time, I couldn't understand why you wanted such a plain dress, but now I do. This puts my work to shame."

"Don't be silly, it's just something simple."

"Something simple? I wish the rubbish stuff I get in was more like this. Instead it's beads and bits of wire that fall to pieces in minutes. 'Exclusive Tiaras', my foot."

Laura's heart began to pound. This was the part where she should offer to show Brid more of her designs. Maybe she might even become a customer, or a business partner even.

But no, she couldn't ask her, not now in front of everyone. It would be too embarrassing and she didn't want Brid to feel as though she had to say yes.

Laura was still her customer and she couldn't put her on the spot like that. No, she'd wait until after the wedding – then she might say something.

Cathy had taken her neckpiece off and the assistant Amanda was examining the detail. "Do you specialise in bridal jewellery only?"

"No, not at all," she replied suddenly embarrassed by all the interest in her work. "But I've never done anything quite so elaborate."

"Really gorgeous," Amanda said, putting down the neckpiece and picking up the earrings, which were basically miniature versions of the neck design. "Where are you stocked? You must be run off your feet."

She reddened. "I am – sometimes I can't keep up with the demand."

She couldn't admit the truth to this woman who was so admiring of her designs.

Laura's pride wouldn't *let* her admit that most of the time, she sat twiddling her thumbs at home.

THIRTY-SIX

THE FOLLOWING WEEK, Nicola and Ken were relaxing in front of the television, Barney sleeping peacefully at their feet, when her phone rang.

"Hey!" she grinned spotting the caller. "I'm so glad you rang. When are we meeting for that coffee?"

"Soon, I hope. But this isn't actually a social call."

"Oh?"

"I couldn't get you at home at the weekend and I didn't want to disturb you at work."

"I was down the country at Laura's wedding ..."

"Well, someone came to see me recently, someone who was asking a lot of questions ... about you."

Nicola took the handset into the kitchen and closed the door behind her. "Who? And what kind of questions?"

"Dan's fiancée. She was pumping for information about when you two were married."

"But you can't be serious. What did she want?"

"Well, she's a cute one. She let on that she was some

kind of solicitor or something. Only for I knew who she really was, I might have been taken in by it. John pointed her out to me one time."

"What? She didn't even tell you who she was?"

"No. She obviously doesn't want anyone, including Dan, to know that she's digging around. Obviously, I didn't say much to her and I told her that the two of us were friends, but only through Dan and John."

"And?"

"And she said she was under the impression that I had been a close friend." She paused. "She was very persistent. I didn't really take to her, to be honest."

Nicola couldn't believe it. If Dan's fiancée was looking for information about her, then maybe she was the jealous type, she thought, recalling how unnerved Ken had been. But surely she'd know there was absolutely no reason for her to be jealous.

"Do you think I should tell Dan about this?" she asked, thinking out loud.

"If it were me, I'd *have* to tell him. I certainly wouldn't want her poking around in my business like that."

"I wonder *has* she spoken to anyone else?"

"To be honest, I kinda got that impression, Nicola. But rest assured she didn't get much from me."

Nicola was amazed. What would Chloe want to know though? Her first guess was that the girl was basically insecure, but why resort to sneaking around?

"Thanks for that. And honestly, we really do need a good catchup, dinner or something."

"Definitely. Maybe I'll pop over altogether. I haven't seen your new place."

"Who was that?" Ken asked easily, when she returned to the living-room.

"What? Oh just Helen, wondering if I could baby-sit Kerry again," Nicola lied.

She couldn't tell him about this. Ken would go mad. *And* she couldn't risk the possibility that he might confront Dan or something.

She sighed inwardly. So much for thinking this was all over and done with.

THIRTY-SEVEN

LATER THAT EVENING once Ken had left, she dialled Dan's number.

"Are you serious?"

"I wouldn't make something like this up."

"I know – that's not what I meant ... crap. What the hell is she playing at?" he asked, voice raised in annoyance.

"I'm not telling you this to cause any trouble, but I have to admit that I don't like it."

"I don't blame you. And I just can't believe that she would do something like that. And pretending to be a solicitor ..."

"Well, why *is* she doing it?"

"I don't know ... I ... well, I know she's been a bit anxious about you and –"

"Why?"

He was silent for a moment. "I didn't ... Nic, she doesn't know."

"*What?*"

"I just couldn't ... I wasn't able to ..." he trailed off.

"Oh come on ..." Immediately, Nicola felt sorry for Chloe. The girl obviously felt threatened and Dan was wrong to keep things from her.

"It's got nothing to do with her, Nic. It's between you and me."

"But that's exactly why she's sneaking around – you're shutting her out."

"It's none of her business," he said again, then sighed. "Look, let me sort it out from here, and to be honest I'm glad you told me. Gives me some idea of the kind of person I was supposed to marry."

Was supposed to marry?

"I thought you two were already married by now," Nicola said, surprised. Their wedding was to take place the day before Laura and Neil's the previous weekend.

"Long story short, but the hotel messed up the booking. We had to postpone and the way things are going, it's a bloody good job we did."

"If Chloe thinks you're hiding something, then you can't blame her for being insecure."

"I know that." He sounded contrite.

The conversation was suspended in silence for a moment, as both remained lost in their own thoughts.

"I promise I'll sort this out but look... can we meet again soon?" Dan's voice was gentle. "Last time we didn't really get a chance to – "

"As I said before, I've moved on – we've *both* moved on." Nicola swallowed hard. "I've got Ken to think of now and there's no point in our going over old ground. As far as I'm concerned, it's ancient history."

. . .

"What on earth did you think you were playing at, Chloe?" Dan raged immediately after Nicola's call. "Sneaking around like that?"

"I'm sorry, really I am. You won't discuss it so I didn't know what else to..."

"I told you before that what happened between me and Nicola is none of your business. We're divorced now and it's over."

"But you're always so cagey about it ... I was just afraid that it was something terrible."

"So did what you find out put your mind at ease?" he snapped. He had no idea what Chloe had learned, so he was particularly interested in how she answered.

She looked away, ashamed. "I know that you and Nicola lost a baby and that ... that she cheated on you." When she saw his eyes widen, Chloe floundered. "I'm sorry, Dan, I had no idea, I thought it might be something else ... oh, I don't know what I thought."

His mind raced. What she had said surprised him, because there were only a few people who would have known about Nicola's little fling back then.

Unless Harris had been shooting his mouth off.

But no, as much as he hated the bastard, in fairness, Harris had been the one to convince Dan that there was nothing between them – that they hadn't been carrying on some torrid affair behind his back.

The guy had been genuinely contrite and although he'd wanted to tear him limb from limb, Dan respected him for his honesty.

Harris had even tried his best to get them back together and for a while it had worked. Anyway, weren't he and Nicola an item now – much as the idea galled Dan and made him sick to his stomach.

So he would hardly go shooting his mouth off.

Who then? Dan thought back to that time, one of the most difficult periods of their short marriage. He never told John anything either. So who else?

Then the thought struck him.

Crap.

THIRTY-EIGHT

"I CAN'T BELIEVE you would blab like that," he raged down the telephone the following morning, once Chloe had left for work. "Why drag all that up?"

"Dan, calm down."

"What? You're telling *me* to calm down. Why did you talk to her in the first place?"

"Look, I didn't know who she was at first, OK? She showed me a business card ... and - "

"You could have kept your mouth shut. I thought you were supposed to be a friend."

"I said I didn't know, OK? Anyway, it's not a state secret that you and Nicola were having problems – you two are divorced, for goodness sake. What's the big deal?"

"I think you knew damn well what you were doing."

She sniffed. "You think I did this for revenge? Because I wanted you all for myself? That one night wasn't enough?"

Dan's stomach contents roiled. He didn't want to have to go through all this again. Bloody women ...

"I think you did it because you were angry that it *was* only one night," he said. "You knew I wasn't myself, that I was going through a tough time yet –"

"Yet I dragged you off to bed," she said mockingly, "Give me a break, Dan, you wanted it as much as I did. What about *my* problems? We needed each other at the time and you know it."

"Man, you're a piece of work. You pretend to be my friend and then at the first opportunity you stab me in the back."

"Stab you in the back? If you had any decency you'd tell your fiancee the truth. No wonder the girl has to sneak around behind your back. *You* obviously don't trust her."

"It's not fair to Nicola."

"Dan, you and Nicola are finished. When are you going to accept that? She wasn't there for you when you needed her; she was too busy feeling sorry for herself. *I* was the one who was there for you, yet you're still carrying a torch for *her.*"

He shook his head. "You have no idea, do you?"

"What?"

"You have absolutely no idea how hard it was. Have you even *seen* her since?"

"Yes, and she seemed perfectly fine to me," she snapped dismissively.

"To think that I defended you ..." He broke off and shook his head.

"Dan, you broke up your marriage all by yourself,

and without help from me or anyone else. You were happy to come to me when you wanted it, so don't you dare try to project *your* guilt now."

"It was a stupid mistake ... I ..."

And it *was* a mistake. He hadn't meant to but he had been so lonely at the time, and he couldn't get through to Nicola – by then he couldn't do anything or say anything right, so what else was he supposed to do...?

"You said you'd tell her. You never did though, did you?"

"I couldn't," he admitted forlornly. "I wanted to but I just couldn't – she'd have been devastated, things were bad enough – "

She gave a short laugh. "It's hilarious, really. Poor old Nicola never had a clue, and the funny thing is she still thinks we're friends. I met her in town a while back and she even asked me to go for coffee."

Dan gritted his teeth. "I promise you," he warned, "if you do anything, or say anything else to Nicola *or* to Chloe, so help me God ..."

Carolyn O'Leary smiled.

"Don't worry," she said smugly, "our little secret is safe with me."

THIRTY-NINE

THE FOLLOWING EVENING Nicola was buzzing around the living-room tidying things away after Kerry's latest sleepover, while a giddy Barney skipped around alongside her, tongue out and tail wagging.

She was so engrossed that only for Barney she almost missed the pasta boiling over on the hob. Hearing his shrill bark, Nicola zoomed into the kitchen and reached the cooker only seconds before the starchy water boiled over.

Thank goodness for that, she thought, reaching down to scratch her conscientious doggy behind one ear. She didn't have time for mopping and scrubbing, particularly when her next visitor was due within minutes.

The doorbell rang, and Nicola looked up at the clock. Just in time. She went out to the hallway and opened the door.

"Hello, stranger," she greeted.

"Great to see you!" Engulfing her in an effusive hug,

Shannon stood back, and gave Nicola the once-over. "How are you doing?"

"Great, great, come on in." Nicola led her through to the kitchen, Barney sniffing curiously at the new visitor's heels. "Don't mind him, he'll be all over you for a bit, but he's harmless." She gave her dog a mock-stern look while she poured wine.

Barney responded by enthusiastically wagging the entire bottom half of his body.

"He's amazing," Shannon said, caressing his silky ears as he nuzzled into her. "How long have you had him?"

"Seems like forever, but he's only been around since I got this place."

"It's great – so well laid-out."

"It needed a lot of work," Nicola handed her a glass of chardonnay. "Luckily I had a very patient builder."

"I can't believe it's taken me this long to pay an actual visit though," Shannon grimaced. "Sorry I should have popped down long before now." Then her expression grew serious. "I hope I didn't upset you with that Dan's fiancee thing. I just thought I should let you know."

Nicola waved her away. "Quite the opposite. I'm glad you told me."

It had been very decent of Shannon to tip her off about Chloe's digging. So far, the girl hadn't yet approached Laura or Helen, and Nicola had yet to find out whether or not she had spoken to Carolyn O'Leary, who'd been her closest friend when she and Dan were married.

But Nicola knew that Carolyn would be the first one to send her off with a flea in her ear. It was such a pity that they had lost contact after her move to the UK. Then again she thought, their friendship had cooled as a result of her relationship with Shannon too.

Nicola had been mistaken in assuming that Shannon was chasing Dan. After a series of complaints that he spent too much time with her, she soon discovered that Dan's insistence he was a shoulder to cry on was actually just that. He eventually admitted that Shannon had been having an on/off affair with John O'Leary before Carolyn came on the scene.

Shannon was in love with his business partner and heartbroken when he married. And the two women detested one another.

Employing her at their new accountancy practice had been a massive flash-point for John and Carolyn, which Nicola now suspected might have eventually led to problems in their own marriage breakdown, and eventual separation.

Which incidentally, she had known nothing about until Dan had told her that day in Bray.

As difficult as it had been, Nicola hadn't said anything to Carolyn about her husband's faithlessness, having been warned by Dan not to.

"There's no point in either of us getting involved," he had said. "I tried to speak to John about it before, and he told me where to go."

"But surely Carolyn deserves to know what a rat he is," Nicola had countered vehemently, after John had wooed and then promptly dumped Shannon for the umpteenth time.

"Well, from what I can tell," Dan had said cryptically, "Carolyn is no angel herself."

At the time, Nicola resolved to keep her mouth shut but her loyalties were torn. On the one hand she hated not telling Carolyn that her husband was being unfaithful, and on the other she felt so sorry for Shannon. The girl had been totally powerless to break free of John's hold over her.

Now Shannon brushed a strand of auburn hair out of her pretty face. "You obviously told Dan about it anyway," she said. "He was straight on the phone, wondering if Chloe had got anything out of me."

"He was?" Nicola was surprised. "Surely he knows you wouldn't have broken any confidences?"

"Well, apparently she already knew about you and Ken – I mean back then before ..." she looked embarrassed.

"What? You're kidding." Nicola's mind raced. Where had Chloe got *that* from? Shannon didn't tell her, and obviously Dan didn't either so who else ...?

"Carolyn," she exclaimed breathlessly.

The other girl nodded. "That's what I figured, and exactly what I told Dan." She hesitated. "I'm not exactly impartial here, and I know you two were friends but I've always known she was a sneaky oul wagon."

Nicola recalled again Carolyn's unfriendliness towards her that day in the cafe. At the time, she had put it down to her friend's discomfort at bumping into her out of the blue after so much time. She knew that a lot of people just didn't know what to say to her since, and was used to it.

But now she knew it was something more.

Carolyn had changed, and like so many others, had obviously preferred to pretend to shut her out. That hurt.

Shannon looked thoughtful. "I've always thought that she resented you, you know."

"Me?"

"Yes." Shannon took another sip from her glass. "You and Dan were so happy and so well suited." She laughed when she saw Nicola's expression. "Well, you were most of the time," she added wryly. "I think Carolyn held your marriage up to hers and knew that it was lacking. She was no fool, she knew that ...." Suddenly, Shannon stopped talking and her eyes danced with amusement as something caught her attention.

Nicola followed her gaze and her eyes widened.

"Oh, Barney, don't." The dog was busily pulling clothes out of Nicola's washing-machine. "You'll mortify me – those are dirty." The dog dutifully stepped back from the machine and apologetically rolled over onto his back, looking for forgiveness. She had to laugh. "You really think Carolyn knew about you?"

"Of course she knew."

Nicola couldn't for the life of her imagine what Shannon had ever seen in John O'Leary, and she certainly couldn't figure out why the lively redhead couldn't find someone else. But she knew too that there was a side of Shannon that didn't want to. She enjoyed the excitement and the danger arising from an affair with a feckless married man.

"I still can't believe Carolyn would blab about that thing with Ken, though," Nicola said aloud. "What would she have to gain?"

"That one always relished dishing the dirt –" Shannon stopped short and looked apologetically at Nicola. "Sorry, I'm probably not the best person to talk to about this."

"Don't worry," she assured her. "That's ancient history now. And Carolyn obviously wasn't the great friend I thought her to be."

FORTY

"LAURA, can you mind my two tomorrow afternoon? I'm going into Holles St for a scan."

On the other end of the phone, Laura bristled.

Why did her sister have to pick this weekend of all weekends to have her scan? The Crafts Exhibition would be running from tomorrow until the middle of the following week. Since the wedding, Laura had been working overtime to get her collections ready.

She and Neil weren't even taking their honeymoon until after Christmas, when the travel business would be that bit quieter, and to give her a chance to prepare for what would hopefully be an encouraging sales period for Laura Connolly Design.

Tonight she had invited the others over for dinner, where hopefully they were going to meet Helen's elusive boyfriend, Paul.

"I'm very sorry – and normally I wouldn't mind, but at the moment I'm way too busy," she said, explaining the situation. Cathy didn't say anything for a long moment and Laura realised just then how like Maureen her sister could be when it came to getting her own way.

"Couldn't you ask Mam?" she offered meekly.

"I was hoping you'd do me the turn. Josh and Dylan are always going on about staying with Auntie Laura in Dublin, seeing as Auntie Laura doesn't visit them very much at home."

There it was, right on cue. The Guilt Trip.

What was wrong with her family? Why couldn't they support her? Laura had had enough.

She was going to make this business work. She was going to display at this Crafts Exhibition and she was going to talk the talk and walk the walk just as well as the rest of them – even better. Why shouldn't she? She was good at what she did.

Why was she always apologising for it? By the time Laura was finished building her empire, she'd have her family *begging* her to design stuff for them.

Even though Cathy was probably long gone, she banged down the receiver and immediately felt a rush of energy, a rush of exhilaration that she didn't think she'd ever felt in her entire life.

Bring on the Crafts Expo – bring them *all* on.

Laura was going to make this business a success even if it was just to shove it down her family's begrudging little throats.

Later that evening, Nicola and Ken arrived, clutching a bottle of wine and a multi-pack of Pringles.

Laura eyed him when they joined her in the kitchen. "You brought crisps?"

"What? I just thought we might be hungry later, that's all." He winked at Neil who was trying his best to stifle a grin.

"Thanks a million. And here's me slaving over a hot stove all afternoon."

"I know," Nicola teased. "That's exactly why we brought the crisps."

"Seriously, Laura, don't mind us – the food smells great," Ken said, sniffing the air approvingly. "When do we eat?"

"Not until Helen and the Famous Paul get here, I'm afraid," she answered. "But I told her dinner was at eight so I'm sure they won't be too much longer."

"Is Kerry coming too?"

"One of Helen's neighbours is looking after her tonight." To Laura's relief, that same neighbour had also been obliging enough to collect Kerry from school the last few days, leaving her free to prepare for the expo.

She hoped this poor girl knew what she was getting herself into.

"So we're not the only eejits at her beck and call then," Nicola said, as she removed her jacket. "Still, I can't wait to get a look at this Paul. Things must be pretty serious there – when was the last time Helen introduced us to one of her playthings?"

"*Play*things?" Ken repeated sardonically. "That's what we're reduced to these days, is it? God be with the days when ye couldn't do a thing without us. Now we're practically redundant."

"Not quite," Laura said, face red as she struggled with a pot of steaming vegetables. "Neil, any chance you could pour some wine for our guests?" she added pointedly.

Still a little wound up from her conversation with Cathy earlier, and unused to cooking for a gang, Laura couldn't keep the frustration out of her tone.

"Sorry, love, better get out of your way," Neil said, picking up on his new wife's spirits. "I'll open a bottle and we'll leave the missus alone to get on with the important stuff." He gave her an encouraging wink and bottle in hand, led Ken through to the dining-room.

"You OK?" Nicola asked.

Laura looked around and almost automatically felt guilty. She was sure Nicola had followed the others into the living-room.

"I'm fine," she answered shakily, "just a little hot and bothered with all this cooking."

"Nervous about the expo, huh?"

Nicola had a knack of hitting the nail on the head. Despite her fighting talk earlier, Laura *was* feeling nervous about the Crafts Exhibition. This was make or break for the business. If her designs didn't go down well or she didn't pick up some new customers, well ... well, then it was all over.

"Oh, I'll be fine," she said. "After all, I've had plenty of time to get ready."

"It doesn't happen overnight, you know," she said gently and Laura's stomach gave a nervous flip. Sometimes Nicola was too damn perceptive for her own good.

She had obviously seen through her false bravado – had known that all wasn't well.

Yet, she had never pushed it, never said a thing because she knew that Laura wouldn't want to admit it out loud that the business might be a failure.

She suddenly felt very grateful to her friend.

"I always told myself that I'd give it a shot, and if it didn't take off, well … at least I tried." She gave a watery smile. "But nobody told me it would be this hard to admit defeat."

"Hey, what's all this 'admitting defeat' business?" Nicola said. "It hasn't been all that long."

"I think you and I both know that maybe I didn't think things through properly. Helen was right – I'm just not made of the right stuff."

"Hey," Nicola put a hand on her arm, "please don't tell me you're thinking of throwing in the towel – not after everything you've done?"

"But that's exactly it. I haven't done *anything*. A few online orders a week and the odd bit of interest from the shops – it's hardly setting the business world on fire, is it?"

"It's something," Nicola countered, "not to mention something to be proud of. Don't lose faith in your abilities, and don't write yourself off just yet."

"I suppose I'll just have to see how the exhibition goes." Suddenly, she didn't want to talk about it anymore.

"It'll be fine. Part of the problem is publicity. Your product is great – you just haven't had enough exposure."

"Maybe," Laura smiled absently.

"Um, Laura?" Nicola sniffed the air, and gestured towards the oven. "I think your roasties might be good to go."

"Oh!" Laura opened the oven door and a thick blanket of smoke rushed out. She looked at Nicola in dismay, her cheeks reddening with annoyance. "Um I think now might be a good time to join the others?" she implored.

Nicola sped off, anxious to make a quick exit.

"And Nicola?" she called after her.

"Yes?"

"Do you think Sour Cream & Onion Pringles are a decent substitute for roast potatoes?"

"With lamb?" she grinned. "They'll be absolutely perfect."

FORTY-ONE

AN HOUR AND A QUARTER LATER, they were still waiting; Ken and Neil having hungrily demolished the crisps between them.

"I've tried her mobile and there's no signal," Laura said, trying to suppress her annoyance. The lamb would be like rubber at this stage too.

"They're probably just running late," Neil said, his tone soothing.

"If they're running late, the least she could have done is phoned," Nicola said, her irritation palpable.

"She'll be here," Ken said, giving her a warning look. "There's no point in our –"

A loud shrill of the doorbell cut short the remainder of his sentence.

"That'll be them," Laura jumped to her feet. "Neil, can you get that, and I'll ready the starters?"

"Sure."

Seconds later, Helen joined Laura in the kitchen looking amazing, her blonde hair swinging freely around her shoulders, and dressed in a stunning black beaded dress, the material clinging faintly to her curves – what few there were.

"Hey," she greeted, moving forward to give her a hug. "Everything good to go here? I'm famished."

Laura was taken aback. She had expected an apology, or at the very least some kind of excuse as to why Helen was over an hour late.

Not a demand to be fed.

"What kept you?" she asked. "And where's Paul?"

"Outside showing Neil his new Audi. The two of them seem to have hit it off already." She grinned.

"Well go on in and join the others. Dinner might not be great after being kept this long," she added pointedly, "but everyone's so hungry they'll hardly care –"

"What others?" Helen interjected, her eyes wide.

"Ken and Nicola of course."

"*What*? You didn't tell me *they* were coming. I thought it was just the four of us – you and me, Neil and Paul."

"What's the problem? Did you and Nicola have an argument or something?" Laura asked.

"No, nothing like that – it's just ..." She bit her lip and looked decidedly panicked.

"What is it?"

She winced. "It's just ... I kinda haven't yet told Paul ... about Kerry. And I was hoping you and Neil might do me a favour by not mentioning her tonight."

Laura's eyes widened. "What? Why not?"

"I know, I know. But we haven't been going out very long and the subject never came up and –"

"Helen, she's your daughter," Laura was incredulous. "That's so unfair. To Kerry *and* to Paul. And he's bound to find out in any case. What did you think would happen?"

"I just thought I'd cross that bridge when I came to it –"

"It's crazy ..."

"I *know*. It's high time I told him but I'm just not ready yet. I really thought it would be just you and Neil tonight and I was so sure you would ..."

"Lie for you?" Laura finished, shaking her head in disbelief. "Maybe you'd better just take him aside now, otherwise –"

"But I can't just drop it on him all of a sudden..." Her voice dropped sharply to a whisper. "Not in public – it wouldn't be fair."

"But you must. It's bound to come up."

"I know, I know. Crikey, Laura what'll I do? Should I talk to Nicola . . . ask her not to . . . ?"

"Rather you than me. But go ahead – "

The door to the living room opened but Helen had her back to it and appeared not to notice.

"Do you need help with anything here?" Nicola asked easily, and Helen nearly jumped ten feet off the ground.

"Hi!" she greeted.

"I see you've finally decided to honour us with your presence ..."

Helen smiled warily. "Um yes, Paul was working late and ..." she trailed off as they heard voices in the hallway and footsteps approach.

"Laura's just in the kitchen," they heard Neil say, and Laura's breath caught as, just behind him, the most stunning-looking guy she had ever seen entered.

Tousled hair, sculpted cheekbones, piercing slate-grey eyes – lucky old Helen.

"Hey," he greeted in a distinct American twang. "Hope you guys didn't start the party without us."

A flustered Helen quickly made the introductions, glancing meaningfully at Laura as she did so.

"Hello, Paul. Welcome," Laura greeted, smiling warmly.

"Good to be here." He grinned back at her, his smile faltering at the sight of Nicola, who simply gave a curt nod.

"Paul was working late," Helen offered quickly, by way of explanation. "So, by the time he got to my place, and then of course our little detour ..."

"I got a bit lost on the way," he admitted bashfully.

"In the metropolis that's Ballinteer?" Neil chuckled.

"I tried to give him directions but you know what men are like," Helen batted her eyelids playfully.

"Hey!" Neil piped up, rising to her bait. "I'll have you know that men are far better orienteers ... orientators ... what's the word again?"

"Exactly my point," Helen jibed. "You know what men are like."

She ducked giddily as he aimed a tea towel at her.

"Can everyone go inside and sit down now?" Laura said testily, deliberately refusing to make eye contact with Helen though she could feel her anxious gaze fixed on her.

Nicola had already headed back to the dining-room, therefore robbing Helen of a chance to have a quiet word. Out of the corner of her eye, Laura saw Neil put a friendly arm around Helen's shoulders and usher her out of the kitchen in Paul's wake.

So not only had Helen landed her in another tricky situation, but she was sick to the teeth of her incessant flirting with her husband. It was the same every time Helen called to pick up Kerry. Laura knew that she just couldn't help herself – get her within two yards of any man and she was batting her eyelids as if she was in a sandstorm and wiggling her backside like Kylie Minogue – even in her current state of tension.

But it was a bit much considering she and Neil were only married a wet week ...

Taking a minute to calm herself, Laura began carrying the first course into the dining-room.

"So, are you a farmer or a forester or something, Paul?" Nicola was asking.

Paul looked at Nicola as if she was on drugs. "No why?"

"Well, since you were working late, I suppose I just wondered why you couldn't get to a phone."

Recognising her tone, Ken nudged her chair beneath the table and Helen shot her a venomous look.

"He misheard the time. He thought I said dinner was at *nine*."

Paul gave Helen a quick glance, which suggested he thought anything but.

"Well, we're all here now, anyway," Laura said,

trying to relieve the obvious tension. "So get stuck in before it goes cold."

"Great," Paul rubbed his hands together. "I'm starving, haven't eaten a thing all day and I'll tell you this, I have one hell of an appetite." He winked at Helen.

"Good thing we waited for you then, isn't it?" Nicola said sweetly but, to anyone who knew her, her tone dripped with sarcasm.

Laura sighed. It was going to be a long night.

FORTY-TWO

NICOLA SAT and watched the gorgeous Paul wolf down his lamb as if he had never eaten before in his life.

What did Helen see in him? OK, that was fairly obvious: he was bloody gorgeous. But still. Where did he think he was going with the fake American accent? All 'hey' and 'wow' and 'guys' this and that.

"So Paul, where are you from yourself?" she asked innocently.

He wiped the side of his mouth with a napkin. "Cork."

Helen shot Nicola another look, knowing exactly what she was getting at. "Paul spends a lot of time abroad on business," she explained.

"What you do?"

He looked pleased to be asked. "I'm an investment advisor – pensions, stocks – things like that."

"He's given me fantastic advice," Helen trilled. "Now I know exactly what to do with my money."

"Oh, shoes are part of a portfolio these days?" Neil

teased. Grinning, he got to his feet. "I'll get some more wine, will I?"

"I'll get dessert." Laura shuffled out to the kitchen with him, leaving the others alone at the table.

Nicola thought it odd that, despite her enthusiasm about her new man, Helen seemed rather ill at ease.

Every time Paul opened his mouth to say something, her friend's gaze kept darting here and there, as if she was worried he might not make a good impression.

She supposed she might have been a bit unfair – it had evidently taken a lot for Helen to work up the courage to introduce him to her friends and it was obvious she was keen they all get along. For her sake, she should make the effort.

"So, you two have been seeing one another for a while now..." She injected some enthusiasm into her voice.

"Yes, she's one hell of a babe." Paul looked at Helen with pure devotion. Yes, men loved Helen; men had *always* loved her but usually didn't have a hope once her friend decided they weren't up to standard. Might Paul actually be the right one for her, the one to banish the ghost of Jamie for good? For her friend's sake, she hoped so. It would be terrific if Helen could finally find someone for her - and Kerry - to love.

"So you've obviously met Kerry then," Nicola continued, just as the others returned from the kitchen. She shot a glance at Helen, who was sitting ram-rod straight in her chair, her eyes pleading with Laura.

Paul looked bemused. "Kerry?"

Nicola watched him curiously. "Well, yes, Helen's –"

"*Dog,*" Helen interjected.

He turned to her, his mouth full. "What?"

"My dog," she said again and Nicola stared at her, shocked. "My dog, a Kerry Blue - I've had her for years." She gave a carefree little titter but her eyes told a *very* different story.

"Oh right." He laughed too. "You never mentioned a dog before."

"Helen? Let's get the coffees and give Laura a little break." Nicola moved resolutely towards the kitchen, her mouth set in a thin angry line.

She heard Ken and Neil engage Paul in mindless chatter, anything it seemed to relieve the tension. But apparently he had noticed nothing amiss.

Alone with Nicola in the kitchen, Helen was shame-faced. "Look, he doesn't know, I just haven't got around to it yet." She studied a piece of carrot that had fallen on the ground.

"You haven't got *round* to it yet? What the hell does that mean? You've been going out with this guy for a couple of months and you've just told him that your daughter –" Helen winced, and looked back towards the dining-room, presumably hoping that Paul couldn't hear, "yes, your *daughter,* is a – a *dog*. What the hell were you thinking?"

"Nicola please – it was the first thing I could thing of –"

"First thing you could think of? Why should you *have* to think of anything? Why didn't you tell him the truth? That Kerry is a sweet, loving child, the most important thing in your life, the most precious thing in all of our lives."

And it was true. Kerry was the child that Nicola had never had, that she might never have and she loved that little girl with all her heart. And as far as she knew, Laura felt the same. The two of them had been there for Helen through thick and thin, and Nicola knew that if she had to, she would fight to the death for the kid. If she felt this way then how could the child's mother, her own *mother,* basically deny her?

"Nicola please, I know it was awful. But it was just a little white lie. And I really didn't mean for that to happen but I wasn't prepared for ... I just ..." She shook her head. "I know it was stupid and I feel so guilty about not telling him, really I do." Her eyes brimmed with tears. "But you don't understand, you don't know how it is. You don't know what it's like trying to find someone, someone decent and nice and ... and I'm just afraid that if I tell him about Kerry it's all over. Men run a mile when they hear about Kerry. I can't let that happen this time. You don't understand – I really *like* Paul."

Just a little white lie...

At this Nicola felt rage rise within her, something she hadn't felt in a long, long time. She took a deep breath and struggled to remember every piece of advice she'd ever heard about anger management. She began to count to twenty but didn't even reach five. Her face hard, she looked one of her oldest friends straight in the eye. She couldn't believe Helen's selfishness, her callousness towards her own child, toward *everyone.*

"Helen, you are a selfish wagon."

"What?" Helen stared at her, dazed. "What did you call me?"

"I called you selfish."

"Nicola, you're my friend. I know you're angry but believe me that is the one reason – the *only* reason I am taking this from you."

"The *only* reason? The only reason, huh?"

"Yes."

The two woman glared at one another, barely noticing as Laura entered the room.

"Are you sure it's the only reason, Helen?" Nicola went on. "Because I'm such a *good friend*? Or is because I know what you're really like?"

"Girls, don't ..." Laura was soothing.

Helen frowned. "What is that supposed to mean?"

"You know damn well what I'm talking about and don't pretend otherwise."

"I really don't know where all of this is coming from, but –"

"No, of course you don't. Because you're so consumed by your own little life, so immersed in what's good for *you,* that you don't know or care about anyone else."

"What? What are you talking about?"

"I'm talking *not* just about denying your own child in front of your latest shag, but doing so on a regular basis. If you're not dumping her on me, you're dumping her on Laura, who goodness knows has had enough to contend with these last few months between planning a wedding and setting up a business without having to babysit a four-year-old."

"Helen, it's OK, I don't mind having Kerry –"

"But you don't care about what she has to contend with, do you?" Nicola went on as though Laura hadn't spoken. "As long as she serves your purpose, you don't give a damn. And she's just too nice and too *loyal* a friend to tell you to stuff it. She's too good to you and we both know you don't deserve that."

"Anything else?" Helen said, her hand on her hip.

"Now that you mention it, yes there is. Kerry needs her mother's attention, she needs you. But you don't give a hoot about that, do you? You'd just prefer to bury your head in the sand and pretend it isn't happening - like you always do."

Helen's expression would have been same had Nicola slapped her across the face. "That's not true ... I do my best; you have no idea how hard I try but –"

"Helen, we've all done our best for you over the years, but you've never been there for any of us in return. Quite the bloody opposite. I *saw* you with Neil earlier and you just can't help yourself, can you? Old habits die hard."

Nicola felt like she was on a runaway train. She was on dangerous ground now but couldn't stop herself – she just wanted to catch the silly wagon and shake her.

"Oh, I get it now," Helen said, her eyes hard as flints. "It's all coming out now, isn't it?"

"Please calm down," Laura beseeched.

"No let her speak, let's allow good old sanctimonious Nicola her long-awaited guilt trip," Helen interjected, glaring. "While you're at it, why not get it *all* off your chest and have a proper go at me – you haven't done that yet, so go on." Now Helen was in full flight too, her voice high and artificial. "I know you're just dying to tell her, you have been for years, so why the hell don't you?"

"*Please!*" Laura implored.

"All that old resentment coming home to roost. Just because I didn't drop everything and come running when things went south for you. Just because I made a mistake – a *single* stupid mistake. Because I wasn't a candidate for best friend of the century. Then again," she added bitterly, "I couldn't possibly beat good ole Laura for that particular prize."

"Don't be so bloody stupid."

"For goodness sake, *will you two stop it!*"

The two spun around finally noticing Laura standing there, tears in her eyes.

"This is my home," she pleaded sadly. "This is my home."

For a long moment a tension-filled hush descended on the kitchen.

Helen looked at Laura and her hand flew to her mouth. "I'm so sorry," she whispered. "I'm sorry, we didn't mean … you don't know what we were – "

"What you were referring to?" Laura finished for her, her expression defeated. "Of course I know, Helen. I've always known."

FORTY-THREE

CHLOE WAS SITTING AT HOME, depressed. She knew now that she had made a very big mistake.

Big. Huge.

She stared at a picture on the mantelpiece of her and Dan taken last Christmas at her mum and dad's.

She loved that picture. She looked particularly good in it and looking at it now, it struck her that she really should wear purple more often. It seemed to complement her skin tone and highlight her cheekbones.

Course, Dan was always equally striking in photographs, his attractive features lit up by that grin. Their wedding photos would be truly spectacular, better than anything in *Hello* magazine.

If the wedding took place, that is.

She had spent what *should* have been her wedding day alone in front of the television, while Dan went in to the office. He didn't have to go in, but Chloe knew that he was trying to avoid her. He was hardly talking to her.

And to top it all off, this whole Nicola thing wasn't such a big deal after all.

Why had she bothered? So what if Dan's ex had a miscarriage that upended their relationship. So what if she had a little fling with her co-worker?

Chloe guessed that most of her so-called friends were laughing behind her back at this stage.

So much for the wedding of the century in The Four Seasons. So much for the designer wedding dress, exotic honeymoon and the supposedly wonderful Amazing Days invites.

The wedding invites ... If it wasn't for the stupidity of that crowd she wouldn't be having any of these problems now. Well, maybe the wedding would still be postponed, but at least her fiancé would be talking to her.

She was losing him and Chloe knew it. Dan was hardly at home anymore. They rarely spent any time together these days – she couldn't remember the last time they had gone out for a meal, or to the cinema even.

She had apologised and explained, and tried to help him understand why she felt the need to go digging behind his back, but he no longer trusted her.

Chloe had focused only on what she might find; not about how it would affect her relationship. In fairness, she hadn't expected the John's wife to reveal as much as she had, considering she was supposed to be Nicola's friend.

And considering what Carolyn had told her about Shannon chasing Dan, she certainly hadn't expected the PA to send her packing.

She knew now that it was likely Shannon that had

spilled the beans. At the time, it was a chance Chloe had been willing to take.

But now, she wished she hadn't bothered. Although, if Dan hadn't been so bloody secretive about all in the first place, she *needn't* have bothered.

The way he carried on, you'd swear the reason for his marriage break-up was the third secret of Fatima.

There was still one thing that was bothering her about the entire situation, and try as she might she couldn't stop thinking about it. It was in the back of her mind all the time and she couldn't leave it alone.

If Nicola had cheated on Dan that time - why had he fought so hard to keep her?

As far as Chloe knew she and the work colleague hadn't run off into the sunset together afterwards – it'd just been a one-off fling.

So what was she missing?

Why had Nicola gone to London?

And more to the point, why had Dan always said that *he* felt guilty?

After all Chloe reasoned, if Nicola had been the one at fault and Dan had done nothing wrong, what on earth did he have to feel guilty about?

FORTY-FOUR

"I'VE ALWAYS KNOWN," Laura repeated wearily slumping down on one of the kitchen chairs. "Did you really think that Neil – my *husband* – would have hidden something like that from me? What kind of a sap do you think I am – both of you?"

Nicola tried to make amends. "Laura, it was nothing, really. It was a long time ago ..."

"I *know*," she repeated wearily. "Unlike you two, Neil thought enough of me to tell me. What kind of a relationship did you think we had? He loves me; there was no way he would have kept anything like that from me. I've known since the very beginning."

The door from the dining-room opened softly, and Neil popped his head around it. "Everything okay, love?" he asked.

Helen looked guardedly at him.

"Everything's fine," Laura answered.

"The lads and myself might pop down to the local – get out of your hair for a while, OK?"

His wife gave a tired nod as the door closed after him.

Nicola remembered the whole thing as clearly as if it happened yesterday.

Christmas – not long after Jamie had abandoned Helen and the baby. Nicola had just moved to London but had come home to see her family, mostly to convince them she was doing OK, but also to attend a New Year's Eve party at Laura and Neil's.

There was a good crowd and everyone had been drinking heavily with the exception of Nicola, who that night was feeling particularly sorry for herself. New Year's Eve was like that.

That night, despite the demands of early motherhood, Helen looked stunning as always with her salon tan, and wearing a jaw-droppingly sexy, gold knitted dress which clung to every curve and emphasised her newly flat stomach. Every inch the social butterfly, she flitted teasingly from one man to the other all night.

Laura had since gone to bed while Neil stayed up mingling.

Deciding she might just go to bed early herself, Nicola made her way to Laura's spare bedroom, trying to remember if she had left her overnight bag there upon her arrival earlier.

The party was already beginning to break up and she suspected Helen might have left already, as she hadn't seen her in a while.

She opened the bedroom door and switching on the light, stopped short.

"What the hell?"

There on the bed, bodies moulded together and kissing passionately were none other than Helen - and Neil.

Eyes glazed, he sat up and horrified, looked drunkenly at Nicola and then back to Helen. Immediately he pushed her away. "Christ," he gasped, "I ... it's not ... I would never –"

"Not what I think? Then what is it, Neil? Because I sure as hell don't know what else it could be."

Helen rolled onto the bed and insolently rested her head on her elbow, watching Neil flounder, not a care in the world.

"Nicola, I swear – I just don't know what happened ... I –"

"Get out of my sight," Nicola ordered, ignoring him. "I want a word with Helen."

"OK, OK, I'm going but ..." He stood up and quickly buttoning up his shirt, looked at Helen. "It was nothing ..."

Nicola flashed him another look and he bolted, swaying slightly as he went.

Her hair and clothes dishevelled, Helen swung her legs off the side of the bed and the two friends faced one another, daggers drawn.

Helen didn't look in the slightest bit guilty – in fact, she looked triumphant.

"What the hell are you playing at?" she spat when Helen didn't say anything. "Laura's your friend."

Helen waved a carefree hand in the air. "Laura,

Laura, Laura," she slurred. "Seems she's just as messed up as the rest of us."

"What?"

"Look at how things turned out," she said as if it all made perfect sense. "*You* get messed up by Dan, *I* get messed up by Jamie – now we're *all* quits."

Nicola was so angry at her she could hardly speak. She knew Helen was finding things hard, but to deliberately ...

"You're telling me that you set out to seduce Neil tonight, just to get back at Jamie?"

"Nope." Helen slumped drunkenly back onto the bed. "To get back at Laura."

"What? But why? What has she ever done to you? She's your best friend, for goodness sake."

"Oh, she's so bloody *perfect*," Helen hissed. "She has her nice little job, and her nice little boyfriend and she never loses her temper, everyone loves her and I'm just so bloody sick of it."

Nicola resisted the urge to strangle her. "Just because you're jealous of her, just because your life is a mess right now doesn't mean that you can go around messing things up for her. She loves Neil and despite what I saw just now, I know he loves her too. What kind of a friend are you, Helen?"

What had happened to her? Was she so full of bitterness towards Jamie that she was no longer able to feel compassion - for anyone?

Helen had given her a look that would cut diamonds before picking up her shoes and exiting the room.

Things changed the next day though. The next day, a

deeply distressed Helen turned up at Nicola's parent's place.

"I'm sorry," she bawled, a sleeping Kerry in her arms. "I don't know what I was trying to prove. I didn't set out to hurt Laura ... I was just so lonely and screwed up and ...."

Nicola wasn't having any of it. "Just promise me that you will never *ever* do anything like that again. Grow up and start taking responsibility for your actions. You're an adult and now you have a child to look after."

"I'm sorry," she said again. "I'm just finding it hard. I miss him so much, and I'm terrified that I won't be a good mother."

Nicola had tried to reassure her that it was still early days, she had just been through a tough time, was still in mourning for Jamie and that everything would eventually fall into place.

And Nicola thought, it had. Helen seemed genuinely contrite, stayed away from Neil and Laura, and began to pick up the pieces after Jamie's departure.

For his part, Neil had been beside himself with remorse and begged her not to think badly of him.

There was no point in upsetting Laura by telling her that her best friend and her boyfriend had had a drunken, meaningless fling on New Year's Eve. Not wanting to think about what might have happened had she *not* interrupted them, she figured it was the best decision.

Apparently, Neil hadn't felt the same way, yet she hadn't anticipated that he would come clean with Laura.

Yet now that Nicola thought about it, it wasn't too

surprising. Neil was a decent man, prepared to sacrifice his relationship and possibly Laura's trust in him by being honest.

She only wished Dan had been the same.

FORTY-FIVE

NOW LAURA LOOKED at them both, her expression stony.

Why is Neil the *only* one who gives me any credit? You," she said, pointing at Helen, "my supposed best friend, tried to mess up my relationship, and you knew about it but never said a word."

"It wasn't like that," Nicola began. "It was just ... a little white lie. We were only trying to protect you ..." She trailed off when Laura held her hand up.

What had happened to the three of them? What had happened to trust, loyalty, support – all the things that made up a friendship, *real* friendship?

How had they let one another down like this?

"Laura, it was all my fault," Helen began. "It was New Year's Eve and I was feeling lonely, and I just wanted someone ... to hold me and to comfort me and –"

"It wasn't just any man, though. Neil wasn't fair game. He wasn't innocent but at least he had the guts to come and tell me about it, at least he respected me enough to do that. I know you two think I'm too soft, too emotional. But I'm not as stupid as you seem to think. I said nothing, because I believed him when he said it was nothing but a drunken fling that had got out of hand. After all, I know what she can be like."

At this Helen hung her head, clearly ashamed.

But then her tone softened. "But I also knew that you were suffering, and I tried to be there for you. I've always tried to be there for you, but you and I have grown apart. You're different, Helen. Ever since you had Kerry, you're different."

"I know," Helen said softly. "I know that. I just ... I just feel so lonely sometimes. You two are so lucky; you don't know what it's like to be on your own without someone to love."

"And what about Kerry?" Nicola asked impatiently. "Don't you love her?"

"Of course I do – but not – not the way I'm supposed to – not the way other mothers do."

"Other mothers?"

Helen looked uncomfortable. "I don't think I feel the way I should – I – I just don't know."

Nicola studied her friend's expression. She hadn't seen Helen let her guard down like this in a very long time.

"But how should a mother feel?"

"I don't know," Helen cried. "That's part of the problem. I love her, but I've never felt that overwhelming maternal thing that everyone talks about. I should feel that, shouldn't I? I should want to kill, to *die* for my child?" She put her head in her hands. "But I don't feel that way, I just feel ... lonely."

Nicola had no idea Helen had been battling with her feelings like this. Yes, she was selfish, always been – but lonely? She would never have used that word to describe her. Not when there was an army of male admirers ready and waiting at every turn.

"I'm not trying to be cruel, but with the way you've been behaving recently, maybe it isn't surprising that you feel lonely."

"I know."

Still, despite her faults, seeing Helen genuinely shamefaced and distressed, Nicola's heart went out to her.

"Honestly, by focusing entirely on what you don't have, you're missing out on what you *do* have. OK, so I have no idea what it's like to raise a child - let alone by myself, but I do have some idea of what I'm talking about when it comes to ... losing stuff."

Helen looked duly shame-faced. "I know, and I'm sorry."

"Time passes by so quickly too," Laura put in, "Keep in mind she won't be this young forever either."

For a long while the three remained silent, unsure what to say to one another.

"I think I should go," Helen said eventually and they watched in silence as she retrieved her coat and bag. "I'm very sorry and I really mean that," she said again, unable to meet anyone's gaze. "Not just for the thing with Neil but ... but for everything."

Saying nothing more, Helen headed to the doorway,

and with an almost imperceptible nod, Laura closed the
door behind their old friend.

FORTY-SIX

CHLOE WAS DAYDREAMING at work when Reception put a call through to her desk.

She wondered if she had heard right. "Are you sure?"

The receptionist sounded hassled. "Line three, OK?"

Her heart pounded. What the hell did *she* want?

"Hello Chloe, Nicola here, how's things?"

She sounded … quite pleasant, actually. But really … what did she want? "Um, hello."

"Look, I won't waste your time. I just wondered if you were free after work this evening?" Chloe's eyes widened as Nicola continued. "I just think that maybe we should meet and clear the air."

"If you're referring to my questioning your friends like that … I'm sorry, I just didn't – "

"It's fine, Chloe," Dan's ex interjected breezily. "Anyway, do you think you could pop over to my place for a coffee or a bite this evening, maybe?"

Now she was really frightened. Was this some kind of trap?

"I'm not sure if ... "

"I'd really like to meet you."

Overwhelming curiosity eventually made the decision for her. She was *dying* to find out what Nicola was like.

Despite what little information she had gleaned there would be no substitute for meeting the ex-wife face to face. Dan mightn't be too happy though.

But what could he say? Nicola had invited her; it wasn't as though she was going behind anyone's back this time.

She swivelled around in her seat. To hell with the consequences. Plus her curiosity was *killing* her.

"OK," she said to Nicola. "Just give me directions and I'll pop down after work, say sixish?"

"Great. Looking forward to it."

So am I, Chloe thought, her thoughts going a mile a minute as she wrote down the address on a post-it note.

So am I.

FORTY-SEVEN

LATER THAT SAME EVENING, Dan drove slowly on the outskirts of Lakeview.

He was looking forward to seeing her again – probably a lot more than he should be, he thought grimacing, reminding himself yet again that he was engaged to be married to someone else.

In any case, he was glad they would have the chance to talk properly this time, and still was ashamed and more than a little embarrassed about the whole situation with Chloe.

He also knew that Nicola would no doubt by now have figured out that Carolyn had blabbed. He would have to try and explain that to her too, although he certainly wasn't going to admit the whole truth – that one time he and John's wife had somehow ended up in the sack.

He didn't know what had come over him that night. It had been a tough, dark period and he'd needed solace. Carolyn had been only too happy to oblige.

And that was ultimately why he had let Nicola go. There was no point in trying to pretend that everything would be OK, that they could pick up the pieces of their marriage and go on as normal. They weren't strong enough for that – *he* wasn't strong enough for that.

Once he had been tempted, Dan was only too aware of his own limits.

No, he had done the right thing by leaving when he did.

Yet after all these years, he was certain that he and Nicola still had unfinished business. They still cared about one another, that was obvious. He didn't know what he had been expecting, when he saw her again, but it certainly wasn't the strong and confident Nicola he had met that day in Bray. She had still looked so well and so *content* that it was almost unnerving.

Then again, Dan thought, he should have known that she would triumph. She had always been stronger, while he was the one who had fallen to pieces, who had let her down in every way imaginable.

But was it possible that she now might be ready to forgive - forget even?

He'd been heartened by her invite and knew this was a breakthrough, so had decided to come a little bit earlier than agreed so he could maybe give her a hand with preparing dinner or what-not. It was something they used to really enjoy when they were married, and might make things a bit more relaxed than him just rocking up when everything was ready.

He was especially looking forward to tucking into his ex-wife's cooking. She had always been a whizz in the kitchen and usually went all out. Dan had really missed that – Chloe could barely make toast.

Suddenly spying the turnoff, he indicated and quickly jammed on the brakes before continuing a little way down the road, recalling the directions she'd given.

Half a mile down, yellow bungalow, third house on the left.

Dan was surprised she had bought a bungalow since she'd always so disliked them; citing their apparent lack of character.

Back when they were married she had fallen in love with a chalet-style place they'd had seen in the Wicklow Mountains, a mammoth house with indigenous stonework, woodwork and tons of personality.

He had been partial to the place too; it was ideal for a dynamic, up-and-coming businessman like himself. Not for the first time, Dan wondered how their life together would have turned out, had things not gone awry.

Seeing a row of houses come into view, he slowed, deciding that he must be almost there. One, two three ... he mentally counted down and then balked as he spied what must be Nicola's place.

Right in front of him, pulling into the driveway, was none other than Chloe's Rav4.

But ... why would she be ... ?

His heart raced with panic as he watched his fiancée park the jeep. She got out and took a quick, uncertain look around as she locked the car door.

Crap. Dan had to reach her before she got to the house. He hit the controls for the passenger window but in his haste, pressed the wrong button and wound down his own instead.

Chloe was now running a hand through her hair, and tottering up the front path. She'd almost reached the door when Dan put his head out the window to call her back, hoping she'd hear him from this distance.

He needed to talk to her first, to explain ...

But when he saw Nicola smiling and welcoming his fiancée from the open doorway, Dan knew that it was already too late.

FORTY-EIGHT

KEN LIGHTLY RAN his index finger over the newly polished diamond.

Would she like it? He certainly hoped so. He was taking a hell of a chance choosing the ring beforehand; he knew that, but he wanted to do this right.

He closed the box and put it back inside his pocket.

He couldn't believe how terrifying all of this felt. Would she say yes there and then, or would she maybe ask for some time to think about it?

He steeled himself for every possible scenario, even one where she might say no. She might not be ready for that yet and of course he would accept that too. He would have no problem waiting – he knew she loved him and she was most definitely the one for him.

He was glad the thing with that other gobshite was finally over and done with too. Ken hated that Dan had sauntered back into Nicola's life lately, as if nothing at all had happened.

Still, the main thing was that she wasn't reciprocating. And he knew she wasn't reciprocating because she was over Dan. Hadn't she told Ken that she wished *he* had been the one she was married to? And that he and Barney were basically her family now?

Well, if things went as well tonight as he hoped they would, they were about to become an actual family.

He began rehearsing the words again in his head and grimaced, almost unable to *look* at the house. Wow, this was nerve-wracking. He had been practicing the build-up over and over, so hopefully things would all go according to plan.

Suddenly, he stopped the car, icy daggers shooting up his spine.

What the hell was *he* doing here? Ken was still a little away, but he could quite clearly make out the other guy's ignorant head.

Hunt was hurrying up Nicola's driveway.

Had she been lying to him all along? Had she been covering up that she and her ex were back on good terms again? After all, she had been secretive about meeting him that time – what else was she being secretive about?

Furious, he wrenched the ring-box from his pocket and flung it onto the floor of the car.

Then, reversing into a nearby gateway, red-faced with anger and tyres screeching wildly, Ken sped off in the other direction.

FORTY-NINE

"IT WAS *AMAZING*," Laura danced excitedly around the kitchen.

She had just returned from a day at the Crafts Exhibition and while Neil had come along to set up the stand, she was on her own once the doors opened to the public. "I must've given out at least two boxes of business cards."

"That's fantastic, love – didn't I tell you it would be brilliant."

Laura beamed at her husband. It *had* been brilliant. Finally her designs were being exposed to the right people – or the right market as Helen would say – and the feedback had been enormously positive.

Helen. Laura's heart lurched again as she thought about her friend. She had heard nothing from her since.

Obviously Helen just didn't want to deal with it, preferring to just ignore it all and cut Laura off when the going got tough, like she had Nicola all those years ago.

That was her way, after all. When faced with unpleasantness or any sign of trouble, she put her head in the sand and pretended it wasn't happening. That was what she was doing with Kerry's stammering too.

Laura certainly doubted that Helen was troubling herself about the bust-up, though she did seem shaken upon her departure the other night. And she didn't think she had ever seen her friend so shame-faced. Nicola's home truths had surely hurt her, but she also knew her friend had said that stuff for Helen's own good, and Kerry's too.

In any case, it was good to have it out. Laura was especially happy that she'd had the gumption to stand up for herself this time, and not let Helen try to paper it over with excuses and pleas of drunkenness.

In spite of everything, in spite of their ups and downs, she didn't want to lose Helen over a little white lie - as Nicola called it. They had been through so much together and life hadn't exactly been all that rosy for her either. Helen, lonely – who would have thought it?

Now she collapsed onto a chair, exhausted after her busy day. "Oh, and guess who I met there?"

"Who?"

"Debbie – from Amazing Days."

Neil looked blank.

"The stationery designer?"

"Oh right."

Laura had bumped into her while rushing off to grab a coffee – trusting the crew across the way displaying handmade fudge to watch over her stand. She had felt a tap on the shoulder while standing in line at the coffee hut.

"I thought I recognised you, earlier," Debbie smiled. "Are you just browsing or ..."

"No, I'm exhibiting," Laura said proudly. Now she was among like-minded folk and getting so much positive feedback, she wasn't in the least apologetic about her work. "I'm a jewellery designer."

"Really? I had no idea. I must pop over for a gander. You already know what my stuff looks like," she added grinning. "Oh, and cheers for the card – do you know you're the first bride ever to send me a thank you?"

"But you did such a fantastic job."

"Mmm, besides the fact that we gave yours to someone else, you mean..." Debbie made a face.

Coffee cups in hand, the two wandered along side by side. Laura pretended she had forgotten about that, not wanting the lovely woman to think that it had been a problem.

But Debbie had something else on her mind. "Actually, I don't mean to gossip, but that other girl was so stuck-up, and you were so nice about it..."

"Oh?"

"Well, it turned out that ..." She paused and stopped mid-sentence when she saw Laura's stand. "Are these really yours? They're fabulous."

"Thanks. But you were saying...."

"Well," Debbie lowered her voice conspiratorially, as if Chloe might pop out from under the pile of Aran sweaters next stand down, "turned out yer woman's wedding was postponed after all."

"Postponed? Why?"

"She didn't say. I know it galled her to have to ring

me and ask for an amended reprint, but the template was made and it would've cost her a fortune to get them from scratch again elsewhere."

So Dan's wedding had been postponed in the end. Interesting ...

"Anyway," Laura said to Neil now, "we went for coffee again when the exhibition closed, and Debbie told me all about how she got started and how it took her ages to get going. To hear her, it was like listening to my own story. Her family were always popping in unannounced when she was trying to get some work done, and she too got landed with baby-sitting her friend's children while they went off shopping and what-have-you. People would send her off collecting laundry, or ask her to wait at their houses to take furniture deliveries, things like that."

Debbie experiences had practically mirrored her own.

"They acted as if I was just sitting at home, with my feet up and nothing else to do but watch telly," the other woman confided. "I was getting nothing done, and being out of the house as often as I was didn't help the business either."

Laura was particularly interested in how she handled that, especially since Debbie seemed pretty no-nonsense.

"Most of my friends understood, but only after I explained that even though I was working from home, I was still *working*. They couldn't just call at the drop of a hat and expect me to be free. After that, they were very supportive. Course, once I got the shop that helped enormously. But I'll admit it wasn't easy."

Laura nodded, thinking about her own situation.

"But in order to keep going, you have to keep believing - not just in your work - but in *yourself.* Condition your mind into believing that failure is not an option. It's not easy and no matter what the papers tell you, there are very few overnight successes and instant millionaires out there." She took a mouthful of coffee. "You just stay determined and keep working away and eventually you'll get the break you need." She gave Laura's hand an encouraging squeeze. "You know, sometimes that's all it takes – just one break. And by being here today, you're definitely on the right track."

Just one break.

If that was what it took, great - but would Laura be ready for that all-important opportunity when or if it came? Or worse, had it already passed her by?

FIFTY

"WILL YOU HAVE SOMETHING TO DRINK?" Nicola asked. "Coffee, tea, a glass of wine maybe?"

"Coffee, please." Chloe looked nervously around. "Um – you have a very nice house," she said without enthusiasm.

Nicola felt sorry for her. It was annoying the way Dan had turned up at the same time like that. She hadn't expected him to arrive until at least an hour later, and wanted to spend some time with Chloe first before he arrived.

But Chloe had been late and Dan had been far too early ...

Now the poor girl looked as though she couldn't wait to get away.

"Do you need help? I could make the coffee," Dan piped up meaningfully.

"Grand."

He followed her into the kitchen.

"What the hell are you trying to prove, Nic?" he hissed.

She checked the percolator and turned to face him. "I'm not trying to prove anything – actually I'm trying to do you a favour."

"A favour? You must be joking."

"Chloe's been curious about me for a while – so I'm just setting her mind at ease once and for all."

"Are you sure that's all it is? Are you sure you're not enjoying this just a little bit?"

"Enjoying?" Nicola looked at him. "What exactly is there to enjoy about it?"

"Why did you invite us here today then – both of us?"

"I didn't intend for the two you to arrive together. I told you not to come until seven, because I wanted some time alone with Chloe first to –"

"Dish the dirt?"

"To explain. Explain what you couldn't, or wouldn't. To let her know that I'm no threat to her. Something you should have done from the very beginning."

"Look, I know that," He ran a hand through his hair, "but I just didn't know what to tell her ... I was afraid."

Nicola shook her head. "When I met you that day in Bray, I thought you'd changed – matured, even. But you're still terrified by this, aren't you? Even though nothing at all is expected of you, you're still afraid."

"It's not that, Nic ... I don't ...I just couldn't –"

"You couldn't deal with it," she finished for him. "You couldn't deal with it then and you can't deal with it now. Fair enough. But what I can't understand is why you didn't tell Chloe."

He looked like a scolded child. "You're right, I know you're right. It's just ... I didn't want to admit that ...oh, I just didn't know - maybe she'd blame me, maybe she wouldn't understand what it was like for me."

"Oh, for goodness sake, Dan, it isn't all about you." Nicola rolled her eyes. "Do you think I enjoyed bringing Chloe here today? Don't get me wrong, I'm not jealous of her or anything like that, but do you think it's easy for me either?"

"I know it must be strange for you, seeing me with someone else, but – "

"Whoa." She made a 'hands off' gesture with her palms. "Whatever you and I had is long gone, over and done with. You're just a little blip on the horizon as far as I'm concerned, and the other reason I'm doing this is because I want you out of my life for once and for all."

"Nic –"

"You have no idea how hard it was to start again on my own," she interjected, annoyed that she was forced to drill this into his idiotic head, frustrated that she had to explain anything. "And I think I'm doing OK – I mean I *was* doing OK until all this reared it's head again. I can go anywhere I want, I have my own house, a job I adore – a man I love very much and who loves *me*. I don't need to rely on anyone, Dan, least of all you."

"I know, and it's brilliant –"

"Don't patronise me." Her eyes flashed.

He looked suitably chastened and for a moment, neither one said anything.

Nicola glanced towards the living-room and her tone softened. "Look, can you just forget about yourself for once and tell the poor girl the truth? All of it."

"I will, I promise. And I'm sorry, Nic, I didn't really consider your side. I was angry with Chloe when she spoke to Carolyn and Shannon but I still didn't get into it. I thought the fact that I was so annoyed would be enough to make her give up." He scratched his nose. "I suppose I just didn't figure how all of this would impact you."

"Same old story," she said. "All you, you, you."

"You're right," He wouldn't meet her eyes, "but I promise now, I'll tell her everything."

"Good." Nicola folded her arms across her chest, but there was a flicker of amusement in her eyes. He looked duly chastened. "Now in spite of my big spiel about independence, will you get that tray for me?" she winked.

"Sure," Dan duly picked up a tray of coffee and biscuits and headed back to the living-room. Then he stopped, frowning. "Where's that noise coming from?" he asked, his gaze moving around the room. "A kind of ... whining?"

Nicola smiled mischievously. "I wasn't sure whether or not Chloe liked dogs."

He shrugged. "She does."

"Great, then."

She opened the utility-room door, and Barney bounded forward, tongue out and bottom-half wagging. He stopped short when he saw Dan and she noticed the hairs at the back of his neck stand up at the sight of her visitor.

Great judge of character as always.

Dan looked wary and Nicola allowed herself a little grin as she made her way back to the living-room.

Barney followed immediately behind her and then spying yet another visitor he raced across to Chloe, sniffing her ankles speculatively.

"Oh, he's gorgeous!" The younger woman forgot her discomfort for a second, and stroked the dog's glossy coat. Barney responded by nosing her palm and nudging himself against her legs, tail wagging all the time.

"I'd be lost without him," Nicola chuckled, pleased that at least she no longer looked quite so uptight. "Will you have a muffin or a slice of cake, maybe?"

"I won't, thanks," Chloe was demure.

"Watching your weight for the wedding, I suppose," she remarked pleasantly. "I'd imagine you're really looking forward to it."

It was obvious she didn't know how to answer that, and now Nicola felt guilty. She hadn't meant for this to be uncomfortable for Chloe – it was her fiancé who needed teaching a lesson.

Just then Dan's mobile shrilled, and in his haste to answer, the phone fell out of his pocket and slid away on the wooden floor. Barney jumped up and immediately retrieved the device with his mouth, offering it to a surprised and more than a little nervous-looking Dan.

"How clever," Chloe exclaimed delighted; Barney's antics setting her more at ease, as Nicola suspected. The Lab never failed to impress people.

"Dan doesn't seem to think so," she laughed, watching her ex distastefully wipe the handset on his trousers before answering the call.

He spoke hurriedly into the telephone. "Can't someone else handle it?" they heard him mutter. "I'm in the middle of something here." He gave an apologetic shake of his head as he retreated to the kitchen and Nicola wasn't sure if the look was intended for herself, or his fiancé.

Seizing the chance to speak frankly to Chloe, she turned to her.

"I'm very sorry for surprising you like this. I didn't mean for you and Dan to arrive together. I had hoped you and I would get a chance to chat a little beforehand."

Chloe nervously cradled the coffee mug in her hand.

"I'm the one that should be sorry," she said, not meeting her gaze. "I shouldn't have gone behind your back like that ... if I had known –"

"It's fine, really it is. I know Dan hasn't been exactly forthcoming."

Clearly troubled, the younger woman shook her head. "I had ... no idea."

"How could you? And I can understand your curiosity about me, especially with my turning up again in his life like this – just before your wedding and everything. But you must realise that I didn't come back into the picture to win Dan back." She gave a short laugh. "There was never any question of that. I'm with someone else now, someone I love very much."

There was a pause. "I did wonder why Dan was so keen to see you," Chloe said, "not to mention so hesitant to discuss your break-up. When it comes to you he can be quite, quite –" she searched for the right word.

"Defensive?"

Chloe nodded. "I felt threatened."

"I can imagine." Nicola reached down and scratched Barney behind the ears. "But Dan's not defensive about *me* – he's defensive about himself. Still, now that we've met, do you still feel that way? Threatened, I mean."

She shook her head, obviously finding it all terribly unnerving. "To be honest, I don't know how to feel. I certainly didn't expect you to be so ... nice." She gave a rueful smile. "I'm sorry, I don't suppose I'm handling this very well."

Dan came back into the room and looked from one woman to the other.

"That was the office," he said flatly. "There's a problem at work – Temple Architects are threatening to move their account. They called and left messages for John four times this week and he hasn't returned any of them. I've tried John's mobile and I can only get his message-minder." He shook his head. "Now I'll have to go and try and sweet-talk Harry Temple into keeping his precious firm with us. I'm so sick of this."

Nicola knew an excuse to leave when she heard one.

"You're going – now?" Chloe asked, the relief in her voice almost palpable. "I'd better be going too." She stood up. "Nicola, it was really nice to meet you. Thanks for the coffee."

"You're very welcome. It was great to meet you too."

"Um, you should come and visit us sometime?"

She tried to keep her expression neutral. "I will – sometime."

"Great."

Dan looked at his watch. "Sorry we have to rush off like this, Nic but we'll talk soon, yeah?"

"Sure."

The couple headed to the hallway and let themselves out; Barney accompanying them to the door.

From the sitting-room window, Nicola watched them retreat to their cars. She knew you didn't need to be an expert in lip-reading to make out what the younger woman was saying to her fiancé.

"Jesus, Dan" Chloe mouthed, her expression horrified. "Why the hell didn't you tell me?"

FIFTY-ONE

A WEARY AND despondent Helen called to Kerry's primary school after work. She was still reeling from events at Laura's.

How could her friend have known all those years and never said a word?

She knew she had taken Laura's friendship for granted, asking her to pick up Kerry from school and look after her while she slipped off for hot sessions with Paul.

She'd taken advantage of her kind heart and gentle nature in the same way she had mistreated Jo, who too had always been helpful and accommodating where Kerry was concerned, to her own detriment.

Helen had finished with Paul that night. What was the point? Nicola was right. She had gone too far by denying her own daughter's existence. No matter how much she wanted a relationship, there was no excuse for that.

That time with Neil – *of course* she had felt guilty about it, realising how nasty she had been in coming on to him. Poor thing, he was so gormless he hadn't a hope, really.

At the time, she hadn't been too concerned. Nicola had interrupted, and it wasn't as if they'd ended up sleeping together, so really it was just a bit of a fumble. Why feel guilty when there was nothing to feel guilty about?

But the fact that Laura knew about the betrayal, and despite this remained her friend - helping and supporting her without question – made Helen felt very guilty indeed. Would she herself have done the same in return? She didn't think so.

How could Laura be so understanding and so forgiving all the time?

She had always thought it a weakness but now she knew she had been wrong. It was actually a strength, a strength of character that no one, not even Nicola, had given her credit for.

And when Nicola too was struggling, when her life was in tatters, it had been Laura helping her pick up the pieces, Laura the one who had stayed with her day in day out, listening to her fears and helping her through them.

Again, Helen felt ashamed that she hadn't been able to do to the same. It was another blight on her character that she had all but abandoned Nicola when her friend was at her lowest. She kept telling herself at the time that she had her own problems, that Jamie was about to leave her, but of course that wasn't it.

The truth was that she was afraid – afraid of what had happened. And much like Dan, she'd run scared, pretty much abandoning Nicola to her fate.

Guiding the car into a parking space, Helen was coming to the conclusion that she was not only a terrible friend and a terrible mother but, all in all, a terrible person.

The school principal looked at her gravely from across the table. Helen knew that the woman was annoyed with her for not coming in before now. Kerry had started here in early September and she knew her daughter hadn't really taken to it.

Mrs Cleary had been trying to arrange an appointment for quite some time, and after a lot of procrastinating Helen had finally decided to bite the bullet.

She guessed what this would be about; Kerry's speech issue was likely impeding her learning and she suspected that the school wanted to consider holding her back and starting afresh next year, when she was a little more advanced.

"Ms Jackson, as I'm sure you're aware, Kerry has a stuttering issue," the older woman began.

"I am – I mean I *do,* of course. She's seeing a therapist but she doesn't seem to be getting any better. I had hoped," she continued, seeing the principal was about to interrupt, "that going to school and being around other kids would help her, although I realise now that she may have problems keeping up."

The woman's eyes widened. "Far from it," she said. "In fact, Kerry is one of the brightest in her class."

"Oh?"

"Yes, though Mrs Costigan – that's Kerry's teacher, by the way," she added, in a poorly disguised jibe, "rarely asks her to read out loud. But she has a keen ear for grammar and from what I'm aware, tries her utmost to keep up."

"I'm confused," Helen said frowning. "I thought you were going to tell me her stutter is causing problems." She certainly hadn't expected her to be complimenting Kerry's progress.

"Ms Jackson, how does Kerry seem at home?"

"At home? Well, she's fine, usually. What exactly do you mean?"

"Does she seem quiet, distant even?"

"Well, Kerry is always quiet. She spends a lot of time in her room playing with her stuff and – now that you mention it – a lot of time perfecting her reading."

"Perfecting her reading – or her speech?"

Helen briefly considered this. "Both, I'm sure."

"Ms Jackson – may I call you Helen?" she asked in a kindly tone. "Because of her stutter Kerry has been the subject of some … teasing in class."

Helen shifted in her seat. "Mrs Cleary," she said evenly, "that doesn't come as any great surprise. Children like Kerry are bound to be singled out. I always knew there was a possibility that she'd be called names and I tried to prepare - "

"It isn't just verbal, and it's a very serious matter. Kerry has been ridiculed and pushed onto the ground, not only by the boys, but indeed some of the girls in her class. It's not just taunting – it's downright bullying. And it breaks my heart to admit that it goes on in my school at all, but especially at that young age. Didn't she show you the marks on her arms?"

For one long moment, Helen felt like she was eavesdropping on someone else's conversation. *Spat at? Pushed over? Marks on her arms?* Why hadn't Kerry said anything?

More importantly, why hadn't *she* noticed?

But Helen didn't have to dig too deep to find the answer. How *would* she? Nicola's words from the other night swam into her brain.

If you focus entirely on what you don't have, you're missing out on what you do have...

"Helen?"

"Sorry – what?" She was so absorbed in her own thoughts, she had almost forgotten the headmistress was there.

"I know this is coming as a bit of a shock to you, and we would have told you sooner but – "

"Kerry didn't want you to," Helen finished for her, shaking her head sadly. "She didn't want to upset me, did she?"

"Actually," the headmistress began, a strange expression on her face, "that's not quite right. Your daughter didn't want you to be *angry* with her. She said – and these are Kerry's words – 'Mummy says I can't talk properly because I don't practise enough. If you tell Mummy then she'll know I'm not practising, and she'll be very mad.'"

"Oh..." Helen's felt a massive knot in her chest. Her hand flew to her mouth and the tears were streaming down her cheeks before she even realised they were there.

What had she done? What had she done to her child? Why hadn't she come in to see the headmistress sooner? Why keep putting it off and putting it off like her daughter's welfare was some kind of ... nuisance? She could just imagine Kerry now, embarrassed and ashamed, begging the teachers not to tell her because she thought that she would be angry with her – that the taunts were all her own doing because she couldn't speak properly.

"Helen, try not to upset yourself over this." The headmistress looked perturbed. "I understand how you must be feeling, but please remember that Kerry is barely four. Children that age have great imaginations. None of the teachers here, or indeed myself, would have taken any notice of such claims.We don't believe for a second that you would inflict blame on Kerry that way. As far as I'm aware, stuttering is a physiological issue, *not* a psychological one. However, Kerry's lack of self-confidence in this regard is bound to affect her progress. I think this is where parents come in. I should add that we've already spoken to the culprits' parents, and will take whatever action is necessary but –"

Helen shook her head. "No, this is my fault, not Kerry's ... I haven't been helping her enough, I haven't done the exercises her therapist suggested in ages. In fact," she paled as the realisation hit her, "I haven't even brought her to see the speech therapist since ..." She buried her head in her hands, shame enveloping her.

"Helen, I'm unaware of your personal circumstances, but from what I can gather you're a single mum?"

She nodded wordlessly.

"There's no denying that bringing up a child on your own is difficult, particularly for a working mother too."

When Helen didn't answer, Mrs Cleary got up and walked around the table, putting a comforting hand on her shoulder. "Helen, please don't upset yourself. I'm sure you've tried your best, but maybe you two now have a few things to sort out."

A *few* things? Helen had never before experienced anything like the guilt that was coursing through her just then. It was like molten lava, burning her insides and destroying her own inflated self-worth. Was there anyone she *hadn't* hurt these last few years in her innate desire to satisfy herself, to make up for the rejection and loss she'd suffered since Jamie's departure?

After a few moments, she stood up and resolutely shook hands with the headmistress. She'd go home now and talk to Kerry about the bullying and the stuttering, maybe try and boost her daughter's self-confidence and actually behave like a good mother, a *decent* mother.

She thought again about Laura - how all her life her friend had bent over backwards to gain her mother's approval, and how it had resulted in her timidity, basically sapping her self confidence.

She didn't want that for Kerry, didn't want her daughter seeking outward validation or approval from anywhere other than within. She wanted her to feel confident, empowered; that the world was her oyster. Like Helen used to.

As she drove towards home, she pictured her daughter's sunny smiling face, then an ugly vision of Kerry being taunted by her classmates.

At this, she felt an overwhelming urge to catch the little bastards and inflict on them some of the suffering her daughter had endured. She'd catch those boys and bang their bullying little heads together and she'd certainly have a thing or two to say to the parents, she'd –

Helen's head snapped up. She pulled over and stopped the car, suddenly feeling like St Paul on the road to Damascus. Was this it? she asked herself, hands shaking with adrenaline. This almost primeval urge to protect – *maternal* urge to protect, nurture, empower. Was this the feeling that had eluded her for all those years?

Helen still didn't know.

All she knew right then was that she had a lot of making up to do.

FIFTY-TWO

"LOOK, just get in the car and follow me down to the village. We'll talk about it then."

Chloe reversed out of Nicola's driveway as if in a daze, and as she did, he saw her cast a questioning glance at the Ford Focus parked outside the house.

He drove off ahead and a little later stopped in the carpark of a local pub.

"I'm sorry," he said simply. "I should have said something."

Before he could say anymore, his fiancée spoke. "That dog – Nicola's dog – he's one of those ... one of *those* dogs, isn't he? Like a guide dog except – "

"An assistance dog, yes."

"But what happened? She hasn't always been that way, has she?"

"No," Dan answered sadly, "she hasn't always been that way."

The dog had been a shock. While aware that over the last few years Nicola had all but resumed her independence, he had been unprepared for the dog's role in that. He recalled the way it had easily retrieved his phone when it fell on the floor just now, and had closed the front door behind them when they left.

Apparently, these dogs could do great things altogether, like switch on and off lights, load or unload washing-machines, all that kind of stuff. He supposed he was a handy guard dog too.

"But why didn't you tell me?" Chloe demanded again.

Dan dropped his gaze to the dashboard. "I'm sorry. But as time went by it was getting harder and harder to bring the subject up."

"What happened though?"

"I just didn't know how to bring it up, you have to understand –"

"No, I mean, what happened to *Nicola*."

Dan cleared his throat. "Well, she and I had been through a lot as you know, with the miscarriage and of course that thing with Harris."

She nodded, waiting for him to continue.

"But we got over it – in fact we got over it better than either of us had anticipated. We loved one another and were both equally determined, equally committed to making the marriage work." He swallowed. "We'd never really spoken about the baby thing, never really shared our grief. And after Harris, we both realised that we were in danger of letting our marriage slip away."

He knew Chloe wasn't comfortable hearing this, but yet there was a strange sense of relief in getting the words out.

"Despite how fragile things had become, we both decided that we still loved one another and there was plenty to fight for. So, we set about doing just that. We knew that if our marriage was to survive, we'd have to make a fresh start."

A new house was to signify a new beginning, a brand new chapter in their life together.

"For a while, it was terrific. Nicola got another job elsewhere – I suppose to reassure me that she wouldn't be seeing Harris again, but I knew he wasn't a problem. All that mattered to me was that I'd got her back – the *old* Nicola back."

He saw Chloe flinch slightly at this.

"I'm sorry, I suppose this is part of the reason I didn't want to discuss it. This kind of thing isn't easy for you to hear."

"Just ... go on."

Dan exhaled. "Right. So the old Nicola was back and – believe me – this turned out to be a bit of a mixed blessing." He chuckled, remembering. "She's always been a whirlwind of energy – flitting off here, there and everywhere. She's no patience and sometimes you can't get her to sit still in the same place for ..." He paused, realising that he was speaking in the present tense. "Anyway, she made an absolute mission out of the house-hunting – I suppose it was something to work towards, something to aim for. I have to admit that I enjoyed it, too – the two of us would take off on our bikes at the weekends to look at houses."

"Bikes?"

Dan suspected Chloe was finding it hard to picture him on a bicycle. He *adored* his car.

"She wasn't a great fan of traffic – had a touch of the old road rage." He smiled, almost affectionately but then his expression became subdued. "But just when everything started to fall into place, just when we were starting to get back on track and things were going well – almost *too* well ..." He laughed, a short bitter laugh. "But, it's true what they say – if you want to give God a laugh, tell him your plans."

"There was some kind of ... accident?"

Dan nodded. "She was out cycling near Glendalough and a tourist who didn't know the road rounded a corner and ploughed into her – bastard was lucky he didn't kill her."

Chloe shook her head. "I'm so sorry."

"The ambulance brought her to Loughlinstown and from there they sent her on to St Vincent's. They set her up in traction but it wasn't long before they came back with a full diagnosis. She'd damaged a certain section of her spine. While she was OK as far as the waist, it was doubtful she'd ever regain the use of her legs."

"The poor thing, what must that have been like for her?"

Dan struggled to speak. This was the part he hated, the part he dreaded.

"However bad it was, I made it worse," he said hoarsely, a huge lump rising in his throat. "I got such a shock when they told us. I couldn't handle it, Chloe - and for a long time I couldn't believe it. Wouldn't believe it. After everything ... I kept expecting someone to tell me that it had all been a sick joke – a candid-camera type thing. I just couldn't handle it."

"What?" Chloe looked at him. "What do you mean? Nicola was the one ... what do you mean *you* couldn't handle it?"

It was seconds before the realisation hit her. She hadn't understood why he had gone to such lengths to hide this from her. But now Chloe knew that it wasn't Nicola's disability Dan had been hiding.

"Oh – my – God," she said, pronouncing each word slowly. "You left her, didn't you? You left her to deal with it all on her own."

Dan said nothing, but he didn't need to. His shame-faced expression said it all.

FIFTY-THREE

NICOLA AWOKE to the sound of the phone ringing in her ears. A quick glance at the clock told her that it was six thirty in the morning. She groaned.

This meant that someone had called in sick and she would need to arrange cover or do the job herself. It took every amount of willpower she had to drag herself out of the bed. She'd had a restless night, waking in fits and starts and had only just begun to drift off again when duty called.

Her car had begun to give her trouble too. The controls, particularly the brakes, weren't as responsive as they should be and Nicola wasn't prepared to take any chances with it so she'd booked it in for a service.

The garage was due to bring it back sometime this week, although judging from past experiences, it was unlikely she would get it back for some time. As she wasn't the best candidate for a courtesy car, she knew she'd be relying on taxis for a bit.

Ken should have been back last night from his few

days in Galway, and would be tired, so she wouldn't dream of calling on him at this hour for a lift.

She hated that, not having the independence to drive where she felt like, whenever she felt like it.

And it wasn't all that easy to get a wheelchair-access taxi in the early hours, which is why she was at that very moment still waiting in her kitchen when she should have been at work.

Not to mention the fact that she would have to use her manual chair instead of her new power-wheelchair.

Poor old Chloe – she had got such a shock when she arrived at the house. Though by now Nicola was well used to that. Most people's reactions to her and the chair generally swung somewhere between discomfort and terror. She let it wash over her now, but it hadn't always been that easy.

She gave a little smile and recalled how difficult it had been to get used to that in the beginning, to get used to people's attitudes.

But of course she'd had a head start on that, because the very first person to panic had been her husband.

At first, she'd been relieved that she was still alive.

"With the speed you were hit and the weight of your fall, it's a miracle that you didn't do more damage," the consultant had said. "It could have been a lot worse."

Throughout the three months she had spent lying on her back in the hospital, she had plenty time to think about how she was going to approach her fate.

She could lie there feeling sorry for herself, and the

loss of her previous way of life (as she did on many occasions) or she could make the best of it. For her there was no choice to make. Of course she would get on with it, of course she would make the best of it. She was still young, and as far as she was concerned she had lost the use of her legs, not her life.

For a time, this was enough to keep her going. Yes, she was flat on her back in hospital – but she was still alive.

Inevitably, there were times – particularly throughout her rehabilitation – that she didn't feel quite so upbeat about her future, but what could she do?

There was no changing her situation, there was no going back to normal, so there was no point being miserable about it. She couldn't turn back the clock, she couldn't change things. She recalled how dark and desolate she had felt after her miscarriage, and how she had all but withdrawn from day-to-day life, consumed by her sorrow. She was determined never to let that happen again.

But Dan was a different story. She could see the change in him; could sense the fear and despair every time he came to visit her. He brushed it off, protesting that he was worried about insurance and hospital bills, but Nicola knew it was something more.

He was losing faith.

Immediately after the accident, he had tried his best to pretend that it was OK, that *they* would be OK, but she could see it in his eyes that he didn't believe it himself.

And soon she found that his sullen visits and stilted

conversation were beginning to wear down her early optimism.

When she was finally released from the Rehabilitation Hospital, she went to stay with her parents – she couldn't possibly stay in their old apartment block, not when she could barely use her new wheelchair.

And at the time she needed full-time care, something that Dan wasn't able to provide and her mum had insisted upon.

Nicola shook her head, remembering those first few weeks in the chair. That was the lowest point on her road to recovery – to normality. She had regained a lot of strength by then as a result of her rehab, but her arms tired easily while trying to manoeuvre, and her bedsores stung – all the stuff the doctors had warned her about. Because she was trying so hard and progressing little, she became easily frustrated and hated the fact that she couldn't do anything for herself – her mother doing all the simple things, carrying her, bathing her, getting her in and out of bed.

Still Dan visited every day, but Nicola knew by then that they had already started to grow apart. They were uneasy around one another; him trying hard not to say the wrong thing, she becoming easily annoyed by what he did say.

She was sick of his self-pity, his lack of support, his glum appearance. She needed positives, she needed her husband to reassure her that she would be fine, that he would be there for her, that of course everything would be OK.

But there was never any talk of what might happen

in the future, where they would live, or what they would do when eventually she regained her independence.

One particular day, Dan called to see her after work. He was tired and harassed-looking, and Nicola accused him of being selfish.

Something in him seemed to snap.

"Did you ever," he asked, pronouncing the words slowly, "ever once think about how all of this might be affecting me?"

"You?" Nicola laughed resentfully. "You're not the one sitting here day after day unable to do anything for yourself, relying on other people to do the simplest things."

"I know how hard it is for you, love, I can only imagine – but it's hard for me too. I don't know how to help. You resent the fact that I'm not here with you, yet you know you couldn't cope on your own at home."

"You could take time off work to help." Nicola knew she was being petulant but she couldn't think of anything else to say to him. She didn't really want that, she would have hated Dan having to do everything for her and she longed for the day she would be strong enough to look after herself. But, at the time, that day seemed very far away.

"Take time off? Do you have any idea how much money we owe the hospital?" Although their health plan covered most of the hospital stuff, it didn't cover the cost of her rehabilitation. "Insurance could take years to sort, if ever. I might have to sell out my share of the company …"

"Money, insurance ... do you think any of those things matter to me right now?"

He ran a hand through his hair. "I don't think I can go on like this," he said eventually. "I don't know what you want me to do, what you want me to say. Of course it's hard for you, I know that, but it's bloody hard for me too. I ... never ... expected things to turn out like this."

Her heart galloped. "What does that mean, Dan?"

"It means ..." he said, his voice almost a whisper, "it means that I don't know what to do anymore. Our life has been turned upside down and I don't know how we're supposed to get out of it. You're coping as best you can, I know that, but there's nothing in the information booklets telling *me* how to cope." He looked at her, his eyes filled with desperation.

"What are you saying?"

"I don't know. I just think that – that maybe we should spend some time apart."

"What?" she whispered, stunned.

"Maybe it might even be easier if I wasn't around. Nic, sometimes you look at me like you hate me. I don't know how to respond to that. I'm not made of stone."

She was crying now, warm tears racing down both cheeks. "What happened to 'for better or worse' – didn't you say those words, didn't you promise to be there in both *sickness* and in health?"

"I'm sorry," Dan said finally, tears glistening in his eyes too. "I just didn't know it would be so ... hard."

And that was the end.

Nicola stayed on with her mother, and his visits

became less frequent until eventually he stopped coming altogether.

Their eventual separation was an epiphany for her though. Although hurt deeply by his rejection, it spurred her on to regain control of her life, and in order to do this, she knew she needed time away – from everything.

She took up an early offer made by her aunt to spend some time with her in the UK.

"It'll do you good to get away," Ellen, a jolly fifty-five-year-old had said, "and I'm sure your mother will be delighted to get rid of you."

That was what Nicola loved about living with her aunt. There was no sitting around and feeling sorry for herself. They talked a lot, slow easy conversations about life, love – and Dan.

Nicola had (a little unfairly she realised) left for London without telling him.

For months she'd heard nothing, until one morning Ellen handed her an envelope with a Wicklow postmark. In the letter Dan tried to explain how he had been feeling, and about how sorry he was that they couldn't make it work. The letter had a kind of cleansing effect, and Nicola sensed it was his way of saying goodbye.

Was it just them, she wondered, or was there a breaking point in every marriage – a point from which there was no going back, no matter how strong the relationship might be?

She and Dan had overcome a lot together, but maybe there was only so much a marriage could take.

A week later she contacted a solicitor.

Of course, getting over him and coming to terms with

a disability was only the beginning, and she'd been totally unprepared for the reaction she got from the outside world.

It was as though she was no longer just a person, but a *disabled* one. The qualifier was of course inevitable, but brought with it connotations that she had never expected.

When she had become used to the chair, and begun going out and about on her own, she had been completely unprepared socially.

People treated her like she had lost, not just the use of her legs but her brain, like Miss Reporter Fidelma that time at work: '*I have to ask – isn't it unusual for someone like yourself to be involved in this type of industry?*'

She had seen the discomfort too in people's eyes at Laura's wedding, when as bridesmaid she wheeled up the aisle ahead of the bride.

At times, people's attitudes were soul-destroying, but at others, they could be quite comical. It wasn't something she thought she would ever get used to, but eventually she had learned not to let it bother her.

And all in all, she couldn't really complain.

Yes, it was a huge blow at the beginning and yes, it was a massive change in lifestyle but she had eventually come to see it as just that – a change in lifestyle. There was very little she *couldn't* do. Sure, she had to put a lot more thought into getting from place to place, and occasionally she missed being so active – missed her bike rides into the mountains and silly things like boogeying on the dance-floor.

But once she had learned to use it properly, the chair

simply became an extension of herself. She had a great job, wonderful friends, her own customised home, and of course, her beloved Barney to keep an eye on her.

Not to mention Ken. Falling in love again was the very last thing she'd expected.

FIFTY-FOUR

HER CAR HAD BEEN on the blink *again,* and she'd been waiting for a taxi home from work. The same day, Nicola remembered, she had been in terrible form. Because the car was out of action, she was using the manual as opposed to her trusty power-wheelchair.

"Waiting for anyone in particular?" Ken had enquired, briefcase in hand as he passed through reception. She was sitting just inside the centre's front porch.

"My lift home," she answered, keeping one eye on the Motiv8 entrance.

"Car giving you problems again? You should have told me, I could have organised a lift for you."

"It's fine. Anyway, he's here now."

Ken followed her gaze. "Ah, I don't think so."

The approaching taxi *was* meant for her, but the driver looked apologetically at his saloon Ford Mondeo. There wasn't a hope of fitting a collapsed buggy, let alone a wheelchair.

"Sorry, love," he said out of the wound-down

window. "I'll ring dispatch and get them to send a van out."

"It's fine," Ken informed him. "It's on my way."

When the man drove off, Nicola glared at him. "I can organise my own lift home, thank you very much."

"Ah, don't be so defensive," he said easily. "You need a lift and I told you that I'm going that way. Will you ever stop your gabbing for once and just say thank you?"

"OK then, thanks," she said, feeling like a bold child.

"Now, do you need any help, or would it be too dangerous for my health to offer?" he said, disengaging the central locking on his car.

Nicola hid a smile. "I'll be fine," she answered, carefully manoeuvring herself onto the passenger seat. Before she knew it, Ken had expertly collapsed her chair and was storing it in the boot of his roomy Citroen Picasso.

She stared at him, surprised.

"What?"

"If I didn't know better, I'd say you've done that before."

He shrugged. "Maybe you don't know better."

She stared straight ahead as he drove away, not knowing how to answer.

"Nothing to say, Nicola? That's not like you."

"Well, what do you want me to say?" Whatever it was about Ken he always seemed to bring out her petulant side.

"OK then, if you must know, my dad's a C4 quad."

"Really?" This time, she couldn't hide her surprise.

C_4 was the one of the most challenging, the worst kind of injury.

"Yes, really. Car accident. He's been in a chair since I was twelve."

"I didn't know."

"There's a lot about me you don't know."

That was certainly true. But thinking about it, Ken's easygoing attitude now made a lot more sense. It was like he didn't even *see* her disability.

"So is he completely paralysed or – ?"

"Arms and legs. He can move his neck and shoulders and has feeling in just one of his fingers. But he's grand."

Nicola suddenly felt ashamed. Here she was feeling sorry for herself and considering herself immobile because her *car* was out of action.

"So does he live with you or –?" She wondered why she was suddenly having trouble finishing her sentences. She wanted to know more, but didn't want to appear nosey.

"Nah, he's home with my mum." He smiled. "She's great with him and has a nurse coming in a few days a week to keep an eye on him, plus I often take him out and about at weekends." Ken flashed her a sideways grin. "So in case you ever wondered why I drive this instead of a flashy Beamer, now you know."

"This is completely out of your way, Ken, you really didn't have to," Nicola said as they approached her road.

"It's not a problem."

"Yes, but I could have waited for the taxi and you could be home by now."

He looked at her. "Nicola, did it ever cross your

cranky little mind that I might actually *want* to drop you home?"

"What do you mean?"

Ken tapped the steering wheel, while the car remained stationary. "We've known each other for years. I'm bringing you home because I consider myself a friend – *and* I want to have a nose at your house."

"OK," she said cheerfully as the traffic moved off again, "I'd be happy to give you the grand tour and, if you behave yourself, I might even make you dinner."

Ken grinned across at her. "Now that," he said, "is an invitation I can't refuse."

Things had happened very quickly after that.

He began spending more and more time at her place, and all too soon confessed his interest in her since that day in his office when Dan walked in on them.

It was wonderful at the time, and it had been wonderful ever since. He was honest, loving and decent and she knew instinctively that he would never let her down like Dan had.

Now, Nicola checked the time on her computer screen. It was almost eight – Ken should definitely be in.

She picked up the handset and dialled his extension, eager to find out how things went with the partners in Galway. No answer.

"Did you see Ken come in yet?" she asked, checking with reception. "I thought he was back today."

"He was back yesterday actually – he called in last night before closing. But he's taken a day off today – didn't he tell you?

Day off? He was so wrapped up in this place he

hardly ever took days off – hell, he rarely even took *sick* days. Oh, well, he was the boss, after all, she thought affectionately, dialling his home number and wondering if, despite the encouraging figures, things hadn't gone as well as he'd expected.

A groggy-sounding Ken answered on the second ring. "Hello?"

"You never told me you were planning on mitching off today."

There was a brief silence.

"Ken?"

"Why would I?" he answered brusquely. "You certainly don't tell *me* everything."

Nicola was taken aback. "What?"

"I can't talk to you right now, OK?"

With that he hung up, leaving her staring open-mouthed at the receiver. What was the matter with him?

Then she realised that it was just gone eight. If he needed a day off then he probably didn't appreciate her interrupting his precious lie-in.

But on her second attempt at conversation a little later, Ken was equally grouchy.

"What's the matter with you today?" she asked easily. It really wasn't like him to be in bad form. "Didn't things go well in Galway?"

"What's the matter?" he repeated. "The matter *is* that I can't quite figure out how you managed to lead me on so easily and for so long."

"What? What do you mean?"

"I mean, when were you going to tell me? That's *if* you were going to bother telling me at all."

"What? Ken ... I really don't – "

"Why spend all that time with me, leading me to believe that we were going somewhere, that we had a future, when you never had any intention ... just why bother?" His voice sounded strange. "I mean, what's the attraction? Do you like being messed around by him – is that it?"

Now Nicola was really confused. "By who?"

"Don't play the innocent. Hunt, who do you think?"

"Dan? But I haven't seen him in ages," She was thrown off-guard. She hadn't told him about her plans to invite Dan and Chloe to her house. It was a spur of the moment decision as it was, and also she knew he'd think she was interfering.

"I saw it," Ken said stonily. "I saw the two of you together at your place. I actually can't believe you would lie bald-face about it."

But how could he have seen? What would he have seen? Oh, why hadn't she told him beforehand?

"Look, love, the thing is, that night I invited –"

"Just forget it. Forget the whole bloody thing. I thought we had something, but all along you were just waiting, hoping he would come back to you. Despite all your bull about wishing I had been the one you married. I don't know why I was so stupid in the first place. After all, you went straight back to him last time too, didn't you?"

With that Ken disconnected.

Nicola stared unseeingly at her desk, her mind reeling.

Obviously he had seen something that night, but not enough to know that Dan wasn't her only visitor.

Now it looked as though she was keeping secrets from him – she'd be annoyed herself, if he'd done the same.

But if Ken wouldn't talk to her, if he wouldn't let her explain, then what was she supposed to do?

FIFTY-FIVE

LAURA WAS RIFLING through a sheaf of invoices and trying to get to grips with her latest VAT declaration. She'd been at this all week and she still couldn't make head nor tail of it.

Not that there was much point in any case. The Crafts Exhibition hadn't been the great success she had imagined at the time. Yes, she had given out plenty of cards and yes, there had been loads lots of compliments thrown about, but still there was nothing concrete – not even the *possibility* of something concrete.

Laura just wasn't selling enough to justify her existence as a jewellery designer. If anything she was losing money, what with all the stock she had to buy and all the packaging and boxes and all the unseen expenses, like phone and electricity and heating and everything. It was just too much.

She had to admit to herself that maybe they had been right; Helen, her mother, all the doubters. She didn't have the tenacity, the confidence, the belief in herself to really make a go of this.

Laura had finally begun to realise that she just didn't have the killer instinct.

"And that isn't exactly something you can fake, is it, Eamonn?" she asked, feeling more than a little concerned that lately all she seemed to do was talk nonsense to the cat.

She got up to make herself a cup of tea and, hopefully, clear her head. On the fridge, Laura caught sight of a wedding snap of herself and Neil at the altar. She studied his earnest expression, the one he had spent ages practising especially for the day. "I can't show off the gap in my teeth," he'd insisted.

But by the time the photographer had arranged and rearranged them all for the shoot, the gap in his teeth was well and truly forgotten. She was pleased. At least in their professional wedding photographs, Neil would look like *her* Neil and not the stiff, uncomfortable version in this one.

How would he feel when she told him she was about to give up her dream? That she was going back to the rat-race, where she would be once again a square peg trying to fit into a round hole?

She heard the phone ring in the workshop and trudged back inside to answer it.

"Laura Fanning?" enquired an efficient British voice.

"Speaking."

Laura sighed inwardly. Definitely not a business call, given the use of her maiden name.

So what else was new ...

"Can you hold the line, please?"

"Sure." Laura listened expectantly to *Candle in the Wind* as she waited.

Then another – Irish – accent came on the line. "Laura?"

"Yes."

"Hi, it's Amanda Verveen here, we met recently."

Amanda Verveen? The *Irish fashion designer* Amanda Verveen? What ... Laura had never met her.

"I'm sorry, I ... are you sure you have the right number?"

"Pretty sure – you're the jewellery designer, right?"

"Well, yes." Laura's thoughts were going a mile a minute. How on earth would someone like Amanda Verveen have heard about her stuff? She wouldn't have been at the Crafts Expo. International fashion designers with customers the likes of Beyonce would hardly be attending crafts exhibitions. She'd be mobbed. And didn't Nicole Kidman wear a Verveen dress at this year's Golden Globes?

This was obviously some kind of joke. Yet, despite her misgivings, her heart kept racing.

"You really don't remember me ..."

"I'm sorry, I really don't."

"I was at Brid Cassidy's for your bridal fitting. She's a good friend of mine, we were at art college together."

Her bridal fitting? Then it hit her. Brid's assistant.

Well, at the time Laura had presumed she was her assistant – she had no idea that 'Amanda' was actually *The* Amanda Verveen. She could pinpoint any of her designs in seconds, but had no idea what the woman herself looked like.

But what ... what did she want with her?

"So I know you're really busy, but I was hoping you might consider a commission for me."

For a long moment, Laura couldn't move. This *had* to be a joke, a dream – *something*!

"For you?" was all she could say.

Amanda laughed again. "I'm sorry but did I catch you at a bad time?"

She quickly recollected herself. "No, no, you're fine. It's just ...well, I'm a little overwhelmed, to be honest."

"That makes two of us then, because I was completely overwhelmed by your stuff that day."

"Really?" Laura could feel the beginnings of tears in her eyes. Then she sat up straight in her chair. For goodness sake stop sounding so bloody pathetic, she admonished herself. "Well, thank you – thank you very much," she replied in the calmest voice she could muster.

"You're welcome." Amanda was all business. "So I was wondering, could you pop over to the Pembroke Street office sometime soon? I'm in London at the moment, but I'll be back in Dublin later this week. Next season I'm doing something with a heavy ethnic influence while at same time keeping my gothic signature, and I'd love to maybe incorporate some of your jewellery for Fashion Week... "

Next season? Was she talking about next season's *collection*? Or London, Milan, Paris Fashion Week?

"No, no, I'd be delighted ..."

"Great." Amanda went on, talking a mile a minute.

"Would you or your staff have any problems working with soft metal as well as silver? It would be great if we could incorporate well, not quite ivory but something equally primitive – wood or stone, perhaps?"

Laura felt her mouth moving, but someone else was uttering the words. "I've already worked with those materials. In fact I've already come up with some black metal and stone variations that might work. I'd have to take a look at your own concepts of course, but I could pop over next week?"

"Terrific. I'll connect you with my personal assistant to make all the details. So sorry I can't chat for longer; I've a meeting with Harvey Nicks which should have taken place ... oh, about half an hour ago."

"No problem."

"But we'll talk soon?" Amanda trilled.

"Yes, thanks for the call."

"Great. I'm really looking forward to meeting you again, Laura. I feel that you and I have a very similar vision for contemporary design and should work well together. Bye!"

They disconnected and Laura sat staring at the receiver for seemed like an age, unable to think, not sure what to *feel*. Amanda Verveen, award-winning and highly revered international fashion designer, wanted to work with her – with *her*, boring ould Laura Fanning from Glengarrah.

She had to be dreaming. This couldn't be real.

She picked up the phone again and with trembling hands input Neil's work number.

"Hey, hon, how are you?"

It was then that it hit her. Hearing him on the other end, hearing her husband's voice like that, so supportive and wonderful, brought Laura out of her awestruck trance.

She bawled into the phone. "I did it, Neil," she gasped. "I finally did it."

FIFTY-SIX

IT WAS A GLORIOUS AFTERNOON, the air was crisp and there was barely a cloud in the sky.

Helen wrapped her scarf tightly around her neck, and savoured the sharp breeze on her cheeks and the sun in her face.

Taking these walks with Kerry in the park close to their apartment building had become a habit lately, and not for the first time, she wondered why she hadn't done it before.

Just ahead, she heard her daughter call after the newest member of the family – a white and tan floppy-eared beagle called Fuzzy.

She was a different child, Helen thought, watching her daughter racing happily along in the grass. While she had made no major inroads with her speech as yet, Helen could see in her eyes that Kerry was becoming that little bit more confident. She hardly stuttered at all in front of her now, innately sensing her support.

It was too early for the taunts at school to have

stopped either, but the physical side of the bullying had – Mrs Cleary taking steps by moving the troublemakers to another class.

And it seemed Kerry had made a friend too, a dote called Fiona, who was also given a hard time and called a nerd in class because she had to wear glasses.

But apparently, Fiona was anything but nerdy – more a tough little cookie who stood up to her tormentors. Some of her daring had begun to rub off on Kerry too; Mrs Cleary having told Helen that she recently had an answer for another brat imitating her.

"If you call that a s-s-stutter," she said, "I think I'll h-h-have to give you l-l-l-lessons."

But the change in her daughter, she knew, was mainly down to the change in her own approach.

Now, she not only spoke to her instead of at her, she actually *listened* to her. She had to admit that Kerry was good fun too, once she'd stopped thinking of her as a chore. She was bright, quick-witted and so very giggly.

She hurried after Kerry and the ever-hyper Fuzzy. He wasn't quite a pup, but he was easily as silly and playful as any young dog. There he was barking and racing after birds that he hadn't a hope in hell of catching, Kerry trying her best to keep up with him.

"Look, Mummy, F-F-F–" she struggled, and Helen wondered again if she had made a mistake calling the dog something that was difficult for her to pronounce, but the speech therapist had advised that this could be beneficial. That way, Kerry couldn't avoid difficult consonants.

So when Helen brought the young dog home from

the local animal shelter and declared he already had a name, she had no choice but to work on her f's and z's.

"Fuzzy w-w-wants to play!" the little girl cried, pointing happily to where the dog was hijacking the ball from a game of soccer already in full swing.

"Fuzzy, no!" Helen ordered, mortified. The dog continued wrestling the ball from the corner-forward, acting as though she wasn't even there.

"I'm so, so sorry." She was all apologies to the other players as lead in hand, she ran out onto the pitch.

"Fuzzy, come *here*," she repeated in a tone that this time had the desired effect. He dropped the ball and – with what Helen could have sworn was one last mournful look towards goal – allowed her to lead him away to the sidelines.

Kerry stood there tittering, hand over her mouth. "Bad dog," the little girl scolded, with no conviction whatsoever, reaching down and tickling him behind the ears.

A spectator looked on in amusement.

"That dog might play for Ireland, yet," he joked.

Helen, embarrassed and more than a little out of breath from running, stood quietly for a moment and watched the play continue.

One player in particular caught her eye. He won the ball in his own penalty area and raced up along the wing, fast as lightning. The spectators rippled with excitement as easily stepping past three defenders, he moved towards goal. Because he was so far wide, Helen was sure he was about to cross the ball to his teammate – but no – this kid checked his man, did a little shimmy and within seconds of striking, the ball was in the back of the net. The little crowd roared with applause.

Kerry too, clapped her hands excitedly. "He's good isn't he, Mommy?" she shouted.

"Spoken like a lady who knows her stuff."

Her daughter looked up at the man standing beside them and smiled shyly, amused – and more than a little pleased – to be referred to as a 'lady'.

Soon they found themselves chatting easily to the bystander. He was tall, wiry with striking green eyes that sparkled when he laughed and somehow instinctively made you warm to him. Kerry must have felt the same as, normally shy, she was now chatting away merrily.

Helen surreptitiously, and almost automatically, checked her wedding ring finger. Nothing.

Interesting.

"That winger – he's terrific," Helen commented.

"Greg?" he replied, in a tone that suggested the lad was local. "He certainly is. And," he bent down towards Kerry, "if you promise you won't say anything, I'll tell you a secret about him – well, you can tell your mum if you like."

She smiled, watching Kerry's eyes widen as he whispered something in her ear. Then she motioned for Helen to bend down, and when she did said, "He's goin to play in the Pwemiership!"

"Ooooh," she replied breathlessly, then fixed him with a questioning glance. "Is that true?"

"True as I'm standing here. United signed him right after his first trial."

"Will he settle there, do you think?" She knew that a

lot of Irish footballers had problems being away from home so young.

"Oh, I'd be almost positive of it," he said knowledgeably, as the referee blew for full time.

"Friend of yours then?" Helen asked over the applause, and then watched surprised as match-winning Greg began to approach them.

"Nah." The man was smiling. "He's my son," he added proudly. Then gave Helen a speculative look. "We're heading off for a bite now to eat if ye fancy joining us?"

Helen shook her head, proud of herself. "Maybe another time."

FIFTY-SEVEN

LAURA WAS STILL WALKING on air.

Amanda Verveen had loved her designs and once they got talking, Laura knew instantly that she could rise to the occasion and produce jewellery that would be simply outstanding.

"It won't be exactly ready-to-wear," the designer had said, indicating a missing breast panel that would have the models spilling out all over the place. "But your stuff truly completes the look."

From what Laura could gather from Jan, Amanda's assistant, most of the catwalk fashion terminology meant little and she wasn't going to start describing her work as Jan had, namely "raw, wild and totally apocalyptic."

She'd like to see how many pairs of earrings she'd sell if she put *that* on her business cards, but nevertheless she had a definite feel for the look they wanted to convey.

Even after that first meeting, Laura felt that she and Amanda were very much on the same wavelength.

By early spring next year her work would be

appearing on catwalks in London, Milan and Paris, something that she could never in a million years have dreamed of.

Not long after the initial phone call from Amanda, Laura had called to Brid at the boutique. She knew instantly from the bridal designer's expression that she had known about the call.

"I hope you didn't mind my giving her your number," Brid began, slightly apologetic. "I wasn't sure how busy you were, but since that day she was raving about you –"

"Are you mad?" Laura cried, enveloping her in a huge hug. "I couldn't be more grateful. I had no idea who she was."

"Amanda keeps a low profile," Brid said. "Thinks it makes her that much more mysterious – like her clothes." She laughed. "It's her image but I find it all a little bit pretentious – so maybe that's why I chose to design wedding dresses instead of haute couture."

The girls had been completely taken aback, Helen in particular. The two had since tentatively reconnected, and Laura discovered that despite the drama, the confrontation at her house had served as a huge turning point for her friend.

She seemed happier and much more content in herself lately - softer, even.

"I have to hand it to you, even when the rest of us – well, me in particular," she added reddening a little, "thought you should pack it in, you kept on going. That takes guts."

"I'm so thrilled for you!" Nicola enthused. "I still

can't believe my best friend is going to be a famous jewellery designer."

"Ah, let's not go mad with ourselves just yet," Laura laughed, although secretly she was enjoying the excitement.

She hadn't yet said a word to her parents though. She wasn't ready to, not until she had met with Amanda and finally convinced herself that yes, this was real – this was actually going to happen. She would never live it down if she told her family, and then the entire thing fell through.

But after the meeting, Laura knew that this was definitely happening, and that Amanda was just as excited about working with *her*.

She and Neil were travelling down to Glengarrah that afternoon to tell them in person. How much better did it get than one of her daughters being asked to work with an internationally renowned designer?

Maureen would get great mileage out of that. They wouldn't be able to shut her up down at the flower club. Oh she couldn't *wait* to tell her!

It was safe now, her mother didn't have to worry about failure anymore – Laura's dreams had come true.

That evening, Neil parked the car outside the cottage and they made their way round to the back door.

"What are *you* doing here?" Maureen looked as though she had just caught an intruder in her kitchen.

"Just in time for dinner, I hope?" he looked longingly at the pots simmering on the stove.

"What's going on, Laura?"

She grinned from ear to ear. "Well, I have some news," she began, looking from her mother to Joe, who was sitting quietly at the kitchen table awaiting his dinner.

Maureen dropped her tea towel. "You're pregnant!" she wailed happily. "Oh thank the Lord."

"Laura's not pregnant," Neil said, when she didn't speak, "but she has some great news about the business."

At this she saw her mother actually roll her eyes in annoyance. She didn't even bother trying to hide it.

"I was going to tell you my good news, Mam," Laura began quietly, her heart constricting with disappointment. "I was planning to tell you that a famous fashion designer has asked me to provide jewellery for her new collection – a collection that will be shown all over the world, in all the magazines, on television and in the newspapers. I was going to tell you that little old useless me with all my notions and talk, have finally succeeded in doing everything I've always wanted to do. I was *going* to tell you that somebody had enough faith in me and my work, to take a chance on me. But judging by the look on your face, I don't think I'll bother."

Laura had never spoken to her mother like that before. In fact, she didn't think that Maureen had ever *let* her speak for that length of time without some interruption or smart comment.

The silence in the small kitchen was almost palpabale.

Neil spoke quickly to fill the void. "The fashion designer is called Amanda Verveen." He shrugged. "I know, I haven't heard of her either, but apparently she's very popular. Irish too – I think she won something on *The Late Late Show* a few years ago – anyway, she wants Laura to work with her – isn't it brilliant?"

Maureen slumped down on one of the kitchen chairs.

"What are you trying to prove?" she asked, flabbergasted.

"To *prove*?"

"With all this nonsense?"

"Maureen, did you not hear –"

"Neil, you're the cause of all this to be honest. She was perfectly happy in her office job before you came along and starting putting ideas in her head."

"But I wasn't happy, you know I wasn't happy." Laura's eyes watered. "Why do you think I spent all those years in Art College? Why do you think I spent every spare minute I had designing and making things – doing what I really love?"

"But you had such a good job ..."

"So my being happy doesn't matter? As long as you can say to the neighbours that Laura has a great job in Dublin – never mind that she hates it – so long as you can say that Laura is doing what she *supposed* to be doing, then *you're* happy. Well, do you know something?" She put a hand on her hip. "I've spent most of my life *trying* to make you happy, *desperate* to make you proud of me, and all I've being doing is making myself miserable because it'll never work. *Nothing* will please you. To hell with what you think, Mam, because I just don't give a damn anymore."

Without another glance at either her mother or her father, Laura raced out of the room, the door slamming deafeningly behind her.

Stony-faced, Maureen lifted her chin into the air. "Did you ever hear such rubbish in all your life?" Then she sniffed. "Well, Joe, after all we've done for her, at least now we know what she thinks of us."

Neil shook his head sadly from the doorway.

"You're a very silly woman, Maureen," he said, "because you really have no idea what you've lost."

FIFTY-EIGHT

LATER, sitting at her own kitchen table, Laura was inconsolable. "I can't believe it," she said, tears streaming down her cheeks as he held both of her hands in his. "Does she take some kind of sick pleasure in making me feel like crap, screwing up my confidence, making me feel unworthy?"

At this stage, Neil too had had enough of the Fannings. They had upset and taken advantage of his wife for long enough and even their wedding day, which was supposed to have been a quiet reserved affair, had been almost ruined by the carry-on of Maureen's family who had made absolute fools of themselves falling around on the dance-floor, and annoying other guests with their over-the-top drunkenness.

No, he too was sick to the teeth of Laura's family, which is why – when he went to answer the ringing door-bell – he wasn't at all happy to see Joe standing in his doorway.

"I wonder if I might have a word," her dad said, in his

usual nervous manner. "I'm on my own," he added seeing Neil glance behind him at the car.

He stood back. "She's very upset, Joe – what happened back there wasn't fair."

"I know that, lad, and believe me I've tried to talk to Maureen, but she's a very stubborn woman."

Slight understatement…

"Dad?" Laura looked up in surprise, but then her expression hardened. "If she's here I don't want to speak to her."

"She's not here, love, I came on my own."

"Oh." Her dad never usually got involved in this kind of thing. Arguments made him very uncomfortable.

Laura wondered if he had taken it upon himself to ask her to go back and apologise to Maureen. Well, he could forget that, for a start.

Her dad cleared his throat. "I wonder if we could have a little chat, Laura, just the two of us?"

Neil's expression was wary.

"It's fine – I've never had an argument with Dad in my entire life, and I'm not going to start now." She gave her father a gentle smile as Neil went into the living-room and closed the door behind him.

"How is she?" Laura asked, wiping her tearstained face with the sleeve of her jumper.

Joe gave a low laugh. "Do you know something, only yourself would ask a question like that."

"I never wanted to upset her." Now that her father was here in front of her, she felt guilty. All the way back in the car, she was glad about what she'd said, but now she wasn't so sure.

"Well, maybe your mother needed to hear some of those things – she mightn't have wanted to, but hear them she should."

"I don't understand ..." Her father always backed her mother, even at her most unreasonable, *especially* at her most unreasonable.

Joe pulled out a chair and sat down. "Laura, I've been working in the factory now for what, nearly thirty years?"

"Well, yes, since I was born . . ."

"And remember I told you I used to work at that local newspaper, *The Herald*?" He gave a wave of his hand. "Ah, it's long gone now, it went not long before you were born."

She knew her dad had worked at the paper, supposedly fixing the machinery and things like that.

"I was a writer at that paper, Laura, I used to do a weekly article."

A journalist? Her father? Was he having her on?

"You wrote for *The Herald*?"

"Not just for the paper." Joe looked away, as if embarrassed by what he was about to say next. "I wrote other stuff too – novels, short stories – that kind of thing."

"*Novels?*" Laura wondered when exactly she had turned into a parrot. But her father wasn't a novelist, he was just an ordinary Joe Soap – a factory worker, she didn't think he had even finished school.

"When I met your mother she was all for it – she'd read some of my stuff and was very supportive. Back then, we were sure that eventually someone important would read them and maybe publish one or two. We used to get a right kick out of talking about it." He smiled at the memory. "We'd be famous, your mother would say, like Brendan Behan, John B Keane and all them lads." He looked away. "Ah, but they were only pipe-dreams, Laura – I was never all that good."

"Have you still got them?" she asked, intrigued as to what her father, *her* dad might have written.

"I think your mother might have tidied them away somewhere but it doesn't matter now."

"So what happened?" she probed when Joe didn't continue. "You didn't just give up, I hope?"

"Well, times were hard back then as you know. There were factories closing, a lot of unemployment and the country was going through a very black period. I married your mother and for a long time we lived on our dreams, well that and the fact that I did a bit of writing part-time at the paper. Because I had a typewriter, some of the local businesses would get me to do a bit of work too."

"But you were waiting for a break with your stories?"

"It was all I wanted, Laura. I was consumed by it, so consumed that I didn't worry enough about putting clothes on our backs or food on the table. I used to lock myself away for hours on end working on my baby, my masterpiece."

"I see." Laura could relate to that, certainly.

"Eventually your mother began to resent me for it and sure, who could blame her? Nothing was happening, and the rejection letters were piling up at the same rate as the bills. Then the paper went bust and to all and intents and purposes I was unemployed – but as half the village knew about my writing and my bits on the side typing – I didn't qualify for the dole. They were all a little wary of me too." He sighed. "Laura, you know Glengarrah as well as I do. The worst thing anyone can do in a small Irish village is try to be different or stand out in any way. As someone who didn't make a 'normal living', I was a bit of an outcast." His voice wavered. "Your mother who of course was born and bred in the village found this hard to tolerate. So when I was let go from the paper, she got a bit of work in the factory, but after a while she couldn't continue. Being around the smell of the sausages made her sick and – "

"She was pregnant," Laura finished, "with me."

Joe nodded. "Things were tight but I was still hell-bent on realising my dream. But one day your mother made me put a stop to it for good."

"What happened?"

"We were badly off, pet - badly off in the old-fashioned sense, not like nowadays when badly off means you can't afford a second holiday or change your car – badly off in the sense that we could barely feed ourselves. So one day, your mother swallowed whatever bit of pride she had left and went to the Kellys asking for help."

Her relations? Laura couldn't imagine it.

"It was a small victory for Joan. She'd been telling Maureen for years that I was only a 'layabout who had notions' and that no good would ever come of my 'scribbling'. She gave her a few bits to keep us going for a little while, but it was probably the worst thing your mother ever did, because they never let her forget their generosity. I'm sure you know as well as I do that by now that charity has been repaid many times over."

Laura tried to put herself in her mother's shoes. Firstly, she couldn't get a handle on how her parents had been that badly off. But Glengarrah was a small village with nothing much going for it back then other than farming or the factories. And her parents weren't farmers. She could only imagine the shame her mother felt then, how damaged her pride must have been.

Laura shook her head. "So that's why she's always so concerned about what everyone thinks of her, of *us*."

"And why she was so worried about you going the same way. She saw it in you quicker than I did. Pet, if you weren't drawing pictures you'd be making things out of toilet rolls and bits of paper. You've been artistic since the day you were born. Maureen was terrified."

"So she tried to stifle me, make me go another direction …"

"She gave in to the college thing – thinking that maybe you might get it out of your system – and for a while you did. And you started what some types call 'a proper job'." He winked. "But I was secretly pleased for you when you started up your business. Of course, I worried too, worried about how you'd manage – what with you being so mild-mannered like myself too. But I never said anything to support you and that was a mistake. I should have. I should have stood up to Maureen and made her see that she had to let you go your own way. Things are different now, young people are more confident, there are greater opportunities and you have so much talent." Then he laughed. "Still, you've more of your mother in you than I thought, love. You went your own way, anyway."

Laura had never truly considered that her parents might have had their own hopes and dreams, dreams that were eventually smothered by circumstance. And yet, how could she *not* have known?

When she thought about it now, it had always been her dad helping her and Cathy with homework – never her mother. He had always been the one with all the answers to the general-knowledge questions on the quiz programmes, the one with nuanced opinions and an open-minded outlook – Joe being one of the few in Glengarrah openly spurning gossip or idle talk.

Laura had never really given it a second thought; she assumed that her father knew things because he read so many books and newspapers. In fact, he was *always* reading. Just then, she had a brief memory of him scribbling things in a notebook, things he found interesting or things he wanted to remember. But she had never thought twice about it.

She would love to read some of his writing. He could have been brilliant ...

"Look, I didn't come here to make you feel guilty," Joe said, seeing her torn expression, "and I hope you don't think that your arrival was the reason for my giving up the writing either. We were mad for a baby and when you came along it was better than anything. No, I just wasn't good enough and over time I came to accept that. Anyway, there were more important things in life. I had to look after my family so I did."

"But haven't you ever pursued your writing since?

OK, I know it wouldn't have been possible when we were young, but the house is very quiet these days. Couldn't you try again?"

Joe's eyes twinkled. "Ah, I do a bit now and again, when your mother's not around," he said. "I enjoy it as much as I've always had, but I doubt it's any good."

"Oh, I'd love to take a look. Will you let me read it?"

He shrugged. "Sure why not? But it's more of a hobby for me these days, love, not something I could do on a regular basis, so don't be getting any mad ideas. We don't want your poor mother losing her mind altogether," he added, chuckling.

Laura had never heard her father speak so much, so *easily* all at once. Then again, when did he ever get the chance when Maureen more than made up for the both of them.

"Look, I suppose I just wanted you to maybe try and see things the way your mother sees them. She's nervous and untrusting of anything she can't understand – anything she can't control. Because of what happened with me, she craves stability and I suppose she couldn't really understand why you would throw caution to the winds and give up a good job like you did. And let's face it, love, sometimes the worst thing an Irish person can do is actually *be* successful."

He gave a wry smile, and Laura thought she understood exactly what he meant. A sense of innate inferiority was at the root of Maureen's problem, and why she worried so much about Laura 'running away with herself'.

"I was so hurtful though, and I tried hard to make her

understand how important it was to me. But she's impossible to talk to and she treats me like I'm still a child ... " Laura trailed off exasperated. "Oh, I don't suppose we'll change her now."

"No, we definitely can't do that," Joe laughed softly. "In a way, I suppose she *does* still see you as child. But pet, what I'm trying to say is that you shouldn't make the mistake I did, and let the begrudgers influence your choices. Your mother can't help herself and in fairness I don't think she realises that she *is* hurting you."

"I know," Laura said, and for a long while she and her father sat in silence, lost in their thoughts.

"Look, pet, it's late and I'd better head back." He stood up and then reached across and patted Laura lightly on the hand. "I'll tell your mother you'll give her a ring tomorrow, maybe?"

"I'll phone her first thing." Knowing what she knew now, she was keen to make up. "Thanks, Dad, thanks for everything."

Giving him a quick hug at the doorway, she closed the door behind her father, and went back into the kitchen.

OK, so it might take a while, but maybe over time, and with Joe's help, Maureen might be won over. And Laura was going to make her parents really proud of her.

Both of them.

She smiled warmly and shook her head as she waited for the kettle to boil.

Her father – a writer! Sometimes, life never failed to surprise.

FIFTY-NINE

"HI," Nicola said, her heart quickening.

Ken stood in her office doorway, stony-faced and tired-looking.

"Did you enjoy your week off?"

He wouldn't meet her gaze. "I just wondered if there were any problems while I was away?" he asked curtly. "Anything you couldn't deal with?"

"No, nothing." He sounded so cold, so distant.

She sat forward, her body taut with anxiety. "Ken, come in and close the door, please. We need to –"

"No," he interjected, his tone brisk. "I know I gave you back your key but I wondered if I might have permission to get some of my stuff from your house? My golf-clubs are still there."

Her permission? Who did he think he was talking to – the Queen? "Well, of course you can – pop round later – "

"I need to go now, actually."

"Sure." Wounded by his dismissive manner, she

reached into her bag and tossed the keys at him. "But can we not ..."

She trailed off in mid-sentence, realising he had already left the room.

Nicola moved to the window and looking down at the carpark below, she saw Ken approach his car, his expression cheery as he got in and drove off.

At this, she felt a burst of annoyance. Who the hell did he think he was, refusing to speak to her for the best part of an entire week and going off in a strop?

Permission to get his stuff indeed. Well, it was about time he did call and collect his crap – those bloody golf-clubs and squash-racquets and gym-gear that had been cluttering up *her* house.

And he could take his blasted *Lord of the Rings* box-set with him too and his other books and video games and ...

She slumped miserably on her desk. Was that it? Was it really over? She couldn't imagine being without Ken – he was such a huge part of her life.

Nicola didn't get much of a chance to think about it much longer, as just then her extension buzzed and Sally put through a call from one of the gym-equipment suppliers.

She groaned inwardly as the rep on the other end tried to explain why seven of the ten treadmills they currently supplied would need to be removed for servic-ing. At this stage, they could take the blasted swimming-pool out of the place for all she cared.

She eventually got back to work but her heart wasn't in it, and she had covered very little ground before Ken reappeared in her office again. And without even looking at her, casually dropped the keys on her desk before turning to leave.

This indifferent gesture, along with his blatant, unashamed rudeness was just about enough.

"Hold on there a second," she commanded.

"What?" Ken answered, all innocence.

"*What?*" she mimicked, doubly annoyed. "I don't know who the hell you think you are, but if you think you can treat *me* like a piece of dog – dog – *meat,* then you've got another think coming. Carrying on like this – sulking and grouching like a spoilt child and making it plain to all and sundry that you're annoyed with me. Refusing to listen or speak to me when you know damn well that I've done nothing wrong."

"You've really done nothing wrong?" he repeated, in a tone that she could only describe as brazen.

"Yes! I mean – no." She shook her head. "I mean, I haven't done anything wrong, yet you won't listen to me, you won't even *look* at me."

"Fine, I believe you," he said and shrugged indolently, a gesture that *really* set her off.

"Don't you dare turn your back on me ..." she called after him, wanted to throw something at the annoying, infuriating, *exasperating* ... "Hey, what the hell?"

She watched in astonishment as Barney sauntered casually through the door, his tail wagging enthusiastically as he sniffed the floor of her office.

"Well, would you look at that?" Ken said nonchalantly, his eyes wide. "He must have sneaked into the back of the car while I was at your house."

"*Sneaked* into the back of the car? For goodness sake, Ken, he's a fully-grown Lab – how could you not have noticed?"

"I don't know. Anyway, he'll be fine with you now, won't he?"

Nicola harrumphed. "This is a leisure centre for goodness sake, you can't have dogs in ..." Barney ambled to her side and she reached down to pat him on the head. "Sorry, Barn, as much as I'd love it, you can't stay here." She glared at Ken. "Ken will just have to drive you back and... now what have you got there ... oh."

Barney dropped whatever he had in his mouth onto her lap, and Nicola stared in disbelief at the small, navy, velvet ...

She looked up and saw Ken watching her, his expression no longer sullen.

"Good boy," he praised and then winked at Nicola "We've been practising that for a while."

"Ken?" she said breathlessly, almost afraid to ask. "Is this ... is this ...?"

"Well, why don't you open it and see?"

Barney flopped down on the floor and put his head on his paws, his dark eyes rising upwards with curiosity as his mistress opened the – admittedly sticky – velvet box to find an ornate diamond ring.

Her hand flew to her mouth and for a long moment, she was unable to think – let alone *say* anything. Was this really...?

"Well?" Ken urged gently, his eyes full of emotion.

Nicola looked from the ring to Barney, to Ken and then back again to the ring.

"I don't know what to ..." She looked at him, still unsure. "But I thought you were breaking up with me – you were so angry ..."

"I was being an idiot. When I saw Dan at your house I was annoyed. Then afterwards, when you denied you'd seen him, I was angry and I thought –"

She knew she was stupid to deny it, but he had put her on the spot. Then afterwards, he wouldn't *let* her explain.

"So, what changed your mind?"

"Well, I went off and sulked for a week, certain that you were going back to Hunt. Then I met Helen in town at the weekend, and she told me what you were up to with the fiancee."

"I could have told you that, if you had let me." She made a silent promise to thank Helen for her intervention. While they'd remained cool with one another immediately after the bust-up at Laura's, they'd recently been in touch to make amends.

Nicola knew she shouldn't have lost her temper, and that accusing Helen of being a bad mother was unforgivable. But she knew they would come through it. They always did.

"I know and I was being an idiot."

"But then why ... this?"

Ken shrugged easily, his eyes twinkling "Bringing Barney here wasn't in the original plan. I'd intended to ask you before now ... actually, I was about to ask you that night."

Now she really understood why he was so angry to

see Dan at the house. But arranging all this and Barney too ... Tears sprang to her eyes.

The dog sighed loudly from beneath the desk, wondering why he was being ignored, and they both laughed.

"So. What do you reckon?"

Nicola looked into Ken's honest brown eyes and didn't have to think too hard about her answer.

SIXTY

ON A COLD AFTERNOON IN JANUARY, dressed in full snow-queen regalia, Chloe prepared to walk up the aisle of St Anthony's.

Her father, dressed handsomely in top-hat and tails, stood back to let the photographer get some shots of the bride on her own.

"Such a shame we didn't get snow," the photographer was saying, and if Chloe didn't know better she'd have sworn he was mocking her.

She turned to the side and gave a beaming smile. At least, it was supposed to be a beaming smile.

Chloe wondered if the lens would pick up on her nervousness, capturing it for posterity. Yet it didn't feel quite the same as nervousness, she decided, it was more like ... uncertainty.

Why was she feeling like this? She had been looking forward to this day for so long and despite the setbacks, her wedding day was finally happening.

Why then wasn't she feeling elated, excited, bursting with anticipation...

She followed the bridesmaids inside. Now, standing at the back of church with her mother and Lynne fussing over the hem of her cloak, she felt ...unsure.

Lynne looked up then and Chloe wondered if she was just imagining the faint anxiety on her friend's face. Was she feeling uncertain too? Had she made a mistake confiding in her?

After her meeting with Nicola, Chloe hadn't known what to think. She knew that there were two sides to every story but Dan had all but admitted that he had abandoned his wife when she needed him the most.

"What's to say that he won't do the same to you?" her friend had pointed out. "So much for better or worse."

It was true that Nicola seemed to have got on just fine without him but then, she hadn't had much of a choice, had she?

"It's not so much his leaving her ... more the fact that Dan had no intention of telling you about it," Lynne had said.

Or had she?

No, Chloe thought, her friend *hadn't* said that, it was the little voice inside herself that had. The little voice that at this very moment was doing its very best to unnerve her.

The opening bars of the bridal march began.

This was it. She felt a sudden rush of adrenaline – or was it panic? Exhaling, she flinched a little when her dad touched her elbow.

"This is us, darling," he whispered, handing her his left arm.

As she followed her bridesmaids up the aisle, Chloe's gaze travelled along the rows of smiling guests, flashing cameras and settled at the altar.

She didn't notice the elaborate flower arrangements, didn't hear the harpist ... she didn't even care how she looked.

Somehow she thought she would be blown away by all the romance and excitement, blown away by being a princess for a day.

But she didn't feel like that at all.

If anything, she felt this was all very, very wrong.

She looked up and saw Dan standing with his back to the congregation, stiffly awaiting her arrival.

She loved him and he loved her. Surely that was all that mattered? And everything that had happened in the past was simply that – the past.

They were getting closer now, and Chloe's heart was knocking hard against her ribs, pounding in her chest. Suddenly, white spots appeared before her eyes and she felt her throat close over and her mouth go ...

Then the bridesmaids stopped walking, and Lynne turned around to relieve her of the bridal bouquet.

Dan was smiling.

Her father was smiling.

The priest was smiling.

Chloe looked up. What was *wrong* with her? *Nobody* knew what the future held, did they? Nobody could be a hundred percent certain.

Could any bride on the day, with all the fuss, pomp

and spectacle – really, *honestly* say that they were completely certain? Could anybody *ever* be absolutely certain?

The bride moved forward to take her place at the altar alongside her groom.

Probably not.

Read on for an excerpt of *The Getaway*, another unputdownable novel from Melissa Hill, out now.

Also available via Kindle Unlimited.

THE GETAWAY

EXCERPT

Another unputdownable book club read from the Irish Times #1 bestselling author.

Careful what you wish for...

Three women routinely take the same coastal train service to the city. All they have in common is that each is desperate for an escape.

Newly-wed Dara would give anything to go back in time and make a different choice. But she's married now and nothing can change that. Can it?

Louise always wanted to be slim, pretty, and popular. So she can't believe it when her luck seems to be changing. But is it all too good to be true?

Widow Rosie has always tried her best to make her children happy. Even though they're both grown adults, they seem to expect more from her than ever.

But one summer morning, a shock incident on the train allows each woman an opportunity to alter life's trajectory. Will they have the courage to grasp it?

ONE

SHE COULDN'T MISS THIS. And come hell or high water, she was *not* going to miss it.

But the rumbling was getting louder by the second, so despite her stilettos and pencil skirt she had no choice but to make a run for it. If she failed to make the train today she was in big trouble. Big. *Huge.*

She wasn't the only one running late this morning either she noted, seeing another harried commuter rush to the ticket booth. Tapping her travel pass, she scurried through the barrier and breathed a sigh of relief to see that the train was still at the platform.

Just in time.

Breathing heavily, she nipped inside the double doors seconds before they shut – nearly catching the hem of her trench in the process. But the person behind hadn't been fast enough, and as the train pulled off she felt bad for the unlucky straggler.

The coastal commuter service to Dublin was a busy route with usually only standing room in the carriages.

Though today there was a precious seat a little way down that no one else seemed to have noticed.

She hurried to nab it, but as she pushed through the standing crowd her handbag slipped off her shoulder, falling awkwardly onto the ground.

Typical. She inelegantly bent down to try and pick it up – forward momentum plus the weight of the briefcase in her other hand, jerking her off balance.

"Here you go." A girl sitting nearest the aisle retrieved the bag, giving it a blatantly appreciative glance while handing it back. "Orla Kiely?"

"Yes it is, and thanks," she replied a little breathless. Sinking gratefully onto the seat, she put her briefcase on the floor and her prized handbag on her lap. The fashion label had since closed and thus these bags were rare as hen's teeth.

Dusting off her skirt, she shuffled exaggeratedly, trying to give a not-so-subtle hint to the guy beside her to move over. She'd noticed some extra padding on her ass lately, but his manspreading was ridiculous.

Catching the eye of an older lady sitting across the way, she flashed a conspiratorial smile. The woman was reading one of those fluffy romance novels and certainly didn't look to be on a work commute. Then again, she thought, catching sight of some guy in a tracksuit and briefcase pushing his way through the crowds, who knew what people might be up to?

Lucky thing, she thought eyeing the older woman's book and trying to remember the last time she had been able to lose herself in a cosy read.

Speaking of which . . . She reached for her briefcase

and withdrew the documents for this morning's meeting. Cosy reading it wasn't.

Her idle musing was cut off by an overpowering, ear-splitting screech. *What the hell?* Heart leaping, she instinctively put her hands to her ears.

Then the carriage began to shudder, her body tensed and the hairs on the back of her neck stood up. She looked wildly around, wondering if everyone else was experiencing the same thing.

Yes, the older woman across from her looked terrified, confused . . . everyone looked bewildered . . . and then there was an almighty roar, a sound so deafening it was unlike anything she'd ever witnessed.

Her heart hammered and her brain flooded with even more excruciating noise . . . then her seat jerked. . . and time slowed to a crawl. Until surreally, the entire carriage lifted and the vehicle seemed to be travelling in thin air.

But that couldn't possibly be, she reassured herself, before a tremendous force winched her out of her seat.

Trains couldn't fly. Could they?

TWO

THE TYPICALLY SELF-ASSURED and flawlessly composed journalist was ragged and white-faced as she looked unseeingly into the camera. In her earpiece, she heard a voice from the news studio.

"Our correspondent, Clare Rogers is now live at the scene of this morning's tragedy. Clare, can you tell us anything concrete at this point?"

"Emergency services have just arrived at the location, so details are sketchy at this time." Clare's voice trembled as she spoke. "All I can confirm is that a train on the morning coastal commuter route to Dublin City has derailed and crashed at Sandymount Beach."

"Any indication as to what might have caused this horrific incident?" the news anchor prompted.

"Again we can't confirm any details at present. Rail Ireland will be making an official statement soon. But I spoke to some witnesses earlier – motorists stopped at the level crossing – who helped me reconstruct the scene. They saw or rather heard, the train braking from some distance, suggesting that the driver may have identified a problem with the signal. The locomotive derailed a few yards from the gates, careered across the tracks and crashed through a stone wall before ending up on the beach here behind us." Clare swallowed hard. "Luckily, there was no southbound train passing at the time," she added solemnly.

"So the driver tried to avoid crashing?"

"Again, we're just not sure. No doubt there will be a full investigation in time, but at the moment the emphasis is of course on the rescue effort."

"Signal failure, something that's unusual for our rail network, isn't it?" Richard went on – intent on getting to the bottom of the situation.

"Correct. Derailments are sadly more common for our neighbours in the UK, given that multiple rail companies operate there. The system is fine-tuned but signals can occasionally be confused. Which," she added, struggling to keep her voice even, "can lead to incidents like this."

"But we have only one rail carrier in Ireland, thus such mistakes are rare."

"Usually. But in recent months, Rail Ireland has been carrying out upgrades throughout the network. Although it is only speculation at this stage – and again, the company will issue a statement soon – it would appear that the signalling system on this particular crossing failed."

"Which would have serious implications for all involved," Richard finished.

"Very serious implications indeed," Clare agreed, her

voice grim. "At this time of the morning, the train is packed with commuters, regular users of this busy city route, and – as I'm sure viewers can tell from our footage – there's likely a high incidence of serious injury and undoubtedly some fatality too."

"Thank you, Clare – we'll come back to you later for the Rail Ireland press conference."

Live footage of the wreck disappeared, and the feed cut back to the newsroom, where the anchor looked somberly into the camera.

"Our thoughts and prayers go out to any viewers at home with loved ones onboard the coastal service this morning. Stay tuned for further updates."

THREE

ROSIE MITCHELL WAITED PATIENTLY at the platform. The train was a little bit late this morning, she noted, checking her watch. Not that it mattered to her. A mid-sixties retiree, she was long past the morning rush.

Thank goodness for the train all the same, otherwise she'd be stuck. Her late husband Martin had always been the one to do the driving and often encouraged her to learn, but she never had any interest.

Luckily her home town of Lakeview was the first stop on the commuter route to Dublin. She and her family had lived for decades in the popular tourist village, centred around the broad oxbow lake from which it took its name. The fact that it had direct train access to the capital made it even more popular with visitors and relocating city families.

Rosie liked the train and enjoyed being able to sit back on the journey and admire the picturesque coastal view, gaze at the birds weaving in and out over the cliffs at Greystones, or stare in awe at the crystal clear waters of beautiful Killiney Bay.

Or if the day was cloudy and the scenery not so spectacular, she would read a book. Sometimes she'd be so stuck in the story that she didn't notice the hour or so journey.

So she wouldn't dream of getting a car. What was the point? The station was a short walk from her house, and with the service running multiple times a day, she had plenty of options. She could nip into the city whenever she fancied and her friend Sheila's new place was close to the rail line, as was her daughter Sophie's house.

For the moment anyway.

The train finally pulled in, and Rosie stood back, patiently waiting until the cluster of younger commuters were seated before she boarded. The upside of this was that she wouldn't get pushed and shoved. Since putting her back out in a badminton match a few months ago, her balance wasn't as sure as it used to be, and she liked to take her time. Course, the downside of waiting was that she was often left without a seat. But Rosie didn't mind. These people all had a hard slog ahead of them, whereas she didn't have a care in the world.

In fact, wasn't she the lucky one – a lady of leisure meeting with her daughter? She'd hate to have to face into work now like her fellow passengers. You could see the stress and strain in their expressions – all preoccupied with whatever awaited them. It was a shame really; the lengths people had to go to these days just to keep their heads above water.

It had been a lot different when she and Martin were

starting out. Neither of them had to spend hours commuting and they were the better for it.

Her husband had worked in his father's gardening business in Lakeview since he was old enough to use a trowel, and Rosie had worked in the tourist office. They'd bought a house close to town so she could walk to work, while Martin went off in his van to wherever he happened to be working that day.

She smiled sadly as she thought of her beloved husband. There wasn't a day that she didn't think of him, or miss him, but she couldn't complain. They'd had a wonderful marriage, two healthy children, and in all their years together rarely a cross word had passed between them.

They'd both known that the day would come when she would be left on her own. High blood pressure was in Martin's family and when he suffered two near-fatal heart attacks in his latter years, it became clear that a simple change in lifestyle or medication wasn't going to save him. But it was lovely that he'd died doing what he loved, tending the roses out in the back garden – the evening sun just beginning to fade when Rosie found him.

Eighteen months ago she had buried the one great love of her life, having made him a promise that she would keep going, keep laughing and smiling and enjoying life, so that it wouldn't seem all that long until she saw him again. At times it was hard but Rosie was doing her best to keep that promise.

Anyway, she was very lucky. Her two adult children were happily married and with good jobs, David to a lovely Liverpool girl named Kelly (there was no sign of kids yet, and Rosie wouldn't dream of asking) and working as a builder in the UK.

Sophie and her husband Robert had toddler Claudia and good jobs too, but were still on the hunt for a house. That was another hardship for the younger generation. House prices in Dublin were obscene.

Today her daughter was taking Rosie to view a house she had her eye on.

"Mum, it's just ... perfect," she'd gushed on the phone the day before. "You've simply *got* to see it."

While she was delighted with her daughter's enthusiasm Rosie couldn't help feeling a little disappointed that Sophie would want to live so far away on the other side of the capital.

Still, it would be nice to see the three of them settled somewhere other than the city centre rental they were in now. There wasn't much space in an apartment, and with Claudia hitting the terrible twos, it couldn't be good for them all to live in what was basically one big room. With luck, this house Sophie wanted her to see today was a tidy semi-d like Rosie's own, with a small garden for Claudia to run around in.

The train emptied some of its passengers at the first city stop, and Rosie sank gratefully onto a recently-vacated seat.

Her back had been giving her a bit of trouble lately, and as much as she tried to tell herself otherwise, there was no denying that she was starting to feel the effects of advancing age.

Despite how energetic and cheerful she might want

to feel, she *wasn't* getting any younger, was she? Rosie smiled. She definitely wasn't one of those glamorous granny types. With their coloured hair, perfect make-up and up-to-the-minute fashion, these women looked for all the world like they were still in the first flush of youth.

Sophie had injections into her face to keep the wrinkles at bay, which sounded horrific, but that wasn't Rosie's way. No, she was going to let her auburn hair go as grey as it liked, and her skin as wrinkly as it wanted – weren't these marks of a life lived? Getting older was nothing to be ashamed of and as much as you might like to, you couldn't outrun time.

But today Rosie wasn't running anywhere, she chuckled, getting off the train at Connolly Station and heading to the nearest bus stop. Shame that Sophie's car was in for a service today, otherwise her daughter could've collected her. Because today's train had been late, Rosie had missed the usual bus connection, but such was life.

She reached into her bag and took out the novel she was reading to pass the time.

The bus duly arrived, and forty or so minutes later, Rosie finally reached her daughter's apartment building.

She took extra care selecting the right buzzer, always afraid that she'd push the wrong one and wake up some poor misfortunate sleeping off night duty or something. Originally from County Clare, and despite living in Lakeview for all of her married life, she still couldn't shake off the 'small village inferiority complex' as her husband used to call it.

Rosie called it good manners and concern for a

fellow human being, but outgoing and confident all his life, Martin didn't understand.

Nor it seemed, did Sophie.

"Mum, I'm just drying my hair – can you hold on for five minutes?" her daughter's voice blared tinnily through the speaker.

"No problem," Rosie replied agreeably, although the coastal chill was making her fingers numb.

"Hi!" It was a good ten minutes before Sophie appeared downstairs, dark hair sleek and shiny, and make-up beautifully applied. Her daughter always looked so stylish, and today she was dressed in a gorgeous fitted suit, something that even Rosie's inexperienced eye could see had cost an arm and a leg.

But it couldn't have cost that much because Sophie and Robert were mad saving for this house. Knowing her daughter's incredible talent for spotting a bargain, she had probably picked up the outfit for next to nothing.

"Sorry about keeping you waiting, but I think you were a little early – I said ten thirty, didn't I?"

Sophie could be a little bit scatty sometimes.

"No, the train was late actually – where's Claudia?" Rosie stepped into the hallway, eager to get out of this cold. Although it was supposed to be summer, the Irish seasons generally set their own agenda.

Sophie linked her mother's arm and steered her back outside. "With the childminder of course. I couldn't bring her with us – we'd have no peace with her wailing and whinging and *touching* everything."

"Oh." Rosie was disappointed. She had been looking

forward to spending time with her only granddaughter. "Maybe we could pick her up after?"

"Ah Tracy offered to take her for the day – she knows I need the break," Sophie answered dismissively. "And of course, she won't say no to the money either." Rosie nodded reluctantly as her daughter chattered on. "Oh, Mum, I am just *dying* for you to see this place – it is truly incredible!"

"I'm sure it is, pet, but don't get your hopes up too much either, OK? You know yourself there's a lot of competition out there and – "

"Mum, this is ours – I just know it is!"

As they ambled towards the residents' carpark, Rosie had to smile at her daughter's enthusiasm. She had been the very same as a youngster, always full of excitement and mischief.

The kids had been quite the handful growing up, and while Martin always insisted that Rosie spoiled and sheltered them too much, she was proud to say that they had both turned out well. 'A credit to them,' her own mother might have said, had she been alive today to see it.

"And I thought we might go for a nice lunch and a chat after – what do you think?"

Rosie was thrilled. A good old gossip with her daughter was long overdue. Although they spoke on the phone, she hadn't seen Sophie in a while, and she wanted to tell her all her news and she wouldn't mind confiding in someone about how her back was starting to give her a bit more trouble and . . .

She was startled when the flashy yellow sports car in front of them beeped noisily.

"What do you think?" Sophie grinned, proudly waving keys.

"Is this yours?" Rosie gasped in confusion. A brand new car? Despite herself, she couldn't help feeling a bit hurt. If her car was no longer giving trouble, why hadn't Sophie collected her from the station instead of having her wait twenty minutes in the cold and then another twenty on the bus? And how on earth would they get a child seat into that tiny thing?

"Yep," Sophie confirmed happily.

"But what about the old one? The one that was giving you trouble."

"I told you it was having a service because I wanted this to be a surprise." Sophie looked a bit crestfallen. "Don't you like it?"

"Of course I do." Now Rosie felt guilty. "It's lovely, pet – I can't wait to get a spin in it."

"Well, you won't have long to wait!" Her good humour restored, Sophie opened the driver-side door and sat princess-like at the steering wheel, while her mother eased herself into the passenger seat. She tilted the rear-view mirror and applied a fresh coat of lipstick. "Ready?" she asked, turning the key in the ignition.

Rosie's back ached from trying to manoeuvre herself into what amounted to little more than a biscuit tin. Sophie's swerving and quick lane-changing all the way to Malahide didn't help much.

About fifteen minutes later, they pulled onto a quiet tree-lined avenue.

Rosie was certain that behind all those expensive wrought-iron gates, intercoms and granite stonework were equally expensive houses – houses way beyond the reach of a part-time insurance clerk and her department store manager husband. There was a For Sale sign outside the one at the end, but surely they couldn't even *dream* of . . .

But Sophie slowed the car in front of the gates, rolled down the window and pushed the intercom button.

"Sophie Morris," she announced in a haughty voice that Rosie had never heard her use before.

"Love, surely you couldn't be thinking of buying a house like this? It must cost an absolute fortune."

"Well, in the scheme of things, it isn't that expensive," she replied airily. "Anyway, I just want you to take a look at it first and see what you think. We'll discuss the rest later."

The rest? What rest? Rosie wanted to ask.

But then it hit her. Just then she realised why Sophie was so eager to show her this house today, why her daughter had been so cheerful and attentive these last few weeks.

She had to give her credit, to be fair. Sophie had bided her time and had waited until well after her father's death before she once again raised The Question.

Now, she felt sad and more than a little used. She supposed she should have known better than to think that her daughter had brought her all the way out here just to get her opinion. Sophie didn't need an opinion – her mind was already made up.

And deep down Rosie knew that this time she probably *would* give in. In truth, she would have that first time too, only Martin wouldn't hear of it. Her husband had been dead set against the idea and that had been the end of the matter.

Until now.

As they approached the admittedly beautiful, but eyewateringly expensive house, Rosie sighed inwardly. Martin would not be happy with her – not happy at *all*.

End of excerpt.

Continue reading THE GETAWAY, out now in print and kindle.

ABOUT THE AUTHOR

International #1 and USA Today bestselling author Melissa Hill lives in County Wicklow, Ireland.

Her page-turning emotional stories of family, friendship and romance have been translated into 25 different languages and are regular chart-toppers internationally.

A Reese Witherspoon x Hello Sunshine adaptation of her worldwide bestseller SOMETHING FROM TIFFANY'S is airing now on Amazon Prime Video worldwide.

THE CHARM BRACELET aired in 2020 as a holiday movie 'A Little Christmas Charm'. A GIFT TO REMEMBER (and a sequel) was also adapted for screen by Crown Media and multiple other titles by Melissa are currently in development for film and TV.

Visit her website at
www.melissahill.info
Or get in touch via social media links below.

Printed in Great Britain
by Amazon